FURTHER PRAISE FOR *VICTORY*

'Two superb novellas full of contemporary resonance...
Extraordinarily taut and compelling'
Leyla Sanai, *Spectator*

'Timely and irresistibly unpleasant... Sure to provoke
passionate discussion... Testifies to the compact virtues of
the novella'
Marcel Theroux, *Guardian*

'Highly conscientious...elegant in its execution and almost
humble in its refusal to grandstand, or to turn a story
about rape allegations into some didactic allegory'
Josephine Livingstone, *New Republic*

'Of the novels to come out of the #MeToo moment to date,
none is more riveting, insightful, and unsettling'
Kirkus Review (Starred Review)

'Darkly humorous and compelling portraits of men
wrestling with guilt and desire... [*Afternoon of a Faun*]
feels very much a novel for our times'
Alex Preston, *Observer*

'Confirms Lasdun as one of the great serio-comic writers
of the age. The writing alternately poetic and razor-sharp
cynical,

JAMES LASDUN

James Lasdun's books include *The Fall Guy* and *Give Me Everything You Have: On Being Stalked*. He teaches creative writing at Columbia University and reviews regularly for the *Guardian*. His work has been filmed by Bernardo Bertolucci (*Besieged*) and he co-wrote the films *Sunday*, which won Best Feature and Best Screenplay awards at Sundance, and *Signs and Wonders*, starring Charlotte Rampling and Stellan Skarsgård.

JAMES LASDUN

Victory

TWO NOVELLAS

VINTAGE

1 3 5 7 9 10 8 6 4 2

Vintage
20 Vauxhall Bridge Road
London SW1V 2SA

Vintage is part of the Penguin Random House group of companies
whose addresses can be found at global.penguinrandomhouse.com

Penguin
Random House
UK

First published by Jonathan Cape in 2019
First published by Vintage in 2020

'Feathered Glory' was published in the *Paris Review*
(Spring 2015)

penguin.co.uk/vintage

A CIP catalogue record for this book is available from the
British Library

ISBN 9781784709419

Printed and bound in Great Britain by Clays Ltd, Elcograf S.p.A.

Penguin Random House is committed to a sustainable future
for our business, our readers and our planet. This book is
made from Forest Stewardship Council® certified paper.

Contents

Feathered Glory

1

The train pulled into the quiet riverside station. A large man climbed out, carrying a battered suitcase. He was alone, a fact observed with puzzlement by the person waiting for him on the platform.

'No Audrey?'

'I'm afraid not.'

'How come?'

The large man sighed.

'I moved out.'

'Oh, Victor!'

'I'll tell you about it in the car.'

'Why didn't you call us?'

'Let me smoke one of these, Richard.'

Victor had taken a small cigar, a cigarillo, from its box, and as the train heaved itself off, he stood inhaling the pungent tobacco while his host for the weekend, Richard Timmerman, waited patiently by his side.

The two were old friends. They had grown up in the same small Massachusetts town and had remained close despite the divergent paths of their adult lives. Richard was now the principal of a private elementary school in Aurelia, a hundred miles north of New York, while Victor lived in Manhattan, on the Lower East Side, patching together a living from music journalism – mostly on esoteric jazz of one kind or another – while leading the disorderly and, in Richard's private opinion, increasingly depressing life of an ageing bohemian.

Recently, however, Victor had married. Audrey, his wife, was fifteen years his junior: an executive at a fashion company; very chic and pretty and efficient. Victor seemed to attract such women. They saw him as a challenge, Richard supposed; a gauntlet thrown down before their powers of cleansing and redemptive orderliness. Few ever lasted more than a couple of months, however, and although Richard had been glad to hear that this one was planning to stay the course, he had also been apprehensive. Now it seemed his fears had been justified.

The story Victor told in the car was brutally simple. He'd met another woman. They'd decided they couldn't live without each other. Victor had abandoned Audrey and their baby daughter, renting an apartment where the new woman, Oxana, was to join him as soon as she'd broken the news to her husband, who was travelling in Asia on business.

'That's it?'

'That's it.'

'My God, Victor. What does Audrey have to say?'

'She's devastated.'

'I would think! You don't seem too happy yourself.'

Victor looked away, saying nothing.

Sara, Richard's wife, had lunch waiting for them when they arrived at the house. She made no comment on the absence of Audrey and the baby; merely looked questioningly at Richard as Victor carried his bag up to the spare room. Richard explained the situation.

4

'What a shame,' she said. 'I liked Audrey.'

She removed a setting from the dining-room table and took away the old spindle-backed high chair which she had brought out for the baby. Daniel, their ten-year-old son, filled the water jug, and the three of them sat, waiting for their guest to reappear.

Fifteen minutes later he still hadn't come down. Richard called up the stairs. Getting no answer, he went up and found Victor asleep, sprawled on the sleigh bed in his shoes, saliva dribbling from a corner of his mouth onto the antique quilt.

He slept till late in the afternoon, and then came down looking worse than before: his eyes bloodshot, his face blotched pink and red.

'Are you all right, Victor? I mean physically?' Richard asked him.

'I'm fine. Is one permitted to have a drink yet, or are the new rules still in force?'

This was evidently an allusion to his last visit, when Richard, in an effort to keep the drinking from getting out of hand, had said that he and Sara didn't usually start before six in the evening. He'd also asked Victor not to smoke in the house because the smell lingered in Sara's weavings. Victor hadn't seemed to mind at the time, and his caustic tone now startled Richard.

'Of course you can have a drink.'

He poured his friend a Scotch.

'Let's go out for dinner,' he said impulsively, handing him the glass. 'Just the two of us. Sara won't mind. I mean, she'll understand.'

Victor brightened a fraction:

'I'm broke ...'

'Don't worry.'

5

They drove to the Millstream, a restaurant at the edge of town with quiet, wood-panelled alcoves.

'All right,' Richard said after they had ordered, 'now tell me the whole story again, from the beginning.'

'It's what I told you.'

'Yes, but there's something missing. You fall madly in love. You're about to start living with the woman. Why are you so unhappy?'

Victor shrugged, turning away.

'You want to go back, is that it?'

'What?'

'You want to go back to Audrey?'

'No.'

'Because that's what I'm thinking. You want to go back to her but she won't have you.'

'Well, you're wrong.'

'You're sure?'

'Don't be a pain, Richard.'

Their dinner arrived.

'Listen,' Richard said. 'I wasn't planning to lecture you, but I'm wondering if that's maybe what you want me to do.'

Victor wiped his lips with a napkin.

'You can lecture me.'

'All right. Look. You're fifty now.'

'Not quite.'

'Almost. You've gone from woman to woman your entire life. You leave them or these days more often they leave you. True?'

'True.'

'Either way, as soon as you're alone you're miserable and immediately go out looking for a replacement. So now finally you've found someone you love – Audrey,

I mean – who by a miracle appears to be able to put up with you. She's attractive, smart, sweet, capable of holding down a job ... You marry her, you have a child together ... Then you just walk out? Aside from anything else what are the chances things are going to work out long term with this ... Oxana? I know I can't speak from experience but it must be quite a negotiation at our age, setting up house with someone new. All kinds of little foibles have to be addressed in the treaty, don't they? Little fine-print details about the snoring, the bathroom habits, all that stuff ... And you're going to put yourself through that – for what? The only thing you can rely on is the law of diminishing returns. *You* know that ...'

He continued in this vein for some time. Victor heard him out in silence. He seemed to be absorbing Richard's words like a chastised and penitent child. But when Richard had finished, he gave him a look of such curious impassiveness that Richard wondered if he'd inadvertently offended him. Even when the large features relaxed into a smile, there was something aloof in it.

'Not bad,' Victor said. 'Not one of your best, but not bad.'

In the small hours Richard was woken by sounds from the back of the house. Going down to investigate, he found Victor slumped across the doorway of the rear porch, his head outside on the stone step, a cigarillo in his mouth, the bottle of Scotch on the floor beside him. He was making a low moaning sound and when he turned around, Richard saw that he was weeping.

'Vic! For Christ's sake! Tell me what's going on.'

Victor gave a groan, raw and loud, like an animal in pain. Richard helped him to his feet, stubbing out the cigarillo on the step. Holding him gently, he steered him into the living room and sat him on the couch.

'Come on now. You have to tell me or I can't help you.'

'Jesus, Richard, do I really need to spell it out?'

'What?'

'Can't you guess?'

'No. Tell me!'

'She dumped me.'

'Audrey?'

'No, you jackass. Oxana. When her husband came back from China. Instead of dumping him she dumped me. Changed all her goddam numbers. Won't answer my emails. Hilarious, isn't it?'

'I'm not smiling at that. I'm just – listen, Audrey's willing to take you back. Right?'

'Yes.'

'Well. So nothing's lost. You go back. Start again. Try to keep things on track.'

Victor blinked.

'But it's Oxana I want.'

Richard tried to keep the exasperation out of his voice:

'Yes, but ... you can't have her. So ...'

Tears welled up in Victor's eyes. And yet Richard found it hard to sympathise: the suffering seemed to him perverse, childish, self-inflicted and utterly unnecessary.

He stood up.

'Come on. Let's get some sleep. We'll talk more tomorrow.'

He woke the next morning with a sense of having been a little hard on Victor. From his experience in the classroom he knew that guidance was best swallowed when the guide was willing to show some kinship with the miscreant: similar desires; a common human fallibility.

That afternoon, he took Victor on a walk along the trail that led into the forest from the end of their road. It was almost April; no leaves or blossoms yet, though the snows had melted and the smell of spring rose from the forest floor.

'I had a similar experience to yours,' Richard began. 'Not the same — I wasn't actually married — but similar. I didn't tell you about it at the time because frankly I was too ashamed.'

Victor gave a grunt of polite interest.

'It was when I was at Ryden College, training teachers. I'd been living with Sara for a year and we'd decided to get married that fall, after she finished her textile classes. I was very much in love with her, just like you and Audrey — that never changed. But I got blindsided by this student. Not one of mine, and not an undergraduate, but a student nevertheless. She was from Ireland, Cork. Francesca Sullivan. She wanted to be a music teacher. She had a lovely voice, played all kinds of instruments — dulcimer, flute, mandolin. I still played the guitar in those days and we met through a group that got together a couple of nights a week to play folk and bluegrass. She was extremely warm and lively, always laughing, joking, making fun of herself. Very attractive, I thought, and in those days I guess I still had the instinct to try to make an impression on any attractive female who came into my orbit.

'So that's what I did, and maybe because there wasn't much competition, or maybe because she was lonely in New York, or maybe, God knows, because she actually found me appealing, it worked, though with a much more powerful effect on *me* than I'd bargained for. I was half in love with her before I knew it. I'd told her about Sara, and that acted as a brake, though it was also a lid under which all kinds of illicit feelings were able to simmer away in secret. First we'd just walk to the subway together, then we started riding the same train downtown even though that meant one of us would have to transfer, then we started grabbing the odd coffee or drink ...

'One evening I stayed on the train with her all the way to her stop. We went to a bar and while we were sitting opposite each other I realised I'd started stroking her hair. I mean, as if that was just the normal thing I did. She had beautiful long brown hair, very thick and wild, and I was just plying my fingers through it without being aware of what I was doing until she started laughing. The next thing I knew we were kissing like a couple of teenagers ...

'At the end of the semester she went back to Cork to spend the summer with her family. We still hadn't, you know, slept together, and we told ourselves the separation would be a good thing – force us to figure out what we really meant to each other, and for a few days I felt almost sane again. But then she sent me a letter, an actual letter, saying, among other things, that she was missing me more than she expected, and I started hankering for her with an intensity that was new to me. I couldn't get her out of my head for a single second of the day. Her hair, her scent, her voice, her face, her mouth ... I started sneaking out of the apartment while Sara was asleep to call her from pay-phones. I'd never felt anything like this in my life, not for Sara or anyone else. It wasn't enjoyable exactly, but it was extremely powerful.

'I did something I shouldn't have done, though in fairness to myself I was barely conscious of doing it. In one of our phone calls I mentioned that Sara was going away for a week. I told Francesca I'd had a fantasy of spending that week with her, renting a car and heading out of the city at random, staying at motels . . . I didn't intend it as an invitation: it was just a way of expressing my feelings. But the morning after Sara left, the phone rang and there was Francesca's voice saying: 'Hi. It's me. I'm in New York.' She'd flown in from Ireland! I was stunned. I've never thought of myself as someone who has that kind of effect on women. But there she was!'

'Let's have a rest,' Victor said, panting from the uphill climb.

They'd come to a clearing in the woods where a farmhouse once stood. Slabs of bluestone from the old foundation had been set up by passing hikers to form a pair of throne-like seats. Victor sat on one, angling his face to a shaft of sunlight. Richard sat next to him, tucking the hem of his jacket beneath him on the cold stone.

'Go on.'

'Well. We spent the day in her hotel room consummating our affair and it was everything it could possibly be. I didn't even feel guilty, strangely enough. I was in a state of, I don't know, elation, or—'

'You were getting laid.'

'Well, it was more than just that. But that evening, when we went out to eat, I had an abrupt change of heart. I can still remember the exact moment: it was when the waiter came and lit the candle on our table. Something switched gear inside me. I tried to hide it, but by the end of the meal I was aware that I'd made a serious mistake. I felt terrible. There was this beautiful woman staring at me adoringly across the table, but all I could think was how to get back to my own apartment, alone, as quickly as possible. Somehow the prospect of spending the night with Francesca seemed a much greater betrayal of Sara than what had already happened. Or at least I managed to convince myself that if I *didn't* spend the night with her I'd be able to salvage something as far as my relationship with Sara was concerned. So ...'

'What?'

'I walked her to her hotel, and then ... told her it wasn't going to work.'

'No!'

'But it was for her sake also. I was from another world, Victor. She was young, nowhere near ready to settle down whether she realised it or not, and my idea had never been to throw away everything I had with Sara for the sake of a fling. That sounds calculating, but it was purely emotional. I wasn't the right man for this woman – I saw that suddenly very clearly, even if she didn't.'

'You're a piece of work, Richard!'

'It was appalling, what I did, every part of it. I know that. That's why I never told you about it at the time. And she – she understandably didn't take it all that well. There was some serious anger. Not screaming and yelling, but some real bitterness. Which I fully deserved. But that's pretty much it. I was offered the job up here that summer. I quit Ryden College, and never saw or heard from Francesca again. Sara and I got married that fall. And that's something I've never regretted. Not for one second. Which is the reason I'm telling you this.'

Victor frowned.

'I don't really see the connection.'

'It's the same situation.'

'No. It's the opposite of me and Oxana. She dumped me. If she hadn't I'd have held on to her whether I thought

I was the right man for her or not. I don't have your self-sacrificing instincts. It's not even a comparable situation.'

'Well, but it could be.'

'How?'

'If you'd just allow yourself to be content with what you have. A lovely wife, a home, a child. That's as good as life gets, Vic. Believe me. Why throw it away?'

Victor said nothing. The melancholy expression had returned to his face. The sun was going down behind the mountains. In shadow, the ruined walls of the farmhouse merged back into the rubble of rocks and scree they'd been built from. Thin grey trees grew out of the old cellar, snaking up over the weeds and brambles like solidified wisps of smoke.

Richard stood up from the cold stone seat, sensing obscurely that he was going to regret having told the story.

'Well,' he said. 'I guess we should get you to your train.'

****

Sara, Richard's wife, had been orphaned at the age of seven when a truck jackknifed across an icy road in Michigan, smashing into her parents' car on their way home from a church supper. Distant relatives – a couple in their fifties – had adopted her, bringing her to their home in rural Minnesota where they ran a mail-order garden supply business. At sixteen, when the local school proved unsatisfactory, she was sent to live with another set of relatives in Scarsdale: a podiatrist and his wife from whose quiet home she graduated from high school and commuted for several years to classes at Parsons and then the Cooper Union.

Each set of surrogate parents had treated her kindly, attending to her needs as scrupulously as if she had been their own daughter. Against the indelible stain of sadness left by her bereavement was a feeling of being cared for, and this peculiar combination had helped to determine a certain unconscious conception she'd formed early on of her own existence: an idea of herself as the concern of others; a belonging whose fate involved two essential gestures: being cherished and being handed on. She had been her parents' in Sioux City, then the Gardiners' in Minneapolis, the Bences' in Scarsdale ... And a few months after meeting Richard in New York, she had become Richard's.

In making herself over to him she had been swayed less by any overwhelming passion of her own than by his forceful certainty that she was the right person for him to be married to. Not that she hadn't considered herself to be in love – she had – but her own feelings had never seemed of great importance to her, and it was largely in deference to the vision Richard presented, of a definite scheme of things in his life, in which a definite place had been created for her, that she had deeded herself, so to speak, into his possession.

At the time she moved in with him she was completing a masters in textile design and had a job waiting for her with a company in Long Island City. Richard was doing a stint training teachers at Ryden College. She had known this was only a temporary stage in his career – part of a larger plan – but she'd been surprised at the abruptness with which he decided, a few months before their wedding, to quit the college. She was even more surprised when he asked her, a little later, how she would feel about moving upstate to a small town where he'd been offered the position of principal at an ailing private school. Despite the job waiting for her in Queens, and despite the fact that she'd never had any particular desire to live in the country, she'd agreed without hesitation.

In her careful, practical way, she had examined her options and decided to take up weaving. Richard's income was enough for them to live on comfortably, but she didn't like the thought of not earning. She'd had a small studio built next to the house they bought, installed a loom, and began producing rugs and hangings, selling them at craft fairs and local stores. In choosing this new occupation she'd had in mind something that would be compatible with looking after a child, and three years later, after Daniel was born, this proved to be the case. As an infant he had slept and nursed and played with balls of yarn in her studio while she worked. As a small boy he'd been her companion as she sat at stalls selling her pieces or went on her rounds to the breeders of the various exotic animals – llamas, vicunas, merino sheep – whose wool she used. This social aspect of her work was from the start more interesting to her than the weaving itself. She had a real curiosity about other people, and enjoyed her contact with the farmers and other craftspeople she got to know. Reticent as she was, she found that, given enough time in her quiet presence, people took to her.

The sudden absence of Daniel from her side, when he started going to school, had been a blow. She'd grown so used to doing everything with her small son that she'd come to think of the weaving itself as a joint occupation. There were the weekends, of course, and the vacations during which, for the first few years, he would faithfully resume his former position. But gradually, inevitably, and under her own conscientious encouragement, he had developed other interests – first soccer, then karate, now basketball – and now that he was almost eleven it had long been clear that that intimately shared phase of their lives was over.

She had gone on with the weaving, partly out of habit, and partly because she felt guilty not using the studio, which, as Richard had pointed out to her in a moment of uncharacteristic bluntness, cost more to build than a lifetime's production of rugs and hangings was ever likely to pay for.

But something in her had moved on, and even as she went through the motions of making new designs and working out their execution on the old wooden hand-loom, she knew that her heart was no longer in it and that for her, too, the time had come to embark on something new.

One afternoon in May the phone rang in her studio. It was Bonnie, one of the volunteers who worked for a neighbouring wildlife rehabilitator. Sara sometimes took in injured animals from the rehabilitator, a woman who'd moved to Aurelia a few years ago.

'Hey, Sara,' Bonnie said. 'Carla has some news for you. Wait one moment, I'll tell her I have you on the line.'

Sara waited.

'Sara?' came a commanding voice. 'We have someone very special for you to meet.'

'Oh?'

'Royalty, my dear. You'll see. Can you come right away?'

'Okay.'

'We'll expect you shortly.'

Sara put down the ball of yarn she'd been threading onto her loom and went outside. It was a mild, cloudless day, and she was glad of an excuse to take a walk. She set off, smiling as she thought how typical it was of Carla to make a mystery of whatever creature she was summoning her to look at now.

Originally she'd agreed to take in these injured animals purely out of a sense of neighbourly obligation, but she'd soon discovered a taste for it. She seemed to have a knack for handling them. Her slow physical gestures and patient manner put them at their ease. They trusted her and repaid her attentions with clamorous attentions of their own that might have been no more than need but felt like affection. She liked getting out of the car when she came home and having a crow she'd nursed to health come flapping across the yard to land on her arm with a squawk, or a pair of orphaned squirrels she'd brought up run chattering down from their box in the horse chestnut tree and follow her to the door. Often the animals stayed around the house or came to visit, long after she had released them. There was a robin that returned every year and would still eat mealworms out of her hand. A buck she'd taken in as a fawn after coyotes killed its mother would sometimes materialise before her in the woods, standing there for a moment as if just to show himself.

The walk to Carla's led through woods of maple and ash. It was cool in their shadow, but currents of warm air drifted through, carrying the scent of leaf mould. A woodpecker drilled into a tree, loud as a jackhammer.

In twenty minutes she arrived at Carla's house, stepping out into the backyard and making her way past the ramshackle outbuildings.

Bonnie, the volunteer, opened a door in the side of the big-bellied red barn, greeting Sara with her usual look of faintly disconcerting mirth.

'Hey there!'

Bonnie was thirty maybe, with hennaed black hair cut in wisps, a notched silver feather dangling from each ear, dark eyes, sharp cheekbones.

'How're you doing? How's Rich?'

Bonnie, Sara remembered, was putting a daughter through Richard's school. She and the girl had recently moved to a cabin here on Carla's property, which Carla let her have for free in return for the chores she did.

'We're well. How are you? How's Caya?'

'She's great. We both are.'

There were two other women in the dimly lit interior of the barn; youngish, semi-indigent wanderers. Rainbow People, they called themselves. A steady stream of them drifted through Aurelia every spring and summer, camping in the woods and hanging out on the village green. Carla often had a few of them working for her. One, a redhead in dungarees whom Bonnie introduced as Tasha, was hosing down cages on the unfloored area at the back. The other, Jo, plump and pale with eyebrow rings and a tie-dye belly shirt, was feeding chopped fish to a family of possums.

'Carla will be right along,' Bonnie said, plugging in earbuds. 'Make yourself at home.' She danced off to the kitchen area where she began mixing seeds in tofu buckets.

Carla was seldom in a room when you entered it, Sara had noticed: it was *she* who had to make the entrance.

Waiting, she wandered from cage to cage in the timbered gloom of the barn with its watchful presences. A fledgling cardinal gaped its mouth as she approached. A rabbit limped to the back of its cage on three legs. Next along was a sleeping barn owl with a bandaged claw; its flat, kabuki-mask face with the strange recessed beak pale

18

and motionless above its perch. Carla claimed that the face of these owls had evolved this way to resemble the disc-shaped scars of paler wood on tree trunks where branches have fallen. Long ago, she had offered this and other observations for publication to a number of scientific journals, without success: part of an ancient conspiracy, she claimed, to 'deny permission' to lay naturalists like herself. Staring at the owl, Sara could half-see Carla's point, just as she could half-believe in the existence of this conspiracy to 'deny permission'. But the other half of her reserved judgement.

She was an odd mixture, Carla, of the down-to-earth and the pretentious. The ex-wife of a state official in Albany, she had arrived in Aurelia five years after Richard and Sara, settling in the farmhouse at the top of their mountain road, where she'd embarked on a fairly public process of self-transformation, from a solitary, forlornly dignified figure still wearing the matronly uniforms of a former political hostess, to what could only be described as a New Age Priestess. She'd stopped dyeing her hair and let it grow long, which gave her broad face, with its sharp blue eyes and prominent, aquiline nose, the look of a cigar store chief. The well-pressed blouses and skirts were exchanged for robe-like outfits accented with large runic bracelets and rings.

She began giving talks at the town hall and the Ahimsa Yogaprananda bookstore – on Tibetan chanting, Siberian Shamanism, Native American healing practices, her own experiences in reincarnation. Flyers with her picture on them, advertising the talks, became a fixture on the town's public bulletin boards. At a certain point she appeared to have decided it was necessary to extend her sphere of influence beyond the sizeable 'spiritual community' (as it called itself) of Aurelia, into the animal kingdom, getting herself certified as a wildlife rehabilitator; a move whose practical utility caught her detractors off their guard, though it didn't diminish their scorn.

Among these detractors was Richard, a fact always troublingly present in Sara's mind when she thought about the woman. He found her ridiculous – a self-aggrandising narcissist, motivated simply by a crude hunger for admiration, and a desire to have people in thrall to her, by whatever means. According to him she had merely identified the easiest route to prominence in Aurelia, with its large number of well-meaning, semi-educated people who regarded themselves as too smart to be taken in by the traditional sources of authority and were thus natural targets for every kind of charlatanism. As it happened, Sara didn't altogether disagree with him, and yet she found herself drawn to the woman nevertheless, and, for reasons she didn't quite understand, fascinated by her.

She claimed to have majored in natural sciences at college, and there was a bookshelf here in the barn full of books on natural history, though the more well-thumbed among them tended to have titles like *Wolves and Other Spirits*, or *The Gospel of the Raven*. She'd given one to Sara as a present once, *Soul Makers*. It was a memoir of a woman's recovery from drug addiction through encounters with various animal 'healers'; very corny and shamelessly anthropomorphic, but Sara had found herself unexpectedly riveted by it, much to Richard's dismay. To placate him she'd agreed to read a book that he said had purged him of the last traces of his own lingering religiosity, leaving him, he claimed, with a paradoxically deeper appreciation of the natural world.

She moved on, listening to the girls talking and laughing, watching Bonnie sway to her silent music as she dipped her scoop into the paper sacks of seed and emptied it into the white buckets, dust and chaff rising up into the high beams of sunlight.

She liked being here – the quiet, easy sociability of people working together at something they enjoyed was a congenial element to her; more so, these days, than the solitude of her studio.

Next to the owl were empty cages, then a groundhog, nervously sniffing at her from behind its bars; a soft-looking smudge of an animal, like a brown shadow. A blowfly infection bulged under its forearm. She gazed in, settling the agitated creature with soothing whispers. A few years ago Richard had caught one of these in his vegetable garden; trapping it in a Havahart live trap. Sara had called Carla to ask what they should do with it. She'd told them to free it at once as it was either a baby that needed its mother, or a parent needed by its babies. When Richard picked up the extension to ask what he was supposed to do, in that case, about his vegetables, Carla had told him to find the burrow and talk to the animals; maybe ask them to just take the first plant in each row and leave the rest alone. She'd offered to come up and talk to them herself, even do a little ceremony in the garden with her bells.

His contempt for her dated from then.

Stepping away from the groundhog, Sara came to the cage where the girl with the eyebrow rings was feeding possums. The girl grinned at her.

'Carla says these babies'll just start eating each other if I stop feeding them before they're done.'

'What happened to them?'

'Some asshole must've ran his truck over their mother – she was squished flat with her eyes all bugged out – but these three guys still alive at the back holding onto her tail. Isn't that so cute? They were the size of my pinkie. Now they'd tear my pinkie right off if I let them near it!'

The girl gave a peal of giggles. The possums cringed back. Looking at them in their steel cage Sara thought of an image in the book Richard had made her read; an update on Darwinian theory in the light of modern discoveries about genes. In it the author invited the reader to regard all living creatures as occupants of a vast mathematical grid in which every combination of the sixty-four 'words' in the universal genetic dictionary had its own niche. Empty niches represented combinations that had failed to create viable organisms. Inhabited ones were those that had succeeded. The 'words' had no meaning: they were just molecular patterns that happened to have this property of self-replication, as other patterns might have the property, say, of adhesiveness. Plants and animals were therefore just complicated pieces of packaging evolved over time by natural selection for the chance advantages they offered in regard to the perpetuation of this arbitrary genetic code: that was all. So that to allow oneself to be 'moved' by them, to experience tenderness or wonder in their presence, was to succumb to an illusion.

Sara had known all this, more or less, from high school biology, but the book's relentless lucidity had brought it home to her with an unnerving force. For a while every time she looked at an animal she'd felt obliged to remind herself that the sympathy rising in her was being stimulated by an object that was nothing more than a mathematical formula applied in a physical universe over a vast amount of time. Eventually she had overcome this depressing compulsion with the thought that since she, by the same token, was also just the result of a mathematical formula applied in a physical universe over a vast amount of time, she was entitled to her feelings. But the image of that matrix or grid came to her often as she looked down the rows of cages in Carla's barn, and there were moments, like this one right now, staring at these otherworldly opossums with their long white tapering faces, eyes close together like the seeds in a halved pear, when she seemed to glimpse the strange, desolate reality described in Richard's book.

The door at the side of the barn opened and there stood Carla.

'There you are,' she said, peering at Sara in the dim space. 'He's ready. Come.'

Her voice was deep, with an imperiousness that people sometimes made fun of, though Sara herself enjoyed the sensation of being ordered around by it. She followed her out of the barn.

'I hope the girls didn't spoil our surprise,' Carla said.

'No.'

'Good.'

Though she was only a fraction taller than Sara, Carla's regal bearing gave an illusion of much greater height. Her long hair hung in two thick, white wings either side of her weather-bronzed face. She led Sara towards the house; a sprawling building with dark-stained cedar plank walls and green-framed windows.

'How is your husband?' she asked.

'He's – okay.'

'Stressed, is he?' Carla said, picking up on the slight hesitation in Sara's voice.

'I wouldn't say that. Just overworked.'

'More than usual?'

'Maybe.'

For some time Sara had felt a desire on Carla's part to draw her out on the subject of Richard. She resisted, scrupulously discreet in such matters, confining herself to the vaguest of comments. But the slight sensation of pressure was not unpleasant. It seemed to bring things into consciousness. She hadn't known, for instance, that she'd noticed anything wrong with Richard, but she became aware of it now. He'd been distracted lately, she realised, and irritable. She didn't know why, but assumed he would tell her when he was ready. He always did.

At the back door, Carla paused to replenish several bird-feeders. The wild birds feeding at them flew off into the bushes but a mass of half-tame ones, released from Carla's infirmary but still being fed, fluttered around their benefactor while she scooped and poured out the new seed; goldfinches, blue jays, scarlet tanagers, indigo buntings, alighting on her shoulders and outstretched arms like so many adoring seraphim.

'I experienced my husband as a greyness towards the end,' she said. She was given to such pronouncements. 'I couldn't admit to myself that he was my enemy. Not in a personal sense, but as a man married to a woman past reproductive age. The relationship is strictly one of hostility, zoologically speaking. I don't think he realised it either. Not in his head, anyway.'

Sara nodded, saying nothing.

'In a context,' Carla continued, sliding the last feeder up its pole and resuming her stately progress around the outside of the house, 'where one no longer has a function decreed by nature, one is faced with a choice between a futile struggle against obsolescence, or changing the context. I changed the context.'

Well, you had it changed for you, Sara thought, applying Richard's sceptical viewpoint again, while nevertheless weighing Carla's words in a silence of her own. Like much of what Carla said, there was something that, despite the grandiosity, aroused her interest.

Coming to a side door in one of the many extensions protruding from the house, Carla put a finger to her lips.

'He may be sleeping. Or she, we're not sure.'

The door opened onto a cement-floored room; wet-smelling, with a vague aqueous sweetness in the dim air. There was a wide galvanised steel pail filled with water and green weeds in the centre, and beyond it a bed of straw on which something white stirred, raising a dark-eyed head on a sinuous, luminously pale neck.

The two women hung in the doorway a moment, while the creature peered at them through the gloom. Then Carla moved slowly towards it, making low, soothing murmurs. 'There, yes, yes ...'

It was a swan. The tall stem of its neck swayed back a little as Carla approached, as if on some soft surge in the air, but it seemed to accept her as she came close.

'There, yes, yes, you know me, don't you? Yes, you do, you do ...'

She lowered herself beside it on the straw.

'He was found on one of those big estates on the other side of the river. His leg was fractured. We think in a fight with a trumpeter swan. He's a mute — you can tell by the bulb on his bill, see? The Fish and Wildlife department have been trying to supplant them with trumpeters for years. They claim the mutes are an invasive species, which is nonsense as I've explained in numerous online articles, though of course they have a long-standing policy at the department to ignore everything I write. It's clear to me they're supporting the trumpeters simply because they're bigger and more aggressive. Which is a drama we seem compelled to enact over and over in this country ...'

It was typical of Carla to elevate whatever she did into an act of resistance in some large battle of good and evil. Richard would have taken the words as further evidence of her insufferable narcissism. And he'd be right, Sara thought; there was something absurdly self-dramatising about her.

'The fracture's healing well. I was thinking, Sara, you might want to take him on yourself at this point.'

'Yes,' Sara said at once. She'd had no experience with a wild creature this size, and was in fact frightened at the idea of it. You heard of people being attacked by these birds; wing-blows hard enough to crack a rib. But the assent had seemed to rise in her of its own accord, voicing itself without hesitation.

'Good. Then come say hello.'

Sara stepped quietly across the cement floor. Again the slight backward surge in the bird's S-shaped neck, this time accompanied by a low sound, part moan, part hiss. Sara paused while Carla calmed the animal: 'Shh, there, it's okay. She's our friend. Yes, she is, she is ... They call them mute but they speak perfectly well, as you can hear. Just not as loudly as the trumpeters. Come, I want you to hold him.'

The bird stared fixedly at Sara as she came over and crouched down.

'Talk to him.'

Sara murmured her own soothing sounds. It seemed to her the animal was taking her measure on some finely tuned instrument of appraisal. Its dark, round eyes gazed directly into hers. Between Carla's flamboyance and the creature's own vivid presence, Sara felt herself to be a subdued figure in the scene; barely pencilled in.

'He accepts you,' Carla said. It sounded, characteristically, more like a decree than an observation.

'Now hold him. Put your arms over his wings – firmly, go on.'

Sara moved swiftly, before her fear could get the better of her. Kneeling above the swan she placed her arms around the boat-like mass of its body. Immediately it rose up on its feet, its folded wings shuddering powerfully against her, the weapon-like hardness of the bones unmistakable under its stiff, crisp feathers. Her heart reacted with its own shudder, but she held on, murmuring softly: 'It's okay, it's okay.'

'Lift him,' Carla commanded.

Surely not, Sara thought; the wings had stopped thrusting out, but she could feel the agitation still bristling through the creature's body. And yet, as she did as Carla instructed, she sensed an effort to cooperate in spite of its alarm; a kind of bracing of itself against her, as if to enlist her steadiness against its own impulse to escape.

Below it the webbed feet hung, incongruously utilitarian in appearance, like little flat-footed rubber waders. Carla took one in her hand and very gently stretched it to its full length. The bird tugged it back from her grasp.

'You see? He's getting his strength back. You'll have him shipshape again in no time. I know you will.'

2

Victor had moved back in with Audrey. He called to tell Richard the news.

'I took your advice. Don't crow about it though. Well, all right, you can crow.'

'Are you happy?'

'Of course I'm happy. I wouldn't be here if I wasn't.'

'I'm really pleased then. How's Audrey?'

'She's wonderful. We're fucking all over the furniture again. It's like having a second honeymoon.'

'Try not to break anything.'

'Ha. By the way, what was the name of that girl you so cruelly jilted?'

'Francesca . . . ?'

'Yeah. Francesca what?'

'Sullivan. Why?'

'She's playing a club in Tribeca next month. Take Five. I saw her name on the schedule.'

'Must be a different Francesca Sullivan. She went back to Cork.'

'Francesca Sullivan, from Cork, Ireland. That's what the listing said.'

'Huh.'

'Shouldn't be hard to find out if it's her.'

Richard heard keys being tapped the other end.

'Are you by a screen? I sent you the listing.'

A moment later a head shot of Francesca, along with the listing details, appeared on Richard's laptop screen.

'That her?' Victor asked.

'Yes.'

'Very nice. You go up a notch in my estimation.'

Richard stared silently into his screen. It was the first time he had seen Francesca's face in more than ten years.

'Think you'll come down?'

'No.'

'Why not?'

'A little hypocritical, don't you think, after my sermon to you?'

'Like I'd give a damn!'

'Well, I would.'

They talked about other things, but it was extremely hard for Richard to pay attention.

The fact was, he had been assailed by thoughts of Francesca ever since confiding in Victor about the affair that day in March, and this sudden appearance of her image on his screen sent a shock of emotion through him. He had kept the episode to himself all these years, not so much out of shame (as he'd claimed to Victor) as out of the simple wish to protect his own peace of mind. Silence had seemed a way of limiting its purchase on reality and, by extension, its power to unsettle him. Extremely turbulent feelings – infatuation, guilt, the sensation of being almost physically torn in two by his split allegiances – had been bound up in the affair. His marriage had required that he lay them to rest; not just in order to conceal the deception, but because he had genuinely wanted to build his life as a father and husband on an uncompromised foundation. He'd succeeded, but it had been an almighty struggle.

It had been stupid of him to reopen the subject. Not that he was superstitious, but there was such a thing as tempting fate, and it had seemed an obvious mistake to expose, even to his closest friend, the emotions of an old affair in which the stakes had been so precisely fateful. He'd regretted it at the time, sensing it almost immediately as a self-inflicted breach in his own defences. And now, seeing Francesca on his screen, he felt even worse. He wouldn't have been thinking about her all these weeks if he hadn't blabbed to Victor, and he certainly would have been spared this disturbing and somehow illicit knowledge that she was back in New York. The internet's power to exhume people from their tombs in one's long ago past was something he instinctively disliked; a kind of necromancy. But here she was; her grey-green eyes smiling warmly back into his, as if she knew he was looking at her.

He exited abruptly from the page.

For a few days he convinced himself he had no interest in going down to see her. Even when he was forced to acknowledge that this wasn't the case, he was able to take refuge in the absolute certainty that he had no intention of actually doing it. Then, as this certainty began to corrode, he took himself more sternly in hand. It was folly to think of seeing Francesca again after all these years, he told himself. Even if by some miracle she'd forgiven him, which he doubted, what could it possibly accomplish? What would he even *want* it to accomplish? He was content in his marriage, loved being a father, enjoyed the tranquil stability of their home. Why jeopardise this? Why do something so purely and obviously destructive?

Two weeks passed. He succeeded in putting the subject out of his mind, more or less. Then one morning he saw a notice of an exhibition of Transcendentalist manuscripts coming up at the Morgan Library. At college he'd made a study of the Transcendentalists, and was still strongly drawn to their aura of dynamic innocence. If he could choose his own epitaph, even now it would be the line from Thoreau's journal: 'I wished to ally myself to the powers that rule the universe.'

He mentioned the show to Sara, casually, adding that he wasn't sure he had the time or energy to go down and see it.

'Of course you should go,' she said without hesitation. 'You should definitely go.'

It was exactly what he'd expected her to say.

On a Saturday afternoon near the end of June he took the train into New York. He'd arranged to have dinner with Victor and Audrey after seeing the exhibition, and he told Sara he'd be home late.

A feeling of faint stealth hovered at the edge of his consciousness as he travelled down. He tried to ignore it, but he was distinctly on edge by the time he got off the train at Penn Station.

The library was quiet, almost empty. Handwritten lecture notes, diaries open on famous observations, autographed letters, were laid out in glass cabinets, along with daguerreotypes of their mild-eyed authors. In a clearer mood Richard might have enjoyed it all. He'd often suspected that his own temperament would have suited him better for that age than the present one, which in his heart of hearts he found almost entirely repellent. Alcott and Emerson, Muir, Fuller, Thoreau, were the figures who spoke to him in his deepest nature. For them the question of active goodness was still crucial; vital enough to restore some actual practical function to the religious instinct, even in the absence of any plausible divinity. Somehow in the company of these figures you could maintain a sense of the sacred, without having to relinquish your basic rationality. As far as he was concerned nothing had come along since them that fulfilled those paradoxical but – for him – elemental needs.

But he was too distracted to appreciate any of this right now. If he hadn't told Sara he was going, he would have skipped the show altogether. Not that she was likely to question him, but he felt obscurely that he owed it to her to follow his own script as closely as possible.

He looked at a letter about the Fruitlands farm, one of Alcott's attempts at building a utopian community. Richard had always been immensely receptive to the idea of these quixotic projects, but somehow he couldn't work up any interest at the moment. 'Plain garments,' he read, 'pure bathing, unsullied dwellings, open conduct, gentle behavior, kindly sympathies and pure minds.' The words seemed inert; remote from him as hieroglyphs from some dead language. He went and sat in a café, and then walked slowly downtown to Victor and Audrey's, stopping on the way to buy flowers.

Victor came to the door carrying his daughter under one arm. He looked great: clean-shaven, his broad red cheeks healthy rather than hectic.

'Come on in!'

With his free arm he hugged Richard, almost crushing the flowers.

Audrey came through from the kitchen, an apron over her neatly pressed blouse and skirt. She greeted Richard warmly, thanking him for the flowers. She looked well too: her dark eyes shining.

She led the way back through the narrow rooms. The place – the same dingy railroad apartment Victor had inhabited since his twenties – was a shambles: toys and books all over the floor, piles of dirty laundry, overflowing ashtrays. Audrey, so spruce in herself, appeared not to notice; either that or she had made an accommodation with Victor's capacity for generating chaos.

At dinner it turned out there were other reasons for Victor's cheerfulness besides the restored domestic harmony. His career had taken some unexpected new turns. He'd been offered a column on New York nightlife for an English newspaper. And he'd been commissioned to write a book on Scandinavian jazz, an old interest of his.

'That's wonderful!' Richard heard himself saying several times.

There was more too. After they'd finished eating, and Audrey had taken the child off to bed, Victor leaned conspiratorially across the table.

'She's pregnant.'

'Audrey?'

'Who else, jackass?'

'That's wonderful!'

'I wasn't supposed to tell you yet, but what the hell.'

'This is great news! I'm thrilled.'

'I'm thrilled too,' Victor laughed, throwing back his large head. 'So's Audrey. She's over the moon.'

'I thought she looked sort of glowing.'

'I didn't think I'd want another little brat climbing all over the place but I seem to be relishing the prospect. I must be getting soft. You approve?'

'Of course I approve, Victor.'

'Good. Now tell me what's eating *you* up.'

'What do you mean?'

'Richard, I can read you like a book. What's going on?'

'Nothing ...'

'Let me guess. The Irish girl. You got in touch.'

'Very funny.'

'Wait a minute. Wasn't it this week she was playing at that club?' Victor took out his iPhone. A narrow smile appeared on his face. 'It's tonight.'

'Oh.'

'Is that why you're in town, Richard?'

'No! I came down for the show at the Morgan. And to see you.'

'Well, what a coincidence.'

Richard frowned. Since he had formed no actual plan to see Francesca's show — hadn't bought a ticket or said anything to Victor about going — he could tell himself truthfully that he had no intention of going. It was necessary, for the sake of his conscience, to be able to stave off any suspicion of premeditation. If he did end up at the club, he wanted to be able to feel that it had come about spontaneously, and preferably under duress.

'Well, since you happen to be here,' Victor continued, 'why don't you go?'

'No. I couldn't.'

'Why not?'

'Oh, you know — I'd feel too strange ... What would I tell Sara?'

'Don't tell her anything.'

'No. I'd feel furtive. A married man sneaking off alone to see an old lover ...'

'Want me to go with you? Make it more of a social thing?'

Richard paused. The scenario he had envisioned, complete with Victor talking him into going, and even offering to come with him, was forming itself almost too easily. He would have liked a few more obstacles in the path.

'What about Audrey?'

'What about her?'

'She won't mind being left behind?'

'Don't be ridiculous.'

'Well ...'

'Come on. You'll regret it if you don't.'

'But I'm very comfortable with regret.'

'Richard. Get your fucking coat on.'

A few minutes later they were in a taxi, Canal Street's cheap stores giving way to the sleeker blocks of Tribeca.

The club, marked by a small awning, was down some stairs in a small, packed room with a spotlit stage at the back. At the centre, seated on a tall stool, was Francesca, wearing a green silk dress.

She was singing in a low voice, with a slow, syncopated beat from the band behind her. It wasn't the kind of singing she used to do in the group she and Richard had played in together back at Ryden College: bluegrass and Gaelic music with its three or four chord changes and correspondingly simple emotions. Either the listing hadn't mentioned it or else Richard had missed, somehow, that she had become a jazz singer.

She glanced through the lights in their direction as he and Victor squeezed through the tables. As he sat down, Richard caught her eye and for a moment a look of shock appeared on her face. Almost immediately, however, she turned the look into one of delighted amazement, dropping her jaw, hamming it up a little.

'Well, well. I've just seen an old pal of mine,' she said into the mike. She smiled again at Richard: 'Evenin' there ...'

He nodded back, acutely self-conscious, but also relieved. He really had been afraid he might get a hostile reception.

From her exaggerated accent, he recognised an old game she liked to play among New Yorkers – 'putting on the Irish', she used to call it.

She looked very self-possessed in her sheath of green silk, legs crossed with a high-heeled shoe dangling from a toe. Her strong, high-cheekboned face was sculpted a little cleaner than he remembered, so that her expressions appeared more sharply drawn. But her hair was the same wild, unruly mass, brown with gold glints in it, tumbling down over her shoulders.

The band had begun playing an instrumental passage to which she was laconically snapping the fingers of one hand. With the other she raised the microphone to her lips and picked up the lyric again. *Couldn't they do away ... with April ... Leave no space ... so there's no trace ... of April ...* The melody, intricately at odds with what the ear expected, flowed from her with the same unaffected clarity as in her Ryden College days. But at the same time the music, with its off beats and diminished chords, was so absolutely strange in relation to the Francesca he had known, it was as if she were revealing some entirely new aspect of her personality. The song petered out, dispersing into broken phrases, snare-drum rustles, stray tinklings on the piano.

Then on some invisible signal the instruments began reconverging, the more urgent beat of a new number kicking in with a slapped thump of bass notes bouncing against a Latin-sounding pattern on the drums ... *I don't know what to think ... About anything any more* ... She grinned, eyes half-closed. *The things I used to enjoy ... A sip of my favourite drink ... A kiss from my favourite boy* ... Her voice itself, Richard realised, while it still carried the unmistakable imprint of her warm-humoured, self-mocking personality, had changed too: deepened in timbre, acquired an expressiveness that gave a precise definition to every shift in the song's rapid flux of moods while at the same time salting each note with a half-amused irony. *Yesterday they thrilled me ... Today I find them a bore ...*

He gazed at her, riveted. What had happened to her? What seas had she swum in since that night they parted company in New York, eleven years ago? He sipped at his drink: a bourbon he'd ordered in deference to the atmosphere of the place, even though hard liquor didn't agree with him.

At the end of the set she came to their table, greeting Richard with what appeared to be uncomplicated pleasure.

'Richard! What a lovely surprise!'

'Well, I saw the listing ... Thought I'd catch you while you're over.'

'Over? I'm living here. Been back almost two years. We have some catching up to do, mister!'

He introduced her to Victor, who had sat expressionlessly through the performance, but now, to Richard's relief (he could be painfully candid) complimented her.

'Nice songs. Some Sarah Vaughan in there, right? One or two I didn't recognise. Did you write them yourself?'

'Aha, yes, busted, guilty as charged. I did, I did.'

She seemed a little giddy; no doubt on a high from her performance. She signalled a waiter, then rested her hand on Richard's.

'You haven't changed a bit, Richard.'

'Nor have you.'

She was looking into his eyes, her own shining with an almost disconcerting intensity.

'Victor's writing a book on jazz,' he heard himself say. 'Scandinavian jazz, right, Vic?'

She turned to Victor.

'Is that right? Funny – I was at the Dyllmar Hotel just last summer with a whole bunch of them fellers. Lars Gullen, Ulf Adgaard ...'

'The jazz hotel?' Victor asked. 'In Stockholm?'

'That's the one.'

'I was there. The same weekend.'

'No!'

'I was. I was there for the Lars Gullen concert.'

'No kidding.' She turned back to Richard. 'Glad you've friends with some taste in music!'

He smiled, not trusting himself to speak. His head felt thick with some dizzying sweetness.

'Too bad they closed the place down,' Victor said.

'What? They did not! Tell me they did not close down the Dyllmar Hotel!' Her hair swung across her bare shoulder as she turned again. Gazing at it, Richard remembered the time he had found himself plying his fingers through it. His hand itself seemed to recall the sensation, with its own strange ache of nostalgia.

'It's a shame, I know,' Victor was saying.

'That's puttin' it mildly! I loved that place.'

'Me too ...'

They talked about this hotel that they both knew — evidently a place of considerable bohemian glamour, and from there they moved on to other subjects: musicians they both liked, new clubs in Harlem and Hoboken.

Richard listened, contentedly. Victor was on good form: always a pleasure to observe. There was never any pretence with Victor. When he was down he looked like a bum. But when he was up there was something splendid about him. His large belly under the spotless cream linen shirt he was wearing, the mottled flesh of his skin bulging over the buttoned collar, gave an impression of bursting vigour rather than excessive weight. His broad shoulders shook frequently with rich laughter. But it was his eyes above all that illuminated his singular spirit of revelry. Like those of mystics or people susceptible to hypnosis, they rolled upward at moments of high animation, with an uninhibited ease that suggested he was perhaps never very far from a state of ecstatic trance. Up they went now, as Francesca finished an anecdote about a dancer who'd done a strip act with a vacuum cleaner at some burlesque evening, sucking the clothes off herself piece by piece. 'Cherry Chakravarti,' Victor said, laughing in recognition, a brief delirious rolling whiteness visible over the lower lids of his eyes. 'I saw her in Vancouver. She's very funny ...'

Smiling along, Richard was conscious of the extent to which he had withdrawn from this cosmopolitan world of theirs with its dense circuitry of entertainments and personalities. More and more, the minds of city-dwellers seemed to him like the buildings they inhabited: strange artifical miracles of integration and compactness. As in the city itself, so in these minds there appeared to be no empty space, no contour that wasn't shaped in response to the lives crowded around it, no tolerance for anything that wasn't purposeful, brisk, decisive. Since moving to Aurelia he had felt the pace of his own mind relaxing, the clutter emptying out. The children at his school kept him abreast of the names of new celebrities and fashions, but beyond that he'd more or less cut himself off from popular culture. They had no TV at home, and only a dial-up internet connection. The books he read were almost all written in the nineteenth or early twentieth century. The only CDs he'd bought in recent years were Smithsonian archival recordings of railroad and mining songs.

Was it possible, he wondered, that he had become a little too complacently detached in his rural retreat? Certainly he would have liked to be able to contribute more to the conversation right now. But on the other hand, there was something that suited his conception of himself, in being perceived as somehow above or beyond these matters … Francesca turned his wrist over to look at his watch.

'Time to get back to work. Can you stick around? We finish at eleven. Maybe have another drink?'

'Definitely,' Richard said as he calculated how much time this would leave him to catch his train.

'Smashing.'

She went back up onstage.

Victor turned to him.

'Want me to leave?'

'No. Why?'

'Well … Put it this way, I think she's forgiven you.'

Richard smiled.

'Stay,' he said.

The music began again. Francesca stood now instead of sitting, casually magnetising the attention of the room onto herself as she moved lightly to the beat. *What was I ever ... but a ghost to you ... a mist of dreams ... the colour blue ...* The silk dress, clinging to the curves of her body, made her look fuller in the figure than Richard remembered; voluptuous almost. Between that and her playful rapport with her band, all men, it seemed clear to him that she had fully embraced, as the phrase went, her own femininity. Not that she had exactly been inhibited before. He remembered the day they'd spent in her hotel room in New York. The room itself had become a kind of charged space in his mind: one that he'd done his dutiful best to keep closed since getting married. It opened now as he watched her, and it seemed to him he was there inside it again, taking in the unmade bed, black dresser, orange velour wingback chair and Francesca herself, not in a green silk dress but an old faded T-shirt, throwing her arms around him as he came through the door, her mouth opening on his, her mass of hair enveloping him in the clove-scented perfume she wore at that time ...

She'd bought champagne at the duty free. She opened the bottle, pouring it into plastic cups from the bathroom — too fast, the foam spilling over onto the dresser top. She was in an exuberant state, just as she had been here in the club tonight; high on the audacity of what she had done. And a little manically intent on seeing that the occasion lived up to the extreme measures she'd taken to engineer it.

No doubt foreseeing some resistance on Richard's part, she had put herself into a doting, worshipful frame of mind. He remembered vividly the effect this had on him. He'd never thought of himself as particularly receptive to the suggestion of subservience in a woman, but the many variations Francesca played on this attitude that afternoon had aroused him like nothing before or since, branding onto his psyche a series of incandescently erotic images. One in particular, in which, whether by accident or design, he'd been confronted by the image of himself behind her in the mirror, her breasts heavy and yielding in his hands, had seemed the promise of an existence founded on pure bliss.

And yet he had rejected this existence. The reasons he'd given Victor for his change of heart — his sudden sense of the disparity in circumstance between himself and Francesca; the tug of loyalty he'd felt towards Sara — were accurate, at least to the extent that they were how he'd explained it to himself. But he'd always felt that they weren't quite adequate to the extreme nature of his reaction; that some other, less rational force must have been obscurely at work. And as he thought back to that moment in the stucco-walled restaurant, when the waiter had lit their candle and the look of pure love had appeared on Francesca's face, and he had felt, suddenly, an overwhelming desire to extricate himself from the situation, it seemed to him they explained nothing at all.

What had he been recoiling from? In hindsight his behaviour seemed to him unnatural, freakish almost, and utterly mysterious. Cringing at his coldness, he remembered the little speech he had made after they'd walked back to Francesca's hotel, where she was evidently expecting him to stay the night. He had been 'impulsive', he told her. He'd put them both 'in danger of making a grave mistake'. He needed to 'step back and think about what had happened …' In an attempt to soften the apparently devastating impact of his words on Francesca, he'd offered to go for a long walk in the park with her the next day, and talk things over. But when he called early the following morning she'd gone: disappeared like the seal maiden in one of the ballads she used to sing.

The second set ended at almost ten past eleven: he had under half an hour to get to Penn Station. Francesca was making her way over to their table. He shouldn't have agreed to stay: better to have left gracefully earlier than put himself in a situation from which he was once again going to have to make an abrupt exit. He was about to stand and make his excuses when their waiter appeared with glasses of champagne.

'This is on me, fellers,' Francesca said, throwing herself into a chair. Her face was flushed, her eyes sparkling. 'All that exercise makes a girl thirsty. Cheers now!'

The three of them touched glasses and drank, Richard glancing uneasily at his watch. He could stay over with Victor, he supposed, but there was no spare room and Victor's sofa-bed, he knew from experience, was filthy and uncomfortable. Anyway, he had to be at work early the next morning.

'So Richard,' Francesca was saying, 'do you think I've come on a bit since the old days?' She turned to Victor: 'Richard and I used to play together in a folk ensemble. I was the damsel with a dulcimer. Richard was our unofficial musical director. Kept us all tidily in step on those old-time tunes of his ...' She waved a pretend baton, singing in a high voice that made people at the next table turn: '*Cumberland Gap is a noted place ... Three kinds of water to wash your face ...* Not that I didn't bring along some pretty hokey stuff of my own. But it was great fun all the same. Was it not, Richard?'

'It was.'

'Those were the days, right?'

'They were,' he answered her. 'But listen, Francesca. I have to go. I feel terrible, but I have to be on a train in twenty minutes.'

'Well, goodness, why didn't you say so, you absurd man? We'll drink up our medicine here, then get you a taxi.'

She knocked back the rest of her champagne. He didn't know whether to be relieved or hurt that she wasn't more upset at his hurry to be gone. 'Come on! Come on!' she was saying. 'Coats. Wallets. Briefcase ...' She bustled him and Victor out through the club. A moment later she was flagging down a taxi on Varick Street.

'Quick. In you get, sir!'

They embraced.

Victor climbed in beside him.

'You can drop me off somewhere.'

Richard stuck his head out of the window.

'Shall we stay in touch this time?'

'Well now, that's your call I'd say, wouldn't you?'

'Give me your number.'

He keyed her number into his phone and waved goodbye as the taxi pulled off.

'Nice person,' Victor said, sprawling back in the seat. 'Talented too.'

'Well, thanks for coming along.' Richard said, vaguely. He was turning her last words over in his mind – *that's your call I'd say, wouldn't you?* – feeling the gentle reproach in them but also, he sensed, the invitation.

****

Sara had installed the swan in her studio, moving the loom to one side, covering the floor with newspaper and setting up the straw bedding next to a zinc water-trough. It liked to dunk its cresses and duck-pellets in the water before eating them. Swiftly, and with a willingness she couldn't quite account for, she grew attached to it, drawn to its presence as if by an enchantment.

Richard had come to see it the first evening, back in May. Despite his dislike for Carla he was usually careful to encourage Sara's involvement with these injured creatures. It seemed important to him to be thought of as a lover of animals, although the truth, as Sara had realised some time ago, was that he was nervous of them – squeamish about feather-mites, deer-ticks, bacteria; afraid of being scratched or bitten. Out of sheer determination he would sometimes force himself to handle one of them; stroke it or even pick it up. She appreciated these gestures, but it was a bit dismaying to observe the effort they took.

Hanging back in the doorway of her studio, he made the usual approving noises, admiring the swan's beauty, even suggesting Sara call Deirdre Wagoner, the science teacher at his school, to arrange for the children to see it. But as he stared across the room at the pale creature sitting motionless on its bed of straw, there was a more than usually guarded look on his face, as if its presence there disturbed him in some way that mites and ticks and germs couldn't quite account for.

The next day he told her, in a studiedly neutral tone, that Deirdre had reacted indignantly to the news that a mute swan was being rehabilitated under his roof. She had participated in a DEP-sponsored 'egg-shaking' programme in which volunteers spent several weekends destroying the cygnet embryos without breaking the eggs, so that the swans would be tricked into trying to hatch them rather than laying a new clutch. It was

45

typical of Carla's amateurish meddling, Richard reported Deirdre as saying, to try to return this animal to the wild rather than have it humanely destroyed, as any responsible conservationist would have done. To prove her point, the teacher had given him a thick sheaf of printouts documenting the many varieties of environmental havoc wrought by this species. Richard knew better than to attempt to lay down the law in his home, but he gave Sara the printouts, and the sense of his opposition was unmistakable. It didn't deter her, but it exacerbated a certain tendency of hers, to withdraw into herself.

Daniel's reaction was more surprising. Unlike his father he had a real affinity for the animals she took in; an easy, affectionate curiosity. He still seemed to enjoy helping her with them. Sitting with him on the porch, feeding a brood of orphaned squirrels or chipmunks with pipettes of warm formula, was a lingering reminder of their old companionship. She'd assumed he would want to help with the swan – take charge of the evening feed perhaps, or collect waterweeds from the stream. More than that, she'd hoped the bird might produce the same delight in him as it had in her. But he had notably failed to rise to the occasion. A laconic 'cool' was all he'd uttered when she first showed it to him, and he'd quickly gone off to play elsewhere.

Why his reaction should be so subdued, she wasn't sure. Maybe it had to do with the size of the creature – too large to pet; too powerfully itself for the kind of half-imaginary relationships he liked to form with these animals. Or maybe it was that her own interest in it was too strong; too nakedly apparent. It did seem to her, as he'd turned to go, that his guileless brown eyes – still those of a child – had a look of puzzlement in them, as though her excitement had disturbed him.

Is there something wrong in my being so moved by this creature? she'd wondered. Something naive? False? Sentimental? She didn't think so, but she was peculiarly moved by it. Its calm acceptance of her; the attentive gaze of its eye as she came close; that curious way in which it seemed to cooperate with her against its own fear when she lifted it up, was a source of undiminishing pleasure. Occasionally with the smaller birds she'd felt glimmerings of a consciousness capable of responding, in more than purely reflex ways, to her own. But this seemed a different order of reciprocal awareness: charged and volatile, as if the creature might be forming as richly strange an impression of her as she was of it. During the daytime, even though there was little she needed to do for it, she found herself reluctant to leave its side. And at night it would flood back into her mind, a soft brilliance, its domed head with the little sharp-angled mask over the eyes, held aloft in the dark or else tucked (as she'd seen it once to her everlasting delight) under a wing. Just picturing it was a source of strange joy. It was as if some benign, otherworldly being had taken shelter in their home. She had felt something like this in the first months after Daniel had been born.

Every few days Carla dropped by to see how the recovery was progressing. Once, noticing the sheaf of printouts sitting on the studio windowsill where Sara had left them, she asked with her customary unabashed inquisitiveness if Richard had given them to her.

He had, Sara said, a little embarrassed. 'But only because his head of science gave them to him.'

Carla looked at her a moment, her axe-hewn features transmitting regal displeasure.

'Deirdre Wagoner,' she said. 'I know her well. She's been an antagonist of mine in more than one incarnation.'

Used to ignoring such remarks, Sara continued:

'I think Richard just felt I should know what I was getting into. I haven't actually read them, yet.'

Gathering the folds of her dress, Carla knelt down beside the swan.

'I've mentioned to you, haven't I, my belief that past a certain age the sexes among higher mammals become not merely indifferent towards each other but in fact functionally opposed?'

Sara nodded, assuming the half-defensive, half-receptive posture she adopted whenever Carla embarked on one of these lectures. One was forced into the role of acolyte, in her company, whether one liked it or not.

'I've published several papers on the subject,' Carla went on. 'You can look them up online. In some of them I speak of what I call the "moil". The moil of sex and money and power. For men between the age of puberty and that of impotence this constitutes their entire image of reality. It is all they are capable of thinking about, biologically speaking. And of course, when one is embroiled with a man, one is also embroiled with this vision of life, along with all its seemingly urgent imperatives. One accepts it as the objective picture of reality. But it isn't. There are other realities, only one must be *un*embroiled, to see them.'

She paused, examining the swan's feet.

Why are you telling me this? Sara was thinking. As always, she bridled slightly at Carla's presumption in speaking to her in this cryptic way about Richard. It seemed a little ignoble, somehow, to hint that you knew or intuited certain things about a person's marriage that they didn't know themselves. After all, what could Carla know? All she knows, Sara thought, is her own marriage, and she clearly has some bitterness left over from that, though she probably wouldn't admit it. It occurred to her that some of what Carla presented to the world as strength, was in fact the opposite: a gaping wound. Was this falsification perhaps what made her seem wooden at times, not quite human?

And yet along with the nonsense she talked there was always a sense of impending revelation that appealed to Sara. What exactly do you mean? she wanted to ask. What other realities? Tell me about them. I'd like to hear … She stood, waiting for Carla to pursue the theme.

The older woman was looking closely at the underside of one of the swan's feet.

'Dammit,' she said, prosaically, 'he has bumblefoot.'

This was a fungal condition, she explained, common in birds and rodents. It had infected the swan's uninjured foot, probably because of the extra weight being put on it.

'You'll have to bring him to the vet.'

Twice a week, then, for the next three weeks, Sara drove the swan to the vet in East Deerfield. For the journey she would lift it into a tall-sided basket which she would place in the front passenger seat of the car. There beside her, it would stare out at the traffic and houses reeling past, seemingly spellbound by what it saw; its long neck stretched up above the sides of the basket, as if it were periscoping up into this world of streets and cars and houses from some hidden world of its own. The urge to watch it as it gazed out was strong; at times so strong Sara could hardly keep her eyes on the road. What did it see? she found herself wondering. What was *its* reality? Not Carla's 'moil', presumably; but what then? Was there really some radically different way of inhabiting the world, or was that just wishful thinking? Do I even wish it? And if so why? Carla's little homilies of recent weeks had begun to insinuate themselves into her mind. Words, phrases, whole arguments would come back to her at odd moments. Questions she'd never thought necessary to ask, began to repeat themselves in Carla's sonorous voice: Have you considered what a woman is *for*, my dear, after she passes the mating age? What position of any importance can such a figure hope to occupy under the predominating vision of reality? How may she grow old gracefully in a world that has no fundamental use for her? What is there to grow *into*? What vital role? What function beyond the purely honorary? What respect beyond lip service? This is the pathos of a woman ageing in our particular culture, my dear. Unlike our ancestors, we live purely in historical time. All the great ceremonies of renewal and rebirth are gone from our lives. Time is absolute — we have no myth of eternal return; no sense that our stay on earth is purely one cycle in a great rhythm of being and dissolution. All we can see in an older woman is an old woman, a crone, a hag. And if she is not careful this is all she begins to see in herself ...

A shift seemed to be occurring in the way Sara thought of certain people. A new set of criteria had begun to prevail. Women, older women especially, were seen increasingly in relation to Carla's 'predominating vision'. Either they had turned their backs on it, or else they were still 'embroiled'. Both categories, in the past, had seemed to present a daunting image of what it was to grow old: the Carla types with their sexless, hardened appearance, or the others, drowning in their cosmetics and hair dye, their garish faces stiffening with the Botox that more and more of them appeared to be using. Each, now, as she thought of them, was like a mask she could try on, and peer through into the world.

All the while there was something tentative, provisional, about the way Sara revolved these subjects. She wasn't sure what bearing they really had on her own life. None at all, she would tell herself. And yet her thoughts kept returning to them, drawn back in, as if to an unsolved puzzle they couldn't stop working on.

By July the swan's fracture had mended and the vet had declared the infection healed. Carla wanted to start reacclimatising it to the water.

There was a good-sized pond in the town land near the municipal offices. In the daytime there were too many people and dogs around to let the swan out safely, but it was quiet in the evening.

'Let me know when you're free,' Carla commanded. 'The sooner the better.'

That Saturday Richard was in New York, where he'd had to substitute at the last minute for a speaker at a conference for educators. There was a reception afterwards and he'd decided to stay the night at a hotel in the city.

Taking advantage of the free evening, Sara arranged to go with Carla to the pond. Daniel, offered the choice, opted for a sleepover with a friend.

It was dusk when the two women set off from Sara's house; a clear, warm evening. Sara sat in the back of Carla's jeep, watching the swan from behind as it peered out. Looking at it, she remembered that in the early hours that morning, she'd woken herself and Richard by laughing in her sleep. The cause of this laughter had escaped her at the time, but it came to her now that it was just this: the swan in its basket staring out at the world with that look of unearthly calm. Recalling it, she felt an echo of the strange hilarity that had surged through her sleeping body; the very pleasurable sensation of tension being released in long ripples of delight.

Richard had woken. 'What? What is it? What are you laughing at?' he'd asked in a kind of muffled panic that seemed to originate deep inside him, before sinking back into his own dreams. Carla would appreciate the little story, she thought, and for a moment she considered telling her, but then changed her mind, shrinking from the small disloyalty it would entail.

They pulled up in the municipal parking lot. There were several beat-up looking trucks already parked there.

'Richard's in New York, is he?' Carla carried the swan along the footpath, one on each side of the basket.

'Yes.'

'Doing what?'

'He went to a conference.'

Carla grimaced.

'My husband was forever attending *conferences*.'

'It's pretty rare for Richard.'

A drumming sound came through the trees.

'Ah, yes. The Rainbow People,' Carla said.

Every year, from June till September, the Rainbow Family of Living Light, along with a motley collection of local sympathisers and hangers-on, would congregate on Saturday nights in one of the old pastures here on the town land, and play their drums around a bonfire.

'Such children,' Carla continued. 'The girls who work for me can barely write their names. But they have the right spirit. There's a great deal they could learn from me if they chose.'

Sara smiled.

Their path took them away from the drumming, across an old pear orchard, and on through woods of white birch and pine, where it descended to the pond.

In the deep twilight the black surface of the water teemed with faint reflections of the birches. Here and there fish rose, spreading circular ripples. The low trill of tree frogs made a continuous soft pulsing.

Lifting the swan from the basket, Carla placed it on the grassy shore. It stood, looking out at the water.

'Go on now,' Carla encouraged it. After a moment it began stepping, with a fastidious, slightly hobbled gait, towards the water; surprisingly ungainly, as if it were in danger of toppling over. Once in, however, it glided effortlessly off towards the centre. The two women watched from the shore. There was no moon yet, but the last of the daylight lingered overhead, a greyish violet glow. In it, the whiteness of the white birches and the swan on the water looked lit from within. The rhythmic beat of the drumming came faintly on the breeze. Closer, there was an occasional bass croak of a bullfrog. A heightened silence seemed to enclose each of these sounds, so that they too seemed lit from within. Nothing felt quite of this world. Even Carla, standing very still at the pond's edge, her thick white hair fanning over her shoulders, seemed a figure in a dream. Sara felt as if she'd stepped outside her life, into some interim space. It occurred to her that she was undergoing some transition. She had no idea where it might be leading, and wasn't even especially interested in knowing.

The swan, close to the shore again, had begun hooping its neck to peer into the water. Abruptly it plunged downward, tipping its tail feathers out of the water, the flame shape of its rear end glowing briefly on the surface like an enormous white water lily before the head rose back up, a strand of pondweed dangling from its bill.

Carla turned to Sara.

'I believe he's ready to go home. His real home, I mean. I'll take him to the river tomorrow. Can you come?'

'Yes,' Sara said, surprised. She hadn't expected to be letting go of the creature so soon.

For several more minutes the swan fed. When it was finished, Carla called to it from the shore, and it swam back to her as if this were most natural thing in the world.

It was almost dark now. Sara had a small flashlight but Carla had a headband with an LED light that cast a blue-white brilliance all around her. She'd bought it from the camping store, she said as she lifted the swan into its basket.

'I wear it at home all the time after dark. It frees the hands for work, and of course, it dispenses with the need for electric light. You should buy one yourself.'

'I will!'

The thought of Carla wandering around her house at night with this Cyclops eye blazing from her forehead was oddly impressive to Sara. It seemed to her majestically, almost transfiguringly, original. Carla had this capacity for flooring one; often just as you were running out of patience with her. In its eerie radiance the swan's masked face, suspended between them, looked like that of some carnival-goer, returning home from unimaginable revelries.

Paradise Meadow, the popular name for the old dairy pasture where the drumming took place, was beyond the woods on the other side of the municipal parking lot. The drumbeats grew louder as the women returned along the footpath with the swan. The red glow of the bonfire appeared between the trees as they reached Carla's jeep. The parking lot itself had filled up; figures in feathered hats and cloak-like garments moved swiftly down the path on the far side of it. As Carla was pulling out, she peered through her window at one of the parked vehicles, a pickup truck with bales of hay in the back.

'That's Bonnie's truck,' she said. 'I wonder what she's doing here. Maybe she came along with those Rainbow girls. Now there's a hard-working woman: does landscaping for half the town as well as working for me. Her daughter's at your husband's school, isn't she?'

Sara was unable to speak for a moment. She had just seen something extremely perplexing. Parked next to Bonnie's pickup was Richard's Saab, the rust-fretted lower edge of the body curving over the wheels like a fringe of rigid lace; unmistakable.

'Yes,' she said, trying to hide her bewilderment. Carla didn't seem to have recognised the car, thank God; at any rate she didn't mention it. She dropped Sara off with the swan. Sara didn't invite her in. She'd come up with an explanation for what she'd seen: Richard's dinner had ended early; he'd come home after all, and remembering that she and Daniel were out, had gone to listen to the drumming. She couldn't recall him ever showing any interest in the Rainbow People or their drumming, but it wasn't impossible that he was curious. He was open to that kind of thing. The position of his car right next to Bonnie's could only have been coincidental.

Leaving the swan in the studio, she went into the house. There was no message on the machine from Richard. She picked up the receiver to call him on his cell phone, but thought better of it: coverage up here was spotty, and if he didn't answer she'd have merely opened herself to further, possibly needless, anxiety. She went to bed.

At around three in the morning she woke up with a jolt, aware that Richard still wasn't home. She dialled his cell phone from the phone by the bed. It rang, but he didn't answer.

She lay in the large bed: unable to stave off the knowledge that something was wrong. He had come back from New York without telling her; had gone to the drumming but hadn't come home afterwards. The possibilities presented themselves with stark clarity. Either he'd had an accident on the way back from Paradise Meadow or else he was somewhere he didn't want her to know about, thinking she believed he was in his New York hotel. She picked up the phone and called the emergency dispatch number. There were no reports of any accidents that night.

She got out of bed, unsure what to do. Drifting into the bathroom, she poured herself a glass of water. A night-light was on above the mirror, lighting her reflection. It was some time since she'd studied her own face for any but the most brusquely practical of reasons. As a teenager, after a certain amount of anguish, she'd settled the question of her looks with the word 'adequate'. When boyfriends, and then Richard, had professed to find her more than that, she'd taken it as chivalrous exaggeration. Her mousey hair had gone grey in her thirties. After she'd turned forty, her complexion had faded. She kept her hair short, and didn't use dye or make-up; assuming (since he never criticised) that Richard liked her the way she was. But looking at herself now, she felt ancient insecurities stirring inside her. Am I attractive? Am I about to be abandoned? Some forlorn childhood self seemed to be rising up inside her as she stared into the mirror. It seemed to her that her face was covered in a layer of dust.

She turned abruptly, went down to the living room. A bright half-moon shone through the windows, lighting her tapestries. These too seemed covered in dust. Worse: they seemed made of it. What are these pallid things I've spent half my life creating? The image of Carla came to her, striding through her house with that headlight. I could use one of those now, she thought, imagining sardonically how Carla might put it: *a third eye to see what is happening to me* ... Well, but there was an insidious persuasiveness in so much of what the woman said. That business about the 'moil' ... ridiculous, like all her pronouncements, but it had lodged itself in Sara's mind nevertheless. The question was whether there was any way out of that tangle of, what was it – sex, money and power? – that didn't necessitate turning oneself into a New Age priestess. That seemed an awful price to pay. A falsification of yourself, it had to be. Even someone as naturally theatrical as Carla must it find wearisome to keep up at times.

Of course, Carla hadn't really relinquished power, had she? Which no doubt added to the sense of something false about her; forced. So perhaps that's my answer, Sara reflected: a more thorough letting go than Carla's ... A white light flickered in the windows of her studio. For a moment she thought it was the swan. Even when she realised it was just moonlight reflecting in the glass, she felt the surge of companionable warmth that the thought of the creature always aroused in her. It struck her that she was going to miss it badly after they returned it to the river tomorrow. She opened the front door and stepped outside. Barefoot, she crossed the dew-dampened grass of the lawn, and as if beckoned by some calming force, quietly entered the studio. The swan was asleep, its head tucked under its wing. It didn't stir. She sat down on the newspaper-covered floor adjacent to it, leaning against the wall.

A few hours later, a sound tugged her out of deep sleep. She was lying on the newspapers. Struggling awake, she remembered tiptoeing in earlier, seeing the swan asleep on its bedding. Her intention, so far as she'd had one, had just been to sit there a while, but she must have nodded off. A trace of something euphoric in her dreams – a sense of wheeling through bright air – was drawing her back into the pleasant oblivion she'd been roused from, when there were louder noises suddenly all around her; violent hissing, the sound of a blow, a cry of pain, and she was wide awake, looking at Richard as he reeled back from the swan, hands up at his mouth, while the swan itself stood stretched up on its legs, hissing and beating its wide, vast wings, overshadowing him like some great archangel.

'Richard!'

'What the hell is going on? Why are you sleeping in here?'

He had his hand to his mouth and there was blood running down his chin.

'Are you all right?'

'No! Your goddamned bird attacked me!'

'Let me look.'

He took his hand from his mouth. Both lips were bleeding.

The swan had stopped beating its wings but was still agitated. Sara spoke to it softly until its rigidly outstretched neck began relaxing slowly backward. She turned back to Richard.

'We'd better get you cleaned up.'

In the bathroom she dabbed the blood from Richard's mouth with tissues. His lips were swelling extravagantly.

'Do you want me to take you to the doctor?'

'No. Thanks.'

'You should ice it though.'

He nodded. 'Sorry to yell at you.'

'That's okay.'

'Beaten up by a bird!' He attempted a smile. 'I guess I should have knocked first. Why were you in there?'

'I don't know. I woke up and couldn't get back to sleep. I thought it might help to move. I guess it worked.'

Richard nodded.

'You're home early,' she said.

Dabbing at his lips, he told her he'd woken early at his hotel and caught the five-twenty train home instead of the six-twenty, which had given him time to come back to the house before morning assembly.

'I'd have called,' he said, 'but I didn't want to wake you.'

Sara caught his eye. He looked away, glancing at his reflection in the mirror.

'Jesus! I look like some eighteenth-century libertine!'

'I'll make some coffee,' she said. She went into the kitchen, absorbing the fact that he had lied to her about the hotel and the train. He'd never, to her knowledge, lied to her before.

****

There was the domestic idea of virtue – kindness, selfless-ness, fidelity – and then there was nature's own idea in which all that mattered was vitality; the feeling of life flowing through you.

For long stretches, years at a time, the two ideas could coincide harmoniously, each enhancing the other. But they weren't the same thing, and their interests some-times diverged; sometimes even became directly opposed. When that happened, as Richard had observed as a younger man, you entered a condition of crisis from which there was no easy exit.

He had entered it again now. Even as the train had car-ried him physically away from Francesca after that evening at the club, his old feelings for her had begun stir-ring again inside him. And within a few days they had regained all their original strength. They were like those seeds archaeologists find in tombs and then germinate; ancient strains of poppy and delphinium breaking back into posthumous life.

He'd started drifting into imaginary encounters with Francesca in which their old intimacy was effortlessly re-established. At school, where his job required an appearance of unwavering attentiveness at all times, it was necessary to resist the inward tug of these reveries. But it was increasingly difficult to do so. The thought of her touched some source of incendiary joy in him. It felt wrong, unnatural, to shut it off. It didn't help that the school's philosophy was all about self-expression, freeing the creative spirit from the chains of conformity and con-vention. Every classroom wall, every poster and notice, every conversation with his eager young faculty, seemed either to urge him forward or taunt him for his restraint. Be Yourself! Dare to Dream! One morning, perched on one of the child-size chairs at the back of the second-grade home room where he was observing a new teacher's class, he saw himself suddenly as a child, or rather had an image of himself frozen in some child-size state of arrest as he sat there, squeezed suffocatingly into the diminutive chair. He stood up abruptly and left the room, the puzzled young teacher staring after him. Striding back to his office, he opened his cell phone, and dialled Francesca's number. She picked up.

'It's me, Richard,' he told her quietly. 'I have to be down in New York again in a couple of weeks. I was wondering if you'd like to have lunch?'

After only the slightest hesitation, she replied: 'That'd be nice, Richard. That'd be really nice.'

He told Sara he had to go for a check-up with a specialist he'd seen earlier in the year about a torn ligament in his shoulder. The ligament had in fact healed, and he'd long ago cancelled the follow-up appointment. He hadn't mentioned that to Sara, and she had no reason to question him.

Francesca had suggested a restaurant in Fort Greene, where she was giving a voice class that afternoon. The place was long and narrow, with salvaged furniture painted in bright oils. Richard felt odd at first, making polite conversation with her. She was quieter than she'd been the other night; subdued almost. But when he asked what had brought her back to the States she told a spirited story about sitting in a pub in Cork surrounded by a flock of girls all bobbing identical blonde ponytails as they chirruped away at each other. 'They're lovely people and I remain devoted to them but that's when I knew I had to get out,' she said, laughing. He didn't really understand the story but after she'd told it, all their old ease with each other seemed to return. She asked about Sara, and Richard spoke affectionately about her and Daniel, making no effort to present himself as a man in an unhappy marriage. At the same time, as he listened to her describe an unsatisfactory-sounding on-off relationship of her own with a musician back in Ireland, he made no attempt to resist the pleasant sensation of being licensed to gaze deeply into her eyes, and of being welcomed into their depths.

It was a nice day, and from what he'd understood there would be time to walk around together for a while before Francesca's voice class. But she had to dash back to her apartment to let in an electrician, she told him, and said goodbye a couple of blocks from the restaurant.

'So good seeing you, Richard. Take care of yourself now.'

'You too, Francesca.'

On the train back upstate he asked himself repeatedly what he thought he was doing. What do I want? It was a surprisingly difficult question to answer. Later that evening, as he sat playing chess with his son, he asked himself again: What do I want? Was it just a matter of lust? 'Getting laid,' as Victor put it. Was that all this was about?

No. Lust, in his experience, wasn't so all-consuming. He remembered one of Daniel's babysitters; a careworn-looking yet oddly alluring Polish woman in her thirties, grey-eyed and ashen, with something at once supple and soft about her figure, who'd washed up in Aurelia for some reason. He had found her acutely attractive, and whether she found him attractive in turn or was just amusing herself, she'd taken every opportunity to flash sexual signals at him, touching and brushing against him whenever they passed by in the house, smiling at him almost mockingly. Once, when he'd come into the living room, she'd bent down in her dress on some pretext with her ass up in the air right where he was standing, holding the pose as if willing or daring him to touch her. He had been tempted, but he'd walked away instead. Almost immediately, the feeling of sharp arousal had given way to relief at having resisted doing something extremely stupid.

That was lust. He'd ignored it and it had gone away. This was something different. His feelings about Francesca didn't seem reducible to a desire to go to bed with her. In fact when he thought of her now, it wasn't in sexual terms at all. It seemed to him that what he felt was something that didn't quite refer to the actual world at all, but to some separate realm of existence, with its own laws, its own dimensions of time and space, in which this rich nameless intimacy between him and Francesca was not only possible but was already actually occurring.

'Are you okay, Dad?'

Daniel was gazing up from the chessboard.

'Huh?'

'You keep frowning.'

'Sorry.'

Sara looked over from the sofa.

'Are you in pain?'

It took him a second to understand why she was asking.

'Well, a little. The doctor gave me quite a workout.'

'Why don't you lie down? I'll get the heating pad.'

'No, no. I'll be fine.'

He looked into his wife's eyes. It was obvious she didn't suspect anything.

A week later, he phoned Francesca again. It was too soon, he knew, but that was partly his reason for doing it.

It seemed to him that he needed to show some forceful-
ness. After all, it was Francesca who had stuck her neck
out last time around, flying across the Atlantic to see him,
only to be rebuffed. Now it was his turn to take the initia-
tive. He thought again of what she'd said outside the club
when he asked if they were going to stay in touch this
time. *Well now, that's your call I'd say, wouldn't you?* Her
words had seemed carefully chosen.

She didn't pick up, but he left a message and called
again the next morning.

'Hello, Richard.'

'Listen, Francesca, I have to come down again in a couple of days and I *really* would like to see you, and to be
honest this may be the last chance for quite a while.'

'Okay …'

'How about a drink somewhere, or dinner?'

'Sure.'

They arranged to meet in Chelsea, near another voice
student of hers.

She arrived twenty minutes late, unapologetic. She sat
opposite him in the dimly lit wooden booth. Her eyes
were conspicuously devoid of their usual mirthful
warmth.

'What's this about, Richard?'

He flinched a little, unprepared for her bluntness.

'It was nice seeing you at the gig,' she continued, 'and I
was glad we made the time to catch up the other day,
though I have to tell you I was thinking it was a bit previ-
ous of you even then, to call when you did. And now here
we are again. What's up?'

A waitress came, but Francesca waved her away. 'Nothing for me.'

'You're not staying?' Richard asked.

'No.'

He lowered his head.

'Well, I'm sorry.'

'Go home, Richard.'

'I was hoping to spend the evening with you,' he said. 'Actually, I think I was hoping to spend the night with you. Since we're being frank.'

She gave a half-smile.

'Is that right?'

'I told Sara I had to go to a conference for educators followed by a dinner and I'd be staying at a hotel.'

'Oh, Richard.'

'Lunacy, right?'

'Well. That's not a word that springs to mind when I think of you ...'

She looped the straps of her bag over her shoulder.

He grabbed her hand.

'Francesca. Listen. I made a mistake that time you flew in to see me. That's what I wanted to tell you. I've regretted it ever since you left. Every single day since then I've thought about how stupid I was, how cowardly, how blind to my own feelings, not to mention yours. Every day for twelve years. I have to tell you this ...' He broke off, dumbstruck by his own words.

She extricated her hand. They stared at each other through the red-lit darkness. She looked away, and then turned back to him.

'I loved you,' she said coolly. 'You rejected my love. You'd do it again, believe me. Anyway —' something seemed to flare in her — 'I'm glad you *did* do it because it wouldn't have taken me long to figure out how wrong I was about you. Only, knowing me I'd have stuck it out out of sheer guilt and niceness. So thank you for sparing me that.'

'God, Francesca—'

She stood up. 'Well, it's true. Now go home, little man, while you're still able. Your wife is waiting for you. And your son.'

She left.

He finished his drink and got the check, not knowing what he wanted to do. His hotel, a Comfort Inn in Queens, was paid for, but it seemed pointless to drag himself out there.

He walked to Penn Station, arriving sticky from the July humidity. There was a train leaving in half an hour and he exchanged his ticket at the office. A black mood settled into him as he stared out the window across the Hudson. The folly of his own behaviour was starkly apparent to him. It seemed to him even that an awareness of this had coexisted in parallel with the behaviour itself, all along. What had he been thinking? What did I really expect to happen? he asked himself. What did I even want? He seemed further than ever from an answer.

It wasn't yet eleven by the time he arrived in Aurelia. Sara would still be awake, he realised. She would ask him about his non-existent conference. The idea of having to lie his way through a prolonged conversation about it filled him with disgust. He pulled into the parking lot of the Chinese restaurant. He wasn't particularly hungry but if he could kill an hour there she'd probably be asleep by the time he got home. She'd wake up enough to ask why he hadn't stayed in the city, but he could tell her the reception had ended early, without the risk of having to invent anything else.

The restaurant was dim and quiet; almost empty. He ordered a beer and some lo mein. The food was slow in coming and he was ready for a second beer by the time it arrived. He was just finishing his food when the door swung open and a woman he recognised came in, carrying a canvas bag. It was Bonnie Fletcher, the mother of a girl at his school. She went straight to the bar without seeing him, propping her bag on the polished surface and greeting the elderly Chinese proprietor with an effusive: 'Hey there!'

From the largely one-sided exchange that followed, it seemed she was selling some kind of water-filtration system. The area had a sulphur problem in its wells. Richard watched from his table as she went through her sales routine. It didn't surprise him all that much to see her working this late in the evening. She was a single mother, not well off but determined to give her daughter a private education, and she often took menial jobs at the school to offset the fees. He'd seen her many times mopping corridors or stacking chairs in the auditorium; her slim figure always half-dancing to whatever music she was listening to on her iPod.

At the end of her pitch the Chinese guy shook his head, giving back the little contraption she'd handed him.

'We don't need.'

'Not a problem!'

She turned from the bar.

'Richard!'

'Hello, Bonnie.' He signalled for the check.

Bonnie came over to his table, eyes flashing in that switched-on way of hers.

'What are *you* doing here?'

'Oh, I was in New York,' he said vaguely. 'I didn't get a chance to eat before my train.' He gestured at her bag. 'I had no idea you were in the filtration business.'

'Hey, whatever it takes! You know me.'

'Right.'

She hovered at the table.

'How's Caya?' he asked.

'She's fantastic. Staying with her dad tonight. My one night off and I spend it hustling! But I'm done now.'

'Well, that's good.'

'Yeah, I'm heading up to the drumming. Have you been?'

'No. I never have.'

'You should come. It's wild!'

He smiled, handing the proprietor his credit card. 'It's a little past my bedtime.'

She gave a raucous laugh, touching his arm.

'Hey, I'll keep you awake!'

She'd always been flirtatious with him. Mostly it just seemed her way. But occasionally he'd felt something more purposeful. Earlier that year, in a meeting she'd requested in order to ask for a deferment on her daughter's fees, she'd seen him wince from the torn ligament in his shoulder and had reached over, gripping the tendons at the side of his neck and probing them gently with her strong fingers. It had felt so good he hadn't pulled away immediately, and she'd taken quick advantage of the lapse to invite him over to her house for a full sacro-cranial massage, at which she claimed to be an expert.

'I'm very good,' she'd said in a low voice: jokily, but he'd felt she was intending to plant a serious idea.

'I'll bear it in mind,' he'd said, standing up. She was extremely attractive, he'd had to admit to himself at that point, with her shining black eyes and fine, sharp cheekbones. He'd dealt with the problem this posed by being always vaguely in a hurry whenever he ran into her.

'I should get home,' he said.

They walked out of the restaurant together. Bonnie got into her pickup truck.

'I'll be there if you change your mind!'

She drove off and he pulled out after her onto the town road. The interlude had distracted him, but it wasn't long before he was brooding on Francesca's words again. *Little man* ... He remembered the vision he'd had of himself in the child's chair the other day, among the boxes of crayons and wooden blocks. Francesca had outgrown him: that had become painfully clear. He felt weighed down; oppressed by his own stalled sameness.

As he approached the centre of town he found himself thinking of a text he presented every few years at morning assembly: Kierkegaard's fable of the wild goose. The wild goose wanted to liberate the flock of tame, flightless geese. But it stayed too long among them and discovered one day that it had lost the ability to fly. A wild goose could become a tame goose, the fable ended, but a tame goose could never become wild.

It was the word 'wild', he realised, which Bonnie had used about the drumming, that had reminded him of the fable.

Ahead of him, her truck turned off towards the town offices, from which the path led up to the meadow known as 'Paradise'. He'd been curious about the drumming sessions ever since they'd begun a few summers back. People of his generation spoke of them approvingly on the whole, pleased that their town had been found suitable as a site for such gatherings. He'd offered to take Daniel once, but the boy had said something sarcastic about 'hippies' and somehow Richard had never found time to go by himself.

Impulsively he turned off, following Bonnie's tail lights. He could spend an hour here, he calculated, and pretend he'd come home on the late train. A faint scruple seemed present in his mind, but he brushed it aside. He was sick to death of his little scruples. He pulled in next to Bonnie's truck in the municipal parking lot.

Her face lit up as he got out of the Saab.

'Hey! Fantastic!'

'Well, I've always been curious about the drumming ...'

She gave a sweet, sly smile, beckoning him with her head. 'C'mon ...'

He followed her to the narrow path that led through woods to the meadow. As soon as they were on the path she lit a joint.

'Want some?'

The last time he'd smoked pot, several years ago, he'd passed out – the stuff around these days was too strong for him. But he didn't want to seem ungracious, or square, so he took a hit. It didn't have much of an effect.

It was dark in the woods but candles in paper bags set out at intervals lit the way. The sound of drumming came through the trees. The narrow trail wound down through clearings with wigwams and tents in them. A figure in a jester's crown jogged onto the path ahead of them, bells jingling lightly. Fireflies wandered between the dark tree trunks, pulsing off and on. A footbridge led across a stream, after which they came out at the meadow, where a couple of hundred people were gathered around a bonfire, drumming or dancing or lying in the grass. Most looked in their twenties or thirties, but there were young children too, in tie-dye shirts, as well as elderly men with bandannas and straggly grey beards, and also a number of more ordinary-looking types. Richard recognised a realtor from one of the offices in town – a man his own age with a big paunch – furiously beating a bowl-shaped drum with his hands. A group of women in their sixties, standing together with small side drums around their necks, also looked familiar, and he realised they were from the food pantry where he occasionally dropped off donations. One of them smiled at him, glancing at Bonnie, who was already doing a kind of shuffle to the beat of the drums; wrists together, shoulders sloping one way then the other, firelight glinting on the silver feathers in her ears. Woodsmoke filled the warm air, and as they drew nearer to the centre Richard caught scents of sandalwood, patchouli, sweat, and more pot. Up this close, the loud pulse of the drums and the sight of a hundred pairs of arms moving rhythmically together in the darkness, roused a feeling of adventurousness in him. He remembered the sensation from decades ago when he used to go to rock concerts.

They came to a trailer-bed piled with instruments.

'Grab what you want, folks,' a bare-chested guy in a round straw hat called out.

Bonnie took a double-ended drum shaped like an hour-glass. Richard picked out a single maraca, intending to limit himself to a token shake or two.

'No frickin' way!' Bonnie cried out. 'You gotta get a drum, Richard!'

She rummaged in the pile, pulling out an enormous cylindrical thing with what looked like the pelts of reindeer hung around the outside.

'Here.'

Richard took it, bemused by her proprietorial manner. He gave it a tentative pat as they joined the circle. It didn't make much of a noise. Bonnie was banging away on hers, already picking up the rhythms of the other drummers around them. He slapped the rawhide skin a little harder. It hurt his fingers but still didn't produce much of a sound.

'You can hit it a whole lot harder than that,' Bonnie shouted. 'It won't break.'

The drummer next to him, a grizzled old guy in nylon running shorts, nodded sagely.

Embarrassed now, Richard attacked the drum with the heel of his hands.

The same flat thud came from it, barely audible in the thundering around him.

'Heart and soul, brother,' the older man said. 'Heart and soul or she won't talk.'

'I don't appear to be a natural,' Richard said, annoyed at finding himself in a situation where, absurdly, some question of manhood appeared to be at stake. Closing his fists he hunched over the instrument and thrashed at it as hard as he could. This time, as if fair-mindedly acknowledging his effort, the drum gave a low, booming resonance. He went on, throwing himself into the beat of the drummers around him. *Chunga chunga chunk. Chunga chunga chunk.* It was surprisingly satisfying; not just for the salvaging of his pride but for the sound itself, a deep boom, but with a bounce to it that made it feel alive and powerful. I must look like a madman, he thought, pounding his fists up and down. But he kept at it, and the self-consciousness gave way to a good feeling of being linked with the other drummers. It was years since he'd played music with other people, and he'd forgotten how enjoyable it was. Bonnie smiled at him. Something warm and tender pulsed in him. It was followed by a censorious impulse telling him he was being an idiot. Which in turn made him pound even more ferociously at the drum. *Chunga chunga chunk. Chunga chunga chunk.* Some degree of self-obliteration seemed possible here. The thought was strangely alluring.

By the time the rhythms began to loosen their grip on the drummers and the noise died away, he was exhausted but exhilarated. Bonnie came back towards him.

'Got some colour in your cheeks there!'

'Well, it was fun.'

They moved away from the drums, walking close together. He felt the back of her hand brush his, then – startlingly – her fingers briefly link and unlink with his. What did that mean? Probably nothing to her, but it sent a surge of desire through him. Gestures of affection had always roused him more sharply than overt sexual come-ons.

She lit another joint, and offered it to him. He was nervous of being seen, but took a drag anyway. There was enough darkness to feel somewhat hidden. He'd smoked half of it before he noticed the effect it was having on him.

'Whoa!' he said, reeling suddenly.

Bonnie grinned. 'Sinsemilla. That other shit was just some home-grown.'

'It's strong!'

'Don't I know it.'

Someone called Bonnie's name. Two girls of around twenty, one a redhead, the other chubby and blonde with eyebrow rings, greeted her with shrieks and giggles. She didn't introduce him and he wandered off. His legs had begun to feel heavy and his head was spinning. He needed to lie down. He found a clear spot near the edge of the meadow and lay on his back in the thick grass, breathing deeply.

The moon had risen, outlining pools of blackness among the clouds. On the horizon, very far off, summer lightning flickered, muffled and thunderless. He closed his eyes but the world immediately began revolving, making him nauseous, and he opened them again. Dreadlocks and patchwork vests drifted on his vision; tattooed shoulders and arms. He remembered a time, long ago, when he'd felt strongly drawn to this world. Its easy-going blend of idealism and hedonism had appealed to him, antiquated as it was even then. As a teenager he used to travel to music festivals with his guitar and sleeping bag, camping out under the stars. For a while after college he'd fantasised about living in a commune: some off-the-grid rural fastness peopled by kindred spirits. There would be pretty girls, a huge vegetable garden, music in the evenings, conversations late into the night.

The fantasy hadn't altogether been extinguished, but it had been put at arm's length; removed from the category of primal yearning into one of mere 'interest'. He 'took an interest' in communes and their history; had read up on Oneida and Twin Oaks, World Brotherhood Colonies and Intentional Communities, the high-minded ventures of the Transcendentalists. It 'interested' him that the only communes that had lasted more than a decade were ones founded on shared religious beliefs, and as a strict atheist this seemed to him a peculiarly tragic fact. But he hadn't lived in one. A dim sense of the longer-term requirements of his own nature – the need to be pursuing active good, out in the world – had drawn him to teaching children instead and he'd gone to grad school and become a teacher. It had been the right decision, and he'd never regretted it.

And yet I am dissatisfied, he thought. Francesca came back into his mind, trailing all the turbulent emotions of their history together. Then came Sara's image, pale and glinting like one of the stars above him. As steadfast too, he felt. But averted from him, somehow, or veiled by some mysterious opacity. He thought of their life together these past years: their conversations at the dinner table, their occasional love-making. It was all ... friendly. They were sensitive to each other's interests and needs. But there was a wan-ness to it all, a docile vagueness. Was this just the natural effect of time on any marriage, or had they always been like this?

He probed back into that earlier period of his life; his training at Bank Street and his first job, at an elementary school in the Bronx. He'd risen to assistant principal there by the time he and Sara had met; the semester before he was hired by Ryden College. Within a few weeks he'd per-suaded her to move in with him. It had been years since he'd thought about that time but as he lay there in the grass its very distinct atmosphere came back to him. They'd drawn something sharp and intense out of each other. Something very different from the pallidly amica-ble selves they presented to each other now. Victor's phrase, 'fucking all over the furniture', came to him, bringing back long-forgotten images of their first months in his apartment on East 6th Street: Sara naked in his arms on the sofa, her lithe limbs gripping him tightly, her breasts flushing pink as she sat astride him, her moans of pleasure as he brought her to orgasm, his own amazed joy at the power of his sensations and feelings. During this time Sara had conveyed something that had a decisive effect on him. It came more through gestures than words; some sense that she'd placed herself in his hands: entrusted herself to him, so to speak, unreservedly. He'd never quite clarified it to himself, but had always known that it was this, above all, that had made him want to marry her.

And yet before I married her I betrayed her.

And he felt as if he were seeing that betrayal clearly for the first time. Not that he hadn't suffered for it in the past: for a while he had made himself almost ill with guilt. But it seemed to him now that that self-imposed torment had been a way, precisely, of *not* examining what he'd done; of enabling himself to consider the deed cancelled, expunged.

Whereas it had continued to exist, and in fact had grown only denser and more monumental over time.

It had been there always, he saw, casting its shadow onto every aspect of his and Sara's life. He had often felt there was something perplexed about Sara; a dreamy, half-unwitting paralysis of bewilderment, as if she were imprisoned in something without knowing it. But he'd never considered that he himself might be responsible for this.

I am though, he thought now. His secret was like one of those accursed objects that keep their victim in thrall until their existence is exposed. In doing what he had done, he had gained an illicit control over her life; spellbound her.

I trapped her, he thought; changed the terms of the life she agreed to share with me, and hid the changes. For the first time he seemed to glimpse the true scale of the harm he had done her.

He sat up. Across the meadow revellers were throwing logs on the bonfire. Sparks whirled into the sky. A drummer banged out a beat and others began to pick it up. Figures started moving back towards the fire. In the shadows he made out Bonnie. She was on her own again, and seemed to be looking for him, peering about her into the darkness. He began to call out to her, but stopped himself, watching her disappear. A pang of wistful affection passed through him. Then bemusement at himself. Then a more fundamental confusion. What did these feelings mean? What were you supposed to do with them?

He lay back down in the grass, still dizzy, his thoughts running on. A documentary he'd seen a few years ago came back to him. It was about a philosopher, a monkish, austere man, not given to frivolous utterance, who'd died aged almost a hundred. Interviewed in his wheelchair at ninety, he was asked if there was anything he regretted in his life. Without smiling and without hesitating he had replied: 'I wish I'd slept with more women. Nothing else matters.'

He'd recognised himself in the old man; some ingrained cycle or sequence that appeared to be destined to express itself through him repeatedly. Desire, restraint, regret. Desire, restraint, regret ... And he was remembering also something his eye doctor had once said, that had acquired a certain talismanic power in his mind. He'd gone in for an examination after waking one morning with a thick drift of silvery spots floating across his vision. After peering into his eye through a tubular lens, the doctor had told him he had a detached vitrius. It wasn't serious, but there was nothing anyone could do about it. The human body had evolved for a lifespan of thirty-five years, the doctor explained. After that it stopped regenerating itself efficiently.

The exchange had played into a certain bleak intuition at the root of Richard's psyche. A lurking sense that this and this alone – the physical body – was what ordained the meaning, such as it was, of human life; that all that mattered to the species was creating the optimal circumstances for perpetuating itself. Up to around the age of thirty-five, it appeared, the benefits of staying alive outweighed the costs. But after that, nature had no further use for you. Modern longevity was therefore nothing but a freakish posthumousness. We filled it with all sorts of pursuits – careers, hobbies, culture, news, accumulation of property, social networking; all that ingenious activity – but none of it meant a thing outside the closed circuit of our determination that it should.

Over the years, with a kind of agonised scrupulousness, Richard had allowed this outlook to supplant all his less rational intuitions to the contrary. He liked to claim that in scouring himself clean of all mystical, spiritual or otherwise aggrandising illusion, he was in fact more open to the true glory of existence than people less rigorous with themselves. But the reality was more often the opposite. The attitude that had gradually become his own grimly denuded everything that came into its purview. It was unbearable, really, at times, and he would have been the first to welcome anything, any countervailing vision or argument powerful enough to demolish it. But he was well aware that there was no such thing, and never would be. Not for him.

3

Victor died. It happened on a November afternoon, three years after the summer of Sara's swan and Richard's evening in Paradise Meadow.

Richard and Sara drove in to the city for the funeral, which was in Washington Heights. They found a parking space a few blocks from the bridge and walked to the funeral home. A wind blew off the river, full of grit, and the streets looked as drab as the sky.

'This was where he moved to?' Sara asked.

'Somewhere near here.'

'He can't have liked it much.'

'Well, it's certainly not the Village.'

'Poor Victor.'

Richard smiled, glad of her uncomplicated sorrow.

She was looking nice, he thought. Her plain grey dress emphasised the trimness of her figure in a way that made him want to put his arm around her waist. The slightly ragged, sea-blue chenille cardigan she wore over the dress brought out the lighter blue of her eyes.

'Will Audrey be here?' she asked.

'I wouldn't count on it.'

'I mean, he's the father of her kids ...'

'Well, I guess we'll see.'

They hadn't seen Audrey since she'd thrown Victor out over two years ago. Victor had been elusive around the time of the blow-up, barely communicating for several months, and Richard hadn't in fact heard the story in any detail until Vic was already at the second or third in a series of changing addresses that had culminated in a one-room apartment up here on 177th Street. Even then, Vic had been a bit vague about the circumstances of his expulsion, though clearly a woman had been involved. After they'd been informed of Vic's death, Sara had left a message with Audrey to say how sorry she was and to call if she wanted to talk, but Audrey hadn't responded.

The funeral home was in a squat building of grey-painted brick. People were making their way in under the faded maroon awning. Richard recognised a few of them, including Victor's older brother whom he hadn't seen since they were all boys. He was the family success, Richard remembered, a chess prodigy who'd gone to Yale and made a career for himself in patent law. He had a smug expression, not helped by a carefully trimmed moustache that looked like a decoration he'd awarded himself.

Polly, the girl Victor had moved in with a year ago, was standing in the vestibule at the entrance to the chapel. She was a dancer, or a dance student, in her twenties and she had the startled look of a commedia clown, with her flopping curls and her big eyes staring wildly out of her white face. Richard had met her once, after Victor and she had started living together, and he'd found her disconcerting. She had a loud, nervous laugh and her conversation consisted of strange non sequiturs. A week ago she'd sent out a mass email to all Victor's contacts saying: 'Please come celebrate your departed chum. Bring songs/dances/

words!' Richard had called her and it had taken him several minutes to piece together what was in fact a brutally simple story: that she had come home a few days earlier to find Vic dead on the couch from a heart attack.

She thrust out a hand as they approached, giving no sign of recognising Richard.

Audrey was there; seated already, right at the front of the chapel with the two children. The little girl, who must have been five now, sat staring at the closed casket. The boy, not yet three, was marching up and down between the rows of chairs.

Sara instinctively made for the chairs next to Audrey, and Richard followed behind. She seemed to flinch as she saw them, but she yielded to Sara's smile and the two embraced. With Richard, however, she remained oddly aloof. He thought she must be displacing her anger with Victor onto him, which struck him as childish, though he was careful to seem understanding. He really had half-expected her to stay away from the funeral altogether. It wasn't as if the children were old enough to get any benefit from seeing their father in a casket while strangers said incomprehensible things about him. And what possible good could Audrey herself hope to get out of it?

The thought propelled him into the contemplation of his own circumstances. How lucky I am, he felt, glancing fondly at Sara. There was a time, not so long ago, when things might have gone badly wrong between them. He was well aware of that. But they hadn't, and instead he seemed to have entered a new phase of happiness in his domestic life.

He thought, as he often did, of his evening at Paradise Meadow. He had fallen asleep, or passed out, in the long grass. When he awoke it was too late to pretend he'd come back from New York on the last train, which had meant he would have to wait till the morning before going home. He'd debated sleeping in the car, but instead drove to a motel in East Deerfield, where he got a few hours' rest. Back at the house, when he'd found the bedroom empty and no sign of Sara, he'd had a brief, irrational and highly uncharacteristic attack of jealousy, wondering if the tables had been turned and it was Sara who was being unfaithful. The idea, which had never entered his mind before, had been amazingly upsetting. Imagining himself the victim of a punitive fate that was about to visit the sharpest imaginable form of humiliation on him, he was in a state of near-panic by the time he burst into Sara's studio, having searched everywhere in the house itself. Of his encounter with the swan he remembered only a dazzle of whiteness out of which something staggeringly violent had exploded. Then he had seen Sara, and despite the blood welling out of his lips, had been flooded with relief. She'd accepted his story of coming home on the early train without any sign of suspicion, and except for the swelling on his mouth (which lasted several days and was a cause of great embarrassment at morning assembly), things had quickly gone back to normal.

It was from then, in hindsight, that he dated the onset of his present marital contentment. This was purely a private matter; not something he felt any urge to talk about to Sara, and in fact he liked thinking of it as a secret. A benign secret, unlike its corrosive predecessor; quietly strengthening the bond between them as they headed together into the late summer of their lives. It took the form of an appreciative calm, a desire to have Sara's opinion on everything, a dislike of being apart from her, and a total lack of interest in other women.

The chapel was filling up. Polly came in, accompanied by Victor's brother, and the room fell silent. Polly looked at the crowded seats, assumed a panicked expression, and promptly sat down, leaving the brother to officiate alone. He did this with smooth assurance, calling on people to come up and speak or read as the spirit moved them. He gave an impression of slumming it a little, here among Victor's motley circle.

The tributes were the usual thing: funny stories, sentimental anecdotes, favourite passages from the books and articles Victor had written. Polly recovered her poise sufficiently to stand up at one point, and for a painful moment Richard thought she was going to do a dance, but she recited a poem. It appeared to be about ponies, though it struck the same note of vaguely religious solemnity as the three or four other poems that had been read, and didn't seem any more beside the point than any of them.

Death, he thought, his attention drifting, was actually not a particularly interesting phenomenon. It was touted as the big subject; the great mystery that poets and metaphysicians were supposed to explore on behalf of the rest of us. But without all the obsolete trappings of immortality and the afterlife, what did it really amount to, in itself?

Nothing. It belonged, at best, with the 'negative concepts': Schopenhauer's term for ideas like Justice or Freedom that can only be known by their absence. We think of it as an occurrence, but really it's the reverse: a cessation of occurrence. What it means, when a friend dies, isn't that something has happened, but just that all kinds of things will stop happening. Instead of having dinner together next week or next month or next year, you won't be having dinner together any of those times. It sculpts itself from the cancellation of all possible future

83

exchanges; from the emails and texts you won't be sending each other any more, the phone conversations you won't be having, the get-togethers you won't be scheduling in your calendar. That's what another person's life is to you. Into the hollow formed by these curtailments we pour our feelings of loss like bronze into a mould, and call the resulting object the death of a loved one. But really, that was a confusion of categories.

He had thought of dredging up some amusing story about Victor's excesses, but in the light of Victor's shiftless and depressing last couple of years, the stories all seemed more like cautionary tales than celebrations of Victor's supposed love of life. Anyway, he hadn't really felt like contributing to the myth Victor's other friends would no doubt be trying to create (and indeed were), of some lovably tragic Falstaffian character. He did love him, he supposed, but he was having a hard time finding the thread of that feeling. For a long time now the thought of Victor had roused something more like angry exasperation than affection. The rituals of their friendship had continued, but the friendship itself had become more like an official alliance between nations than a living bond between human beings. In all candour, he had written Vic off as a lost cause after that second break-up with Audrey, and the news of his death had just seemed to confirm the judgement.

So he had looked for something to read instead, trawling through the copiously marked-up copies of his beloved Transcendentalists. In the end he'd chosen a passage from Thoreau arguing that the death of a friend compels us to 'fulfill the promise of our friend's life' in addition to our own. He wasn't sure he really agreed with the sentiment but at least it managed to be uplifting without caving in to pseudo-religious palliatives. Anyway, he'd shown Sara the passage and she'd said it was perfect.

Polly finished her poem and crumpled back into her seat.

Seeing that no one else was going forward, Richard stood up. His plan was to ad lib for a few minutes after reading the passage. He had the seasoned schoolteacher's confidence in his ability to extemporise.

Turning to face the audience he was struck by the number of tear-filled eyes glistening before him. He hadn't picked up on the emotion in the room. It filled him with an odd mixture of shame at having failed to rise to the occasion himself, and a querulous wish to remind everyone of the shortcomings of the deceased.

He introduced himself and in his mildest, most affable morning-assembly manner announced that he was going to read something from the great Henry David Thoreau, a text he was sure many of them were familiar with.

'"On the death of a friend,"' he read, '"we should consider that the fates through confidence have devolved on us the task of a double living, that we——"'

He broke off. He had seen something so inexplicable and so disconcerting that for a moment he was unable to speak.

It was Francesca, sitting at the back of the chapel. The sight seemed to require a degree of mental agility to make sense of, that he was simply unable to summon. It was as if some very strange spatial or temporal anomaly had occurred, and either he or Francesca or the chapel full of mourners wasn't really there.

He looked back down at his sheet of paper, and read on mechanically:

"'... have devolved on us the ... the task of a double living, that we have henceforth to fulfill the, uh, promise of our friend's life also, in our own, to the world ...'" He struggled to understand the phrases he was repeating. As he made his own off-the-cuff remarks he felt as if he were talking underwater, and he returned to his seat with the sense of having spoken more or less gibberish. He smiled apprehensively at Sara as he sat down. She smiled back, though he wasn't sure if it was out of approval or pity.

After the ceremony, coffee was served in the anterooms between the chapel and the lobby. Leaving Sara with Audrey, Richard moved off through the crowd, edging through the packed rooms until he saw Francesca. She was standing alone, wearing a soft-looking black leather jacket with a russet silk scarf. Seeing him approach, she lowered her cup of coffee to the saucer in her other hand; very slowly, as if afraid of spilling it.

'Francesca!'

'Hello, Richard.'

'What are you doing here?'

She held his glance a moment.

'Ah. Vic didn't tell you.'

'Didn't tell me what?'

She cleared her throat.

'We had sort of a – fling.'

'My God.'

'Well, it wasn't a great success. But we stayed friends.'

'My God. My God!'

'I thought he must have told you.'

'No!'

'I'm sorry. He told me he was going to. He's not – he wasn't the most dependable man though, was he?'

86

She gave a smile, but Richard ignored it.

'I'm stunned,' he said.

She nodded.

'I imagine it would be rather stunning. I'm sorry.'

'How did it come about – if I can ask?'

She looked away, pursing her lips as if unsure whether she wanted to tell him, then shrugged.

'He came to a gig. We had a chat, a drink. We met up a few times after that; purely social at first. Then just, you know, the normal ...'

'The normal! I wouldn't—'

'Richard, don't be upset with me, please.'

'It's not you I'm upset with.'

'Ah. Well, him either. He cared heaps about you, you know that.'

'Heaps. Do I?'

She put her hand on his arm. They were standing close, speaking very quietly.

'Don't be upset, Richard. You're happy in your life, aren't you? Vic said you were blissfully happy. Actually, the last time I saw him he said you were nauseatingly happy! And you looked happy sitting down next to your – to Sara. That was her in the blue, right? I watched you together. You looked like the happiest couple, even from the back!'

He frowned.

'I'm in shock, I guess.'

She nodded, withdrawing her hand.

There didn't seem to be much else to discuss. Besides, he didn't want to linger. Sara might see them and wonder who she was, and he had no wish to make up any more lies.

'Well, good seeing you,' he said.

'You too, Richard. Take care.'

Later, driving home, Richard realised he wasn't actually
as injured as he'd first thought. Disappointed, yes, though
it was hardly a surprise to discover Victor was capable of
making a move on his best friend's ex-lover. But not, after
all, deeply wounded. He didn't feel hurt or angry so much
as faintly scornful of them both, as if he'd caught two
pupils misbehaving in some foolish way. He was even able
to go back, very calmly, over the evening the three of them
had spent at that club in Tribeca, examining it for traces
of some spark between them. In hindsight, it seemed to
him the only real surprise was that he hadn't seen the
whole thing coming. But even this didn't arouse any great
feeling of betrayal. And just now, being with Francesca
again, so unexpectedly, hadn't had anything like the effect
on him he might have predicted. He felt a nostalgic fondness, and a dim sense that she represented some large
failure or shortcoming on his part, but there was none of
that old anguished hankering. No feeling of old fissures
reopening.

I must really be over her, he thought.

He glanced at Sara, who was gazing out the window.
How grateful he was for her calmness and quietness, her
steadfast dependability. Her undemonstrative, wifely
love – a matter of scrupulous attentions to himself and
Daniel year after year after year – seemed to him infi-
nitely more desirable than any number of romantic
gestures or passionate declarations. She had always been
indispensable to him in a practical way, managing their
household, running Daniel, but only recently had he
become fully aware of how emotionally indispensable
she was too; how linked her serenity was to his own peace

88

of mind, his happiness. He had come to think of her as an immense piece of luck that had fallen miraculously into his hands and which, even more miraculously, he had managed not to lose despite his carelessness. He still cringed, thinking of those idiotic, clandestine trips to see Francesca in New York, and that strange interlude, or non-interlude, with Bonnie at the drumming. Bonnie, thank God, had never made any allusion, by word or manner, to his presence there or his disappearance. She was very sweet, he thought, very *cool*, as she herself would have no doubt put it, and this too seemed a part of his luck.

Well, those days were over. He knew that with absolute certainty. He had entered a new phase of his life, one that seemed to stretch before him like a broad, sunlit river, and he intended keeping Sara by his side as he sailed along it. Thirty-five might be the age of obsolescence as far as evolution was concerned, he reflected, picking up a familiar thread, and it was undeniable that a certain air of futility hung over the activities of men and women as they grew older, but one persisted nevertheless, and one could hardly be blamed for wanting to pass the time in a state of comfort and companionship. Even if that comfort and companionship were founded on something artificial, or at least not comprehended by the strict axioms of survival and procreation ... Victor perhaps hadn't been able to accept this, preferring to take his chances with loneliness and *dis*comfort, which perhaps, Richard was willing to concede, made him a more courageous man, or truer to his essential self. But even if he'd gotten what he wanted, which Richard doubted, he had paid a price for it, and others had too. Marriage undoubtedly curtailed aspects of one's nature, but better that than the mayhem Victor had inflicted on everyone around him. Better anything, really, than the feral squalor of a man growing old on his own.

In the pleasantly self-congratulatory mood brought on by these thoughts, it came to Richard that perhaps even his affair with Francesca had played a necessary role in the formation of his present happiness. *I betrayed Sara before I married her so that I wouldn't have to betray her afterwards . . .* Was that possible? It seemed so. Everything, in that moment, seemed mysteriously balanced, well aligned, at least in his own existence. He was modest enough not to attribute this to any special quality of his own. It was luck again, pure luck, and the only position to take in regard to it was pure gratitude. Yet it was impossible to stave off the feeling of being in harmony with something more profound than simple luck; some deeper principle of order.

All Nature is but Art, unknown to thee . . . The words of the poem came back to him as he drove on up into the twilit mountains: *All Chance, Direction which thou canst not see . . .* Another illusion, of course, the rationalist's reinvention of God; Jehovah refurbished as a deist version of Intelligent Design, but how hard it was to resist sometimes (and how little inclined he was to do so these days), even down to the particular childishness of cloaking that already childish fallacy in an aura of mystical benignness: *All Discord, Harmony, not understood; All partial Evil, universal Good . . .* Then something else, he forgot what, ending in *-ight*, and then that wondrously shocking little one-line manifesto for eternal complacency: *One truth is clear, 'Whatever IS, is RIGHT"* . . .

A surge of love came into him; a strong desire to say something romantic. He tried to think of some words that wouldn't sound too sappy. He glanced at Sara in the mirror but she was still looking out at the sombre hills flanking the throughway. He put his hand on her knee. After a moment she laid her hand reassuringly over his.

4

Something had happened, but she wasn't exactly sure what it was. In an effort to get some purchase on it, she was going over the progression of events that had just occurred.

At the end of the service she'd lingered in the chapel talking to Audrey while Richard disappeared off into the reception. After a while she and Audrey had left the chapel with Audrey's two kids following behind, squeezing through the crowded vestibule to the room beyond, where the refreshments had been laid out. While Audrey poured herself a cup of coffee, Sara had been staring absently through an archway that led into another, longer room. A knot of people under the arch broke up and she'd glimpsed Richard at the far end, talking to a woman in a black jacket with a silk scarf. Richard, who was facing away from Sara, was rubbing at the bald spot at the back of his head, which was something he did when he was agitated. The woman was smiling at him in a way that seemed appeasing, or anyway actively sympathetic. She'd looked faintly familiar; her striking features and long brown hair evocative of some far-off occasion, though Sara couldn't place her.

Audrey had come up, with her coffee. Just then the woman had put her hand on Richard's arm and said something that made him rub his bald spot furiously.

'Do you know who that is with Richard?' Sara had asked.

Audrey turned. At once, a look of acute distress had appeared on her face.

'It's Francesca,' she said. 'I didn't realise she was here. I'm leaving.'

She looked around for her kids.

'Wait – who is she?' Sara had said.

Audrey seemed not to understand.

'Huh?'

'I mean, who *is* she?' Sara repeated.

'You must know who she is!'

'I don't.'

'She's the woman your husband introduced to Victor. It's who he left me for. The second time. Though I think she dumped him pretty quick. I assumed you knew, Sara.'

Two bright patches of red had appeared at Audrey's cheeks.

'No,' Sara said. 'I had no idea.'

'I can't believe she came. Anyway, I'm leaving.'

Abruptly she'd gathered her kids and led them off.

Sara had turned back towards Richard, but he was standing with Victor's brother now and the woman had disappeared.

An elderly man had come up to her as she was trying to remember where she'd seen her before.

'Wasn't that a moving tribute?' the man said. 'I thought that was the *most* moving tribute . . .'

She'd had no idea who he was, but tried to look politely attentive as he spoke to her, though in fact it was impossible to pay any attention at all. The things she had just heard and seen seemed to require urgent processing, as certain dreams do on waking. Nodding and smiling, she'd found herself probing blindly into fifteen years of memory for the woman's image.

Then Richard had come up, looking agitated.

'We should get going,' he'd interrupted unceremoniously.

Not wanting to offend the old guy, she hadn't immediately responded, and Richard had stood there looking increasingly impatient while the other man rambled on. After a couple of minutes, Richard had interrupted again, this time too forcefully to ignore, and they'd made their way out.

She hadn't liked being hustled out like that, and did what she did when she was annoyed, which was to retreat into herself. It wasn't exactly characteristic of Richard, to order her around, though she'd noticed recently that he was more focused on her than he used to be. More attentive, she had to acknowledge, as well as more demanding, which was nice, she supposed, though occasionally she couldn't help feeling oppressed by it. He'd started accompanying her on her afternoon stroll in the woods if he was home, something she'd always taken for granted as a solitary interlude in the day, and she'd found herself resenting the intrusion.

By the time they'd reached the car, he seemed to have gotten over whatever was bothering him.

'You okay?' he'd asked.

'I'm fine.'

'You're very quiet.'

'Just thinking.'

She'd been about to ask him about the woman he'd been talking to, but had stopped herself, not wanting him to ascribe her taciturnity to some fit of possessiveness.

They'd driven in silence for half an hour, when she felt his hand on her knee and, ever obliging, she'd laid her own hand over his. She could ask him now, she thought. But still she held back; silenced by a foreboding that he might lie to her. In a sense he'd lied already by volunteering nothing about this woman, either today or back whenever it was that he'd introduced her to Victor. But an omission wasn't quite the same as a direct lie and she realised she very badly didn't want him to lie to her directly.

What am I afraid of? she wondered, lifting her hand from his. She thought of that other time he'd lied to her, pretending he'd caught the early-morning train when she'd seen his car next to Bonnie Fletcher's in the municipal parking lot. She'd never confronted him, waiting instead for him to explain himself. Even when it became clear that he wasn't going to, she'd refused to allow herself to speculate or interrogate him. Accustomed to her own privacy, she was wary of probing other people's. It wasn't that she couldn't imagine the questions another woman might have asked. God knows she'd had plenty of general guidance on that front, from Carla. She'd even picked up what had seemed a more specific hint one afternoon near the end of that summer when she'd overheard one of the Rainbow girls in Carla's barn saying something that included the phrase 'Sara's husband', only to be shushed by the other girl as Sara immediately made her presence known. Bonnie had just driven off somewhere. She'd wondered even then about this reluctance of hers to probe. Am I afraid of what I might learn if I push too hard? Is that why I don't question him? But no sooner had the thought articulated itself than a vehement, almost bodily repudiation of it along with all its demeaning implications had risen in her, and she'd angrily closed the subject.

She stared out through the passenger window. Had she been deluding herself? Was it possible, after all, that there'd been something going on between Richard and Bonnie? Merely coupling their names seemed to entail an act of violence against her own sense of reality. Richard, pushing fifty, sensible, responsible, wryly amused by people who differed in any serious way from himself – and Bonnie, barely thirty, with her patchouli scent, her silver feather earrings, her iPod in its moccasin case at her hips, her look of being permanently a little high on something …? No, it wasn't plausible. Too much that seemed solid and incontrovertible would have to turn out to be pure illusion for that to be conceivable.

Anyway, she wondered, puzzled by the turn of her own thoughts, why was she even thinking about that now? What did Bonnie have to do with this other woman, Francesca, or whatever her name was? She seemed to have caught herself in a curious labyrinth of things past and present, remembered and forgotten. Again, more concertedly now, she tried to recall where she'd seen the woman before, struggling to light up the dimmest of distant occasions for some clue; rummaging through Richard's professional acquaintances, his more distant relatives, the handful of people he kept in touch with from his home town …

'Who was that woman you were talking to?' she asked him at last, exasperated by her memory's refusal to cooperate. 'The one in the leather jacket?'

Richard frowned, as if trying to think who she meant.

'Oh, her. She was one of Vic's girlfriends from way back. Before he married Audrey. I only met her once or twice but I guess I was the only person she knew there. I couldn't remember her name though ...'

He's lying to me. Sara felt the knowledge enter her: sharp and hard.

'She looked familiar,' she said, still unready to challenge him more directly.

'No, not possible. This would have been before you and I met.'

She sat very still, staring forward.

And then, as if the reverberations of the lie had removed an obstruction from some delicate mechanism full of gears and springs and flywheels, she felt the memory of Richard's abrupt, unexplained wish to get out of New York all those years ago shift inside her, and with a quick sense of things uncoupling and regrouping, she realised where she had seen the woman.

It was at Ryden College. She'd gone there to meet Richard, who was practising with his folk group. Hearing music she'd wandered down a corridor from the lobby and seen them through a glass panel, six or seven of them strumming and plucking and singing, among them the woman with that unmistakable head of hair, sitting over a dulcimer with a look of dreamy absorption in her instrument.

'Well? Do you know it?' Richard's voice cut in. He had been talking to her.

'I'm sorry – what?'

'Baucis and Philemon. Do you know the story?'

'No.'

'This old couple who love each other so much the gods turn them into two trees intertwined around each other when they die.' He smiled at her lovingly in the mirror. 'I was thinking of it for some reason.'

She looked away, unsure whether the fear gripping her was of the future or the past.

'Are you okay, Sara?'

'She was at Ryden College, wasn't she?' she said, turning back to look at him. 'In your folk group.'

Richard's face tensed.

'What? Who are you talking about?'

'I saw her there. Audrey said you introduced her to Victor. He had an affair with her, just after their second child was born. Her name's Francesca. You must have kept in touch with her over the years.'

Richard frowned exaggeratedly, opening his mouth as if to ask again who she was talking about. But he closed it instead, swallowing.

'All right', he said. 'All right. I was just trying to make a complicated story simple.'

'You told me a lie.'

'Christ almighty! All right. I'm sorry. But it's totally innocent. Good God, Sara! I'd be happy to tell you the whole story in all its extremely boring detail if you really want to hear it.' He gave a sidelong glance.

She turned away.

'Do you want to hear it?'

'I want to know why you told me a lie.'

'All right, I'll tell you. It's very boring, so be warned.'

Richard paused, and then sighed, rather theatrically. 'I mean, okay, it's embarrassing too, mildly, as well as complicated. Because it does have to do with me having been vaguely attracted to her at one time, ages ago, so there's that. But it's innocent; I give you my word. Do you want me to tell you, Sara?'

She said nothing. The thought of that other lie had brought back the whole episode of the swan, and the creature was in her mind again, brightening there, drawing her inward like a source of some mysterious strength.

'Okay, I'm going to tell you the whole thing. I don't want you having any suspicions about me ...'

Through the window the forested grey slopes flanking the throughway were tinged with gold light at the top. She thought of the day she and Carla had driven with the swan to the river. They'd arrived late in the afternoon. A handyman had unchained the gate and they'd continued down to the boathouse, where a wooden dock jutted into the water. A few hundred yards out into the mile-wide expanse of the river was a long, thin island with a fringe of cattails where other swans nested. She and Carla had carried the swan out of the car in its basket and set it down at the end of the jetty, stepping back to let it free itself when it was ready. For several minutes it had sat in the basket, not moving. Sara had wondered if it wasn't after all going to seize the opportunity to free itself. She'd half-hoped it wouldn't.

'He's taking the measure of things,' Carla had declared. 'They do that.'

Beside her in the car Richard had launched into some convoluted story to which she was barely listening. Something about not wanting to tell her he'd known Francesca from Ryden College precisely in case she did get the wrong idea, a fear he seemed to be attributing to the fact that, yes (he kept saying *yes*, as if strategically conceding some point in a legal argument), he had been attracted to her, and yes, he might even have been tempted to have a fling with her if he hadn't already been head over heels in love with Sara, and that, yes, on the basis of this attraction he had irrationally feared that Sara wouldn't believe he'd run into Francesca years later entirely by chance while he was walking down Third Avenue with Victor. None of it seemed real to her. She let herself slip back into that summer afternoon.

'You see?' Carla had said, when the swan stood up at last in the basket. And in spite of herself, Sara had felt a sharp joy travel through her. With a brief shudder of its wings as if awakened suddenly to the memory of freedom, it had stepped out of the shallow basket, and hobbled to the edge of the jetty. Holding its wings forward it had let itself fall into the water with a soft splash and glided off towards the island.

Richard was talking more calmly now; the story he was telling having apparently settled into a congenial form in his mind. 'So yes, I was attracted to her. I'll admit it. But there was never any possibility of my getting involved, even though she'd made it clear she wanted ... you know, that she wanted that. But it wasn't easy and it certainly wasn't comfortable seeing her every day in the classrooms and corridors. And yes, that's frankly why I quit. I never told you about her because telling you would have made it seem as if there was something for you to be concerned about, but there was nothing. Absolutely nothing. I only wish for Audrey and the kids' sake I hadn't been with Victor when I ran into her on Third Avenue. I introduced her to him, just to be polite, and I think she said something about working as a singer, maybe even mentioned a club where she was performing. I wasn't paying any attention myself, though I guess Victor was. But that's Victor, right? Of course, he never told me anything about it. Anyway ...'

It was the image of the creature moving away from her that had lodged itself in her mind. Moving away as effortlessly as if it had let go of something and was free-falling into its own future.

Richard was still talking, though his words might have been in a foreign language, for all the effect they were having on her. Something seemed to be crystallising inside her; something clear and bright though not yet ready to put in words, its form as yet indistinguishable from that of the swan gliding away from the shore; cutting a wake of light as it moved further and further out across the river, undaunted by whatever lay ahead.

Approaching the island it had merged into the glare of sunlight, becoming invisible. A few seconds later the sun had sunk behind treetops on the far shore and the glare had gone, but by then the creature had vanished into the reeds.

Afternoon of a Faun

Part One

1

'What he appears to have done — and I'll admit I'm as astonished as everyone else — is turn this election into a referendum on whether it's okay to objectify women and, frankly, assault them. I can't help noticing how frighteningly well he illustrates a phenomenon many women who've been assaulted describe, which is the double nature of the attack. First there is the physical assault, and then there is what I would call the epistemological assault, by which I mean the brazen denial that anything untoward took place. It isn't enough to violate the woman's bodily autonomy. Her version of events must also be seized and subjugated. In many cases it is this secondary attack, the seizing of a woman's reality, so to speak, that proves the most traumatic in the long term ...'

The speaker, a woman in mauve tweed, was giving the lunchtime talk at the Irving Foundation, to which my friend Marco Rosedale had brought me. Her subject was rape, specifically the relationship between rape and memory. She herself had been raped thirty years earlier (she told us this in a tone of studied neutrality that seemed intended to spare us from having to react), and recently she'd curated a travelling exhibition consisting of several installations in which the circumstances of her own and other women's assaults were reconstructed in whatever detail memory could supply, and with whatever distortions of scale memory lent those details.

The striking thing about most of these exhibits, judging from her slides, was their seeming innocuousness. No scary dungeons or sketchy back alleys, no vans with blacked-out windows; just ordinary domestic spaces. There was a student dorm room with ashtrays and plastic cups; a pool house with tiny people swimming in the pool outside; an office mail room with a frozen waterfall of huge envelopes spilling from a box. There was a comfortable-looking bedroom in which a man's suit and shirt were folded neatly over a chair. The man was in bed asleep while the woman lay beside him with her eyes open, staring at a crack in the ceiling. The two had matching wedding bands on their ring fingers.

The speaker mentioned a trend reported by therapists in a recent newspaper article. 'It's purely anecdotal,' she told us, smiling pleasantly, 'but it interests me greatly.' Large numbers of women patients had apparently begun talking to their therapists about long-ago episodes of harassment that they'd either forgotten or considered too insignificant to be worth discussing.

'It appears to be a kind of spontaneous collective impulse ...'

Marco glanced up from his lunch plate, catching my eye. He'd become interested in these subjects lately — harassment, memory, the public reverberations of private conduct — ever since getting caught up in a drama of his own in which these topics featured prominently. The drama had ended before any serious damage was done, but he was still unnerved by the experience, and hungry for any kind of elucidation.

I knew what his glance meant, more or less. Imitation had become a topic of particular interest to him, and it was predictable that he'd seize on the speaker's anecdote as proof of his theories about his own accuser. 'Why did she only come out with it *now*?' he'd begun asking in recent weeks. 'Why not thirty years ago? Why not *forty*, for Christ's sake, when it happened, or rather didn't happen? Was it just because suddenly everyone else was doing it? Was it some copycat cultural meme thing she'd succumbed to? I'd have thought Julia, of all people, would do anything to avoid seeming unoriginal ...'

I'd make some non-committal noise. I wasn't required to answer Marco, mainly just to listen, and not irritate him with comments suggesting he perhaps didn't acknowledge the full extent of the wrong done by men to women over the centuries, because he did acknowledge it; he'd just never considered himself one of those men, and even now, when his ordeal appeared to be safely over, resented the threat of being stigmatised as one when he'd done nothing to deserve it.

At any rate the speaker's anecdote about women suddenly discussing harassment en masse with their therapists clearly played straight into his suspicions about Julia's timing, even though that was hardly the point the speaker was trying to make. She was actually offering the report as a sign of newly awakening female strength (and I'm sure Marco understood this as well as I did): a silver lining to the cloud threatening the country in the form of a serial harasser of women having won the Republican nomination for the upcoming presidential election.

Marco had grown up in the same London world as I had. His father was a barrister and the family belonged to the same circle of professionals and artists as mine; left-leaning bourgeois bohemians with large houses in Islington or Holland Park or Notting Hill Gate. He was a few years older than me, which meant we weren't friends as children, but I was always aware of his existence: he was one of those boys who exude a magical charisma of good looks and easy confidence that marks them in the consciousness of their generation as people to watch. He had a striking face, hawkish but epicurean, with eyebrows coming in at an angle like arrow fletchings, giving his eyes the *mira fuerte* – 'forceful gaze' – of macho movie stars from that distant era, and strong lines either side of his slightly abbreviated-looking nose, curving out in a belling flourish around a firm-set but sensual mouth. His mother had been a model in Milan before she married, and his looks came mainly from her. From his father came the ruddy colouration of his cheeks, which added an appealing look of wind-blustered vigour to the general effect. We overlapped for a year or two at the same school in London, after which he went off to Cambridge, emerging a few years later as a precociously assured young talent in British television. Longish news features were what he first became known for, usually about political conflict and almost always pervaded by an atmosphere of danger that, intentionally or not, cast him in a glamorously intrepid light.

His first big coup came when the British ambassador to Uruguay was kidnapped by the Tupamaros guerrillas. Marco's parents had a weekend cottage near the ambassador's family farm in Sussex, and Marco was able to get an early interview with family members, blinking in shock outside their oast houses a few hours after news of the kidnapping reached England. On the back of this he got a commission to make a programme about the guerillas themselves. Footage of Héctor Pérez distributing stolen food in the slums of Montevideo, along with a lingering close-up of the 'People's Prison' where the ambassador himself was possibly being held at the very moment of filming, provoked spasms of scandalised indignation in the right-wing press, ensuring Marco's success with the left, and providing the formula for future triumphs.

From the Tupamaros he went on to embed himself for periods with insurrectionists and paramilitaries across half the world. He was in Northern Ireland in 1975, filming a programme that upset even some of his admirers, when the actions he was accused of decades later were alleged to have taken place.

The footage in question, of a young Catholic woman being tarred and feathered, had no direct connection with the private scene that occurred, or didn't occur, in Marco's hotel room a few hours after he filmed it, but a certain affinity exists between the two (or does in my mind); and I found myself thinking of both as I listened to the tweed-clad woman at the lectern speaking about rape and memory, imitation and repetition, while Marco sat nodding, frowning, jabbing at ragged chicken bones on his plate, tilting his face this way and that in his usual unguarded fashion; every word seemingly triggering some reflex of warm approval or restless annoyance.

2

His 'ordeal' (as he'd taken to calling it) began with, of all things, a private message on Twitter. He'd never used Twitter for private communication. For that matter he'd never tweeted. The only reason he had a Twitter account at all was to search for tweets about himself (he told me this with an only mildly embarrassed grin).

'@Marcorosedale,' the message read, 'desperately need to get hold of you. Can you contact me asap?'

The sender, a Mel Sauer, included his email address, the server for which was a British national newspaper. I'll call it the *Messenger*.

It depressed Marco a little to think he'd dropped so far off the map that a major newspaper couldn't track down his phone number. But the message itself seemed to him to bode well. He wondered if it might have something to do with his current project, a pilot for a series combining travelogue and crime reportage, provisionally titled *A Crime and a Place*. The idea – by his own admission more gimmicky than anything he'd tried before – was to attend trials at county courthouses across the US, and look at the crimes through the lens of local cultural issues. 'I'm thinking *Artisanal murder* for the tagline,' he'd joked; 'or else *Marco Rosedale sells out for one last gig ...*' Somewhat to his surprise, early reaction to a rough cut of a domestic violence trial in Maine had been positive, and he was already in talks with cable companies and independent financiers. Was it possible, he wondered, that the *Messenger* had got wind of the project and wanted to run a puff piece of some kind? Marco didn't like to think he cared about such things any longer, but he admitted feeling a minor stir of excitement. It was years since he'd had any serious attention from the press.

He made himself wait a couple of days, and then sent a laconic note with his number in Brooklyn.

The phone rang almost immediately.

'Marco? Mel Sauer here. So good of you to get back to me. We're running an excerpt from a memoir by one of your old girlfriends, and I wanted to have a quick word with you about the contents. Take your temperature, as it were.'

So much for the puff piece. The man's tone – glib, presumptuous, a little nervous – put Marco on his guard.

'Which girlfriend?'

'Julia Gault.'

The name surprised him – their affair had been brief, and he'd never actually thought of her as his 'girlfriend'.

'Julia's publishing a memoir?'

'She's written one. I don't know that she has a publisher, necessarily, at this point, but we're keen to run the excerpt regardless. You're in it, which is why I want to talk to you.'

'What does she say?'

'Well, it's very candid, and somewhat ... intimate.'

Marco, who'd already been rifling his long past for an incident in his personal life that could possibly interest an

English newspaper, and drawn a complete blank, blurted out the only thing he could think of.

'You're going to inform me I have a secret illegitimate child – is that it? All grown up presumably, given how long ago our little fling was ...'

Sauer chuckled.

'No, nothing like that. Why don't I email you the relevant passage, Marco, then you can read it and we can talk again?'

'Okay.'

'You may dispute one or two details, in which case we'd certainly consider running something in tandem by yourself. We'd be very open to that, in fact.'

'Send it over,' Marco told him.

An email arrived a few minutes later: 'Here you go. Like I say, just taking your temperature at this point! Let me know your thoughts. Yours ever, Mel.'

The passage from Julia Gault's memoir was attached.

I should mention that the name Julia Gault was familiar to me, and had been for almost as long as I could remember, though it was years since I'd heard it spoken. There was a time when I thought I might write a long novel, even a series of novels, about that distant English world of ours, in which Julia's recurrent appearance at the periphery of my life as she transited through the many phases of her own, would form a significant motif. I can't say I knew her in any way that properly qualified me to write about her. I was a shy teenager in the period when she was a regular presence in our house, and I don't think I ever had a private conversation with her. But she made a strong impression on me, and as an adult, qualified or not, I spent many hours over many years making notes and sketches for what, in the grandiose ambition consuming me, was intended to be a portrait of her in the monumental manner of Proust's Odette or Anthony Powell's Pamela Flitton.

I hadn't realised she and Marco had had a fling, though it didn't surprise me to hear it. She'd been something of a media star herself for a short time, a current affairs presenter on a popular but serious TV show (the combination existed once), though from what I knew her own decline had been steeper and harder than Marco's. The last news I'd heard of her involved money troubles stemming from a messy divorce and a house-sitting stint in the home of friends that had ended badly when she refused to leave.

The passage from her memoir that Sauer had sent began as a reminiscence of the sexual mores of the 1970s in general and the behaviour of men at that time in particular. Marco read it aloud from his phone to me and my wife when he visited us that spring to talk about his situation. The gist of it was that men were more overtly sexist then; more unabashedly condescending, imperious, entitled, aggressive and preeningly lustful, than they were now, and that young women like herself had been duped into thinking that a reluctance to play along was evidence of a prudish spirit. Marco was offered up as a characteristic specimen of the period, strutting about the globe in his leather jacket and jeans, with a fixed grin of libidinous intent on his handsome face and various phallic items of photographic equipment slung over his shoulder.

Despite the note of ridicule, it was, on the face of it, an affectionate portrait, and I believed Marco when he told me that on first reading it, he'd thought it pretty harmless. He wasn't sure why the *Messenger* considered it worth publishing, but his feeling was that if Julia could make some money out of it, then good luck to her. He knew vaguely about her straitened circumstances, and was sympathetically disposed. The leather-jacketed stud stuff didn't bother him; in fact, he told me, it had made him briefly nostalgic for his younger, cockier self.

He'd been about to email Sauer that he had no objections to the article, when a dim misgiving made him reread it. Only on this second reading did he take in the potentially damaging part. It was packed into a relatively small space; just a few sentences two thirds of the way through, easy to overlook, or at least mis-gauge. In them, Julia described an incident that occurred while she was working as the research assistant on his Belfast film. They'd been drinking at the bar of their hotel after a difficult shoot. At one point he'd kissed her, and after a while they'd gone upstairs to his room. She was in a serious relationship with someone else at the time – a university boyfriend whom she was planning to marry. Upstairs with Marco, she'd had an attack of fidelity and told Marco very apologetically that she didn't want go to bed with him after all.

'Did he take any notice?' her piece continued in its oddly jaunty way. 'Not a bit of it! Next thing I knew, my buttons and buckles and fasteners were being undone by what felt like about a hundred pairs of exceedingly powerful if also exceedingly nimble and well-practised hands, and I was lying naked underneath him on the bed. If memory serves, it was all over very quickly.' From there the piece swerved back into affectionately lampooning mode, teasingly describing the long row of sharp-toed leather ankle boots lined up in the corner of Marco's hotel room, along with its grimy corner washbasin and fly-specked ceiling light, but also praising his TV programmes, and declaring that 'in spite of everything' she was proud to have started her media career working with someone so talented and dynamic.

The accusation he'd missed the first time around hit him square-on this time. She was saying he had assaulted her. Regardless of the cheery tone, regardless of the decades that had passed since the night in question, it was a statement that could cause him serious harm. It was the kind of thing that, once said about you in public, rendered you permanently suspect – at best.

He emailed Sauer, telling him he considered the piece malicious and defamatory, and that he was astonished the *Messenger* would even consider publishing it. Sauer wrote back, suavely placating, assuring him that nothing was set in stone yet, repeating that for now he was just interested in, as he put it, 'taking your temperature', while also asking if Marco could be more specific about what he found 'defamatory'. Reluctantly (unversed as he was in these matters, Marco sensed that to repeat an allegation, even if just to defend oneself against it, was a sure way to increase its weight and substance), he directed Sauer's attention to the scene in the hotel bedroom.

Sauer replied: 'Are you suggesting you didn't sleep with her that night?'

'No,' Marco corrected him. 'I probably did sleep with her that night. I'm not disputing that we had a fling. But it certainly didn't happen the way she describes it.'

That 'probably' of his was a mistake; at any rate it gave Sauer a little crack to slither through. 'Do please correct me if I'm wrong,' he emailed back, 'but it sounds as though there's some uncertainty in your memory about the events of that night. Is that in fact the case?'

To which Marco retorted impatiently: 'Of course there's some uncertainty about that night! It was forty years ago! But I'm damn sure whatever happened was fully consensual.' Already he was beginning to feel pestered; angry at being drawn in even this far.

'I understand of course,' Sauer wrote soothingly. 'Memories can be slippery, can't they? As I said, we'd be very open to something by you presenting your side of the story. We're always terribly concerned to be balanced. Do please let me know if you'd like to write a riposte of some sort. Perhaps you might want to remind people that all kinds of behaviours we condemn now were considered perfectly acceptable in those days. I think that's a point of view many of our readers would sympathise with.'

Enraged, Marco typed: 'Go fuck yourself, you slimy sewer rat. All I have to say is that if you print this I'll sue you and your shitty excuse for a newspaper for every penny you're worth.'

He deleted the words, however. He wasn't the son of a barrister for nothing; he understood the dangers of emailing abuse and threats to a newspaper features editor who already appeared to be out for his blood. Instead he wrote: 'Thanks, but my point is that I never indulged in those "behaviours": never wanted to, never needed to, never felt they were "acceptable" even in "those days". As I said in my first email, the article is defamatory. Really, I have nothing further to add.'

There was no immediate reply, and after a while Marco began to feel cautiously hopeful that his point had been taken. Libel laws being stricter in England than the States, he knew the *Messenger* would have to be careful. It seemed possible this man Sauer had genuinely thought he might not mind the article, and that Marco had scared him off just by showing that he did. Sauer's response, when it finally came, didn't entirely dispel this optimism:

'Thank you for this, Marco, enormously appreciated. As I say, just wanted to take your temperature. Will discuss with my senior editor tomorrow. Have a good night!'

Marco slept reasonably well (he remembered this because it was the last good night's sleep he got for several weeks), but in the morning he found an email from Sauer in his inbox. 'Hello Marco, we do feel Julia has a right to tell her side of this important story and are inclined to press ahead on the basis of that, but we equally feel you should have an opportunity to defend yourself. I'm attaching a suggested snapshot about you, listing your considerable accomplishments in I trust acceptable terms, though do please feel free to revise as you see fit, and we are more than happy to offer you equal space with Julia to comment however you choose, within reason. Greatly looking forward to your thoughts about this.'

The 'snapshot' described Marco in ingratiating terms, making him sound far more successful than he really was. He was flattered for a moment, but soon realised that in the context of the proposed article itself, the flattery would merely make readers dislike him even more than they were going to anyway. What really unsettled him, however, was the opening: 'Marco Rosedale, son of eminent barrister Sir Alec Rosedale QC ...'

Having lived half his life in the US, Marco sometimes forgot what a considerable personage his father still was in British cultural and political circles. Even now, in his nineties, the old man was something of a public figure, lending his name to progressive causes and occasionally appearing as a guest on TV shows, where he cut a figure of simple dignity: white-haired, mild-eyed, his mind as alert as it had ever been, his sympathies for the downtrodden undimmed. Marco revered him, but preferred not to define himself in terms of his distinguished paternity, and it was always a bit of a shock to him when other people did. On this occasion, along with the shock, came a sudden suspicion of why the *Messenger* was so interested in publishing Julia's tale. Dirt on a well-known, well-respected name. Just the kind of sleazy exercise English newspapers liked to indulge in on behalf of their readers; the more respected their target, the better.

I'm not sure I agreed this was their sole motive. Julia had had her own celebrity moment (albeit briefly and long ago), and Marco himself was not a totally unknown commodity, so there was some scandal mileage in each of them in their own right. But no doubt the connection to Sir Alec helped. Either way, the thought of his father getting dragged into this was upsetting to Marco for all sorts of reasons. He'd always had a sense of himself as somehow questionable, dubious even, compared to his father: generationally inferior you could say; condemned, by historical forces if not personal inclination, to be looser and loucher. So the accusations touched a nerve. Then too, he was just plain mortified; ashamed at the prospect of his father seeing him engulfed in this miasma that seemed to be moving towards him, wafting like a bad smell out of Sauer's emails.

He steeled himself for battle, resolving not to trouble his old man's peace, even though he could have used his advice.

3

The first I heard of all this was in May of 2016, when Marco called me upstate and invited himself for the weekend: 'I need to talk to you about something ...'

He was wearing one of his usual casually dapper outfits when I picked him up at the train station – dark jacket over a mustard polo neck, English cords tapering to grained leather boots. But he looked pretty ragged all the same: eyes bloodshot, grey-brown stubble blurring the normally clean lines of his chin and cheekbones.

'I haven't slept for a month,' he said, catching the look on my face.

'How come?'

'Tell me something. Have you been following these sexual harassment dramas in the news?'

'You mean like ... Bill Cosby?'

'Cosby, Assange, DSK, Jian Ghomeshi ... Do you follow them?'

I felt a shade apprehensive.

'Some, a little. Why?'

'What interests you about them?'

'I mean, they're all very different from each other, aren't they?'

'In what way?'

'Well ... I suppose with some it's just the fascination of hearing about appalling behaviour ...'

He nodded gloomily. 'And others?'

'Maybe something more like a suspense novel? Guilty or not guilty? The mystery of what happens between two people in a room. I think I prefer that kind.'

'Why?'

'I guess because there's no basis for an objective judgement, which means the onus of belief is entirely on the believer.'

I had a foreboding, as I spoke, of what he was about to tell me; the gist of it if not the details. It stirred an odd mixture of reactions: empathy, but also something more like self-protectiveness. Certainly I didn't want to indicate any willingness to be recruited in support of some defunct male prerogative, if that was where this was going.

'The onus of belief ...' Marco repeated, thoughtfully. 'What does that mean, "the onus of belief is on the believer?"'

I'd blabbed out the words without thinking, but I did my best to make sense of them.

'Well, you make a judgement one way or the other, because that's how the mind works. It's geared towards judgement, presumably because life requires decisions to be made, constantly and rapidly. But in these kinds of situations there's no solid basis for judgement other than your own assumptions and prejudices. So you're forced up against yourself, your own mysteries. I like that kind of story.'

We drove in silence for a bit. The wooded mountainsides either side of the state highway were coming into leaf: powdery sprays of pale pink and green. I'd always thought these spring colours, subtler than their fall equivalents but just as varied, weren't properly appreciated, but I refrained from comment. Marco clearly hadn't come up to talk about the scenery.

I want to be accurate about the nature of our friendship. It had begun ten years earlier, when I'd recognised him at a party in New York. I still had some vestige of my old teenage sense of him as a heroic figure, which made me deferential, which in turn seemed to make him comfortable. Anyway, we hit it off. The fact that I was no more successful in my sphere than he was in his, probably helped: he could be prickly with people doing obviously better than he was. For my part I was always glad, in my somewhat isolated life, to make a new friend. More positively, I liked his cast of mind, which was detachedly curious and cheerfully unillusioned. That our fathers had both been prominent figures in the London we'd left behind (mine was a well-known architect), gave us plenty to talk about. Also, we'd both been Englishmen-on-the-make in New York at one time, and some of the old fun of that game revived itself when we were together.

I began spending Wednesday nights at his house in the fall, when I taught in New York. These weekly stayovers were something I looked forward to, and I think he did too. In return for his hospitality I'd take him out to his favourite restaurant on Gates Avenue where they kept a taleggio risotto with chicken liver on the menu just for him (or so they told him), and we'd usually be nattering till long after they closed the kitchen. So in that way we were good friends; pals. On the other hand we'd connected too late in life to form the kind of really deep bonds that transcend all other considerations. There were limits — we hadn't tested them, but they surely existed — to what either of us might be willing to endure or sacrifice for the other. It wasn't an elemental relationship, in other words, though in a way this made it more interesting. One gets a taste for impure things, as one gets older.

'Well, anyway,' he said as we turned off the highway, 'I have one of those stories for you. The mystery kind. Starring me.'

4

He'd sketched the outlines by the time we arrived at the house. Caitlin, my wife, was in the dining room, sorting through a delivery of wine. Rows of freshly unpacked bottles stood before her on the table, glittering in the sunlight. She liked organising things and she liked wine, so she was in excellent spirits. She liked Marco too. His good looks and slight air of dissipation brought out a sort of answering rakishness in her. She'd had a wild youth herself, before we got married, and she enjoyed being reminded of it.

'I'm plotting out the drinks menu for today and tomorrow,' she said. 'I thought we'd build up to something really stellar. Maybe these Volnays?'

Marco was always pleased to see her, though I sensed he was wary of discussing his situation in front of her. He hadn't told Hanan, for instance, his girlfriend of four years. 'You don't know how people are going to react,' he'd explained in the car. 'Hanan especially. She may be supportive or she may decide she has some obligation of sisterly solidarity with Julia. I don't want to put her to the test if I can avoid it.'

We talked about other things at lunch, mainly what Caitlin was going to do with her life now that our kids had left for college and the demands of motherhood were tapering off. Marco, who'd always seemed genuinely intrigued by her decision to become a full-time mother, participated valiantly. But as he was quizzing her on her various pre-motherhood jobs, she interrupted him, putting her hand on his arm.

'It's nice of you to be interested, Marco, but what's going on with you? You don't seem happy.'

He hesitated, before nodding.

'You're right. I'm not. I'm about to have my life destroyed.'

The three of us spent the rest of the day talking about it. When it grew chilly in the kitchen we moved into the living room and lit a fire. At intervals Caitlin went over to the dining room table, and, after carefully reinspecting the bottles, chose one to suit the drift of conversation, and refilled our glasses.

In concrete terms, what had happened since Sauer's email inviting Marco to write something to 'defend' himself, was a protracted stand-off.

'The invitation smelled like a trap to me,' he said, 'a way of getting my implied consent to publish the excerpt. My instinct was still to say no. They're nervous of being sued, I could sense that, and I didn't want to do anything to make them less nervous. Also I didn't want to give any legitimacy to the idea that there really are two sides to this story, which there are not. I know I can't expect anyone, including you guys, to just take that on trust. You can't *not* have doubts. I understand that. I'm not asking for belief anyway, just advice. And maybe some pity! But *I* certainly wasn't going to give any ground on it. On the other hand, I felt I should keep my options open in case they decided to print the fucking thing anyway ...'

126

He'd skirted the issue, ignoring Sauer's invitation and simply restating that the article was defamatory. His curt email produced another promising silence. Two whole days passed, and then Sauer wrote: 'Marco, I hear your concern. Definitely don't want to publish anything defamatory. Running the piece through legal and will get back to you. Thanks ever so for your patience!'

'He sounds kind of creepy,' Caitlin said.

Marco nodded.

'Anyway, a couple more days pass and then he sends this.'

He read from his phone: 'Marco, Legal feel the piece is not defamatory and so we want to go forward with publication. Have you by chance given further thought to writing something from your side? We want to offer you every opportunity to put your own case if you dispute Julia's version of events. Think our readers will find the two perspectives on this fascinating. As said, we're happy to give you equal space, and can assure you we won't edit (though just bear in mind we're a "family" newspaper!!).'

'How could their legal department just unilaterally decide it wasn't defamatory?' I asked. 'It's not like they have any way of proving it, I assume?'

'Of course not,' Marco said, frowning. 'Frankly, I thought they were bluffing. I still do. It doesn't make sense. This is the kind of thing juries award millions in damages for. I might come out of this a pariah but there's a good chance I'll be an extremely rich pariah.'

'You could move up here, Marco,' Caitlin said. 'We'd still socialise with you.'

He smiled. 'On the other hand maybe there's something I'm just not seeing. I'm not a lawyer, after all. I'd have asked my dad for his advice, but I don't want him dragged into this ... But I did draft a long email to this outfit in London that deals with complaints against the press. I haven't sent it yet because I don't want to spread the story around, even to them, if I don't have to. But I thought it wouldn't hurt to drop their name to Sauer, so I emailed saying I was going to ask Ipso — that's their name; Independent Press something or other — what they thought about my writing this riposte, and that I'd get back to him.'

'Good move,' I said.

'Well, it did seem to rattle him.'

Sauer's reply offered a minor concession: after further consultation with 'Legal' he'd asked Julia to take out the sentence about lying naked underneath Marco on the hotel bed, and she'd agreed. 'Less explicit that way,' Sauer wrote, 'and we hope you feel that makes it acceptable. Planning to go to press end of month so you have another three plus weeks. Very hopeful you'll send us something to accompany this light-hearted but important article. Think it over!'

There'd been a few more rounds of brinkmanship since then, but that was more or less where things stood that weekend. No commitment from Marco to write a response; no further concessions from Sauer except for an attempt at financial enticement ('fee could be negotiable if that helps') to which Marco hadn't deigned to respond; and a clock apparently ticking.

I haven't conveyed the discomfort Marco was in as he recounted all this. Despite the sardonic humour he maintained, it was clearly intense; present in his wracked expression, in the pitch of his voice, in the flinching, frowning, jerking-back motion that periodically seized him: a sort of excruciated recoil, as if from some unsavoury presence continually encroaching on his private space. He'd convinced himself that Sauer was acting out of purely cynical, gutter-journalism motives; that his claim to believe Julia's article was 'important' was hypocritical crap; his proof being the half-heartedness with which Sauer actually made this claim. He believed this half-heartedness was intentional; a deliberate, jeering signal that Sauer didn't in fact give a damn whether the piece was 'important', or even true; that along with the prospect of a juicily salacious story, he was enjoying himself making Marco writhe. There was the business about knocking his father also, Marco believed, and bound up with that, possibly, a class-war element, with Sauer, definitely not a beneficiary of a private education judging from his writing style, revelling in having got a son of privilege into his grimy clutches. Again, I wasn't sure I agreed with every aspect of the analysis – Marco was always a little quick to read class warfare into his exchanges with other Brits – but I could see how Sauer's oily pretence of concern could get under his skin.

'Almost the worst of it,' he said, 'aside from not being able to sleep, is not being able to think about anything else. As you can see I've become a complete monomaniac. Even if my friends and colleagues don't shun me for being a sexual predator, they'll do it for being a crashing bore. Listen to me! I haven't even asked about your kids! How are your kids?'

'They're fine,' I told him, wincing at the sound of him using that terrible phrase 'sexual predator' about himself. It was as if he were trying to get used to it ahead of time, and I felt a burst of real sympathy for him. 'And you're not being a bore.'

'Christ! What the hell are those?'

He was pointing towards the window. I looked out.

'Wild turkeys.'

Two toms and a hen, part of a large flock that often came out of the woods for the spillage from Caitlin's bird-feeders, had wandered onto the meadow beyond our lawn.

'They look like dinosaurs!'

As they came close to the lawn, the larger of the toms raised his black tail feathers and fanned them into a tall, bronze-ringed semicircle. The three of us watched as he began moving in short, suave bursts towards the hen.

'Speaking of sex ...' I said.

The hen moved off a few paces, seemingly indifferent, while the smaller tom hung back, observing. After a moment the big tom glided again towards the hen, tilting his enormous fan now this way, now that, while she wandered off again, pecking nonchalantly in the grass. The tom appeared to be readying himself for his next pass. His neck had turned bright blue. Stretching it forward, he made a tender, crooning, putt-putt-putt sound. The hen paused, faltering in her indifference. The smaller tom looked from one to the other, with an air of studious fascination. Then the hen stepped forward a few paces, and very matter-of-factly lay down in the grass. At once the big tom sailed forward, puffing out his chest feathers, fanning his dark tail like some strange satanic peacock, and climbed onto her back, his curved spike of beard waving at his throat as he trod her, the wattled skin above his neck engorged and red, his head gone entirely white, the long appendage of flesh over his bill dangling weirdly, his whole body swollen and immense, as if dilated into some billowing, fantastical and irresistible idea of itself. Scooping the hen's tail feathers to the side with his own, he lowered himself and began thrusting. After a few seconds he stepped off and walked uncertainly away. The hen stood up and did the same.

A silence descended on us; some minor awkwardness in it that was perhaps our own voyeurism catching us unawares, or perhaps just the slightly too blatant connection to what we'd just been discussing. I made another joke, quoting from Julia's article.

'"It was all over very quickly ..."'

Marco laughed good-naturedly. 'Now, now ...'

Caitlin got up to open another bottle, a thoughtful look on her face.

'But so what actually did happen that night?' she asked when she came back. 'Do you remember it at all?'

Marco looked at her, taking in the slight change of tone, and then nodded, as if to say he welcomed the question.

'I've been trying to. It was a long time ago, so it's never going to be crystal clear. It wasn't the first time we slept together, I know that for sure. We'd done it before, in London, at least once. I remember because I remember her telling me she had a boyfriend who she was serious about, and we agreed it was just going to be a one-off. Belfast was maybe a couple of weeks later. We'd had a stressful day shooting with an ex-militia contact who'd brought us to a flat overlooking this back alley where a Catholic girl was going to be punished by some Provos for consorting with a British soldier. It was extremely gruelling to watch. They stripped her half-naked and tarred and feathered her, and we got the whole thing on camera. Julia and I and the camera crew went back to the hotel and had a few drinks to decompress. At some point the crew went off to eat but she and I stayed in the bar.

We were drinking whisky, I remember that, and she was matching me shot for shot. We kissed a bit in the bar and like she says I invited her up to my room where I'm sure, knowing my twenty-something-year-old self, I was fully intending to get her into bed. I don't recall her mentioning her boyfriend that time. I'm not saying she didn't, but what would have been the point, since I already knew about him? But let's say she did, and let's say she did express some misgivings about being unfaithful again, even some outright reluctance, there's still no way I'd have coerced her, and more to the point there's no way she'd have let herself be coerced. *You* knew Julia in those days ...'

He looked at me, and I nodded.

'She was a force, right?'

'She was.'

He turned back to Caitlin.

'I mean, not in the sense of being extrovert or boisterous – she could seem quite reserved sometimes. But once you got to know her you'd realise she was someone who knew how to handle herself. She wouldn't have submitted to anything she didn't want to do, not without putting up a fight. She certainly wouldn't have spent the entire night with me if I'd made her do anything remotely against her will, but that's what she did. I remember that part very clearly, because we were both so hungover in the morning we almost missed the taxi to the airport. The cameraman had to drag us out of bed.'

'Are you still in touch with him?' I asked. 'The cameraman?'

Marco thought for a moment.

'No. But I could probably track him down ... That's a good point.'

'Not that it would prove anything even if he remembered,' I said.

'True, but still ...'

'And by the way, your word "reluctance" ... I know you were just using it hypothetically, but it's a dangerous word, at least in my world. If a student was accused of assault and admitted the girl was reluctant, he'd be toast.'

'Oh, that's ridiculous!' Caitlin broke in. 'People have sex reluctantly all the time. I certainly have.'

I looked at her, wondering whether to feel stung, but decided to ignore it. She was more than a little tipsy, as we all were.

'Well, anyway,' Marco said, 'the point is she wasn't reluctant and I wasn't coercive. I can't prove it any more than she can prove the opposite, but that's the nature of these things. As you say, the onus of belief is on the believer ...'

'Why do you think she's doing this,' Caitlin asked, 'if it's not true?'

'I assume to make money. She's broke, I know that. Her career didn't turn out the way it was supposed to. But whose does?'

'And that was the last time you slept together, that night?'

Marco tilted his head. 'Actually, you know, I'm not sure. We weren't exactly a couple, so there was never a formal break-up. We just stopped at a certain point. But I have no idea if that was the last time. Maybe it wasn't!'

'But either way you went on working together?' I said.

'Absolutely. For at least another year. That I could prove, I imagine, for whatever it's worth.'

'And no bad feelings between you?'

'None I was aware of.'

133

'Have you tried contacting her directly?' Caitlin asked.

'No!'

'That would be intimidation,' I said.

'Seriously?' Caitlin asked. 'Just calling her up to ask what's going on?'

'It's a risk.'

'Wow.' She shook her head. She was, is, somewhat unworldly in her interests, my wife, and as a result constantly being amazed by the world.

'But does she actually know she's harming you with this story?'

'She has to know,' Marco said.

Caitlin frowned into her wine. 'I'm not getting a very clear picture of this person. Could you tell me more about her?'

Marco gave the same grave nod. I had a sense that, for him, the conversation had something of the quality of a rehearsal: an informal dry run for some sterner version of itself likely to occur somewhere down the line.

'Well, she was this quiet girl from the Midlands. Grew up on a housing estate. No father around, mother worked for the council. Got into Oxford where she was apparently very shy and retiring. Came to London as a freelance journalist and began to realise she had something that made people want her around. Worked in print and radio for a couple of years, before moving into TV.' He turned to me: 'Didn't your mother help get her that TV job?'

'That's right, she did.'

'Anyway, that's when I met her. She was assigned to me as a researcher. Actually, what she told me was she'd finagled the assignment. I was a desirable commodity then, professionally speaking. We worked very closely together, and we'd often go for a drink at the end of the day. She seemed a bit Sphinx-like at first but she turned out to have strong opinions and we had a sparring, mocking relationship that kept me on my toes. She used to call me a closet colonialist because in her opinion my embrace of third-world politics was just an update on Kipling — White Man's burden, etcetera, with journalists as the new pukka sahibs. I'd defend myself furiously, but she was right, in a way, and I knew it, which was part of what attracted me to her. I was physically attracted too, obviously. I mean, she was gorgeous. She looked like a lioness, I used to think. She had this wide, wide face with a sort of distant smile as if she was dreaming about something simultaneously enjoyable and highly dangerous. I'd say for sure we both knew we were going to end up in bed sooner or later ...'

The sun was going down behind the woods as Marco talked; lighting the hillsides opposite. I was half-listening, slipping off into my own memories of Julia. I mentioned that she'd been a presence in our house during my teens, but for a period she'd actually been something more in the nature of a fixture. My mother had befriended her, 'taken her up', as they used to say; inviting her to dinner in London or for the weekend in Sussex, connecting her with influential friends, bringing her along to first nights and private views. She was friendly to me, in the amused way of worldly young women with tongue-tied teenage boys. I didn't see anything lion- or lioness-like about her. Physically, she reminded me of the Flora figure in Botticelli's *Primavera*, with that inward look expressive of both bashfulness and sensuality, but there was certainly a fierceness about her — an air of intensely but privately pursued pleasure — that always intrigued me. And beyond this there was a radiance about her that, whatever its real cause, existed for me in my generally befogged condition at that time, as an idea of reprieve. It's not an exaggeration to say that for me she incarnated the idea of joyous freedom that I believed life consisted of once you came through the long tunnel of adolescence. I had a crush on her, also.

5

Marco had planned to spend two nights with us, but the next morning at breakfast he asked me to drive him to the train station right away. He'd decided to fly to London. He'd already bought a ticket from JFK online, and just needed to pick up his passport in Brooklyn.

He'd had an idea in the night, as a result of our conversation. He wouldn't tell me what it was as he didn't want to jinx it, but he promised to give me the full story after he got back.

He was in a jittery, distracted state as we drove to the station, talking in non-sequitur bursts about his Crime-and-Place project, his daughter's new partner, Hanan's visa problems, anything but his 'ordeal', though it was obvious he'd been up all night thinking about it. He'd shaved, and splashed on some of the cinnamon-scented cologne he sometimes wore, but a sheen of exhaustion clung to him; a sort of manic optimism shot with dread.

'There's a quiet car on the train,' I told him. 'You should get some sleep.'

'Not a chance.'

I didn't hear from him for a while. The spring turned mild and showery, with waves of blossom rolling through the woods, and birdsong bubbling everywhere like some naturally occurring spritz in the air. But it was melancholy too: our first with no child at home. I worked on a book, fitfully; breaking off regularly to remember, as if from yesterday, how I used to sit at this same desk, watching our children laughing and squabbling as they played on the swing set that stood unused now out on the empty lawn. The paradox of memory — being able to traverse in an instant the chasm of time that had taken all these years, all these thousands of days, to inch across in the first place — never ceased to fascinate me, and if I was lucky the fascination would supplant the feeling of sadness. Caitlin, less metaphysically disposed, took it harder — or maybe just took it straight. I'd see her in a doorway, staring at some haunted corner, her eyes moist, a look of bewilderment on her face as if she were trying to recall why she had ever opened herself to this inevitable desolation in the first place. I'd put my arm around her, remind her what happy, functional, unfucked-up kids our parenting, and hers especially, had produced; how they'd always be coming back to us, one way or another ... Obvious platitudes, but they seemed to comfort her, at least temporarily, and she'd cheer up, or pretend to; go off to the hospice where she volunteered, or re-pot some plants, or take a stroll with her birding binoculars, or work on a proposal for another travel book in the series we'd started before the kids were born and set aside when they were too old to pull out of school. We were tentative with each other; each of us aware of the need to establish a new basis for our marriage, or re-establish the original basis, if such a thing were possible.

One minor incident occurred, of relevance to this story. The old dairy pasture beyond our lawn was getting overgrown and in danger of reverting to forest. I rented a brush-hog from the hardware store and spent a day of pleasantly mindless labour dragging the squat, all-devouring machine back and forth by tractor across the scrub of brambles and baby pines, leaving satisfying stripes of stubble in my wake. Halfway through the job I saw a turkey hen sitting in some tall weeds. She looked up as I cruised by but she didn't move, and I realised she must have made her nest there. I steered around her, leaving a small island of brush to keep her hidden. Caitlin was alarmed when I explained the situation. She had a gift for immersing herself in the lives of whatever creatures, human or otherwise, lay closest to hand, and these ungainly birds had joined the ranks of this fondly tended menagerie. She got it into her head that, having drawn the creature here in the first place with our birdseed, we were now responsible for the successful hatching of her eggs. To that end, and with encouragement from an article in one of the many wildlife publications she read, she decided she needed to camp out in the meadow at night for the four-week incubation period, to keep the foxes away.

I don't sleep well alone. I did try sleeping in the tent with her, but after a couple of uncomfortable nights I resigned myself to a period of solitary slumber, doing my best not to complain. Anyway, it rained fairly often and on those nights, if the rain was hard enough, Caitlin felt it was safe to stay inside. By some miraculous dispensation of the powers that preside over marital harmony, we entered a phase of frequent lovemaking. Our wedding anniversary fell during this time, and we went out to celebrate at our favourite restaurant. It happened to be a dry evening, unseasonably warm, and we had a candlelit dinner on the restaurant's creek-side terrace. I wasn't thinking about the turkey as we drove home, and Caitlin said nothing about her. We went to bed, made love and fell asleep in each other's arms. Early the next morning I heard a cry from the meadow, and ran outside. Caitlin had gone to check on the nest and was standing in front of it, in a state of extreme anguish. The hen was gone, and all her eggs had been broken. It wasn't Caitlin's style to blame other people for things that went wrong, and she didn't say anything directly reproachful to me, but as we stood there looking at the wreckage of the nest with its glistening smashed eggshells spotted with blood, I heard her muttering furiously to herself: 'I should've just done what I wanted to do! I shouldn't have given in! I always give in!'

I turned and went back into the house, upset and confused. Guilty too, though I had no sense of having forced or even subtly pressured her into sleeping with me. Should I have actively discouraged her, though? Was it my responsibility to think through the situation from her point of view as well as my own? I couldn't help remembering that comment of hers about people having sex reluctantly, herself included, and of course I couldn't help thinking about Julia's accusation against Marco, and wondering if I'd just been accused – albeit within the entirely private precinct of our home – of the same thing, and if so how I should react.

The episode faded fairly quickly and we moved on, but I imagine it affected the way I viewed Marco's plight, his 'ordeal', as it continued evolving over the next several months. I don't know whether it made me more sympathetic or less. But it certainly made me more interested.

6

He called me after his return from London.

'Victory!' he shouted into the phone.

Was I momentarily dismayed? I can't think why I would have been, but memory persists in noting a split second's shadow falling before the appropriate response rose to my lips.

'That's wonderful, Marco!'

He told me the full story a couple of weeks later when I had a meeting in the city and decided to make a night of it.

I dropped off my things at his house, and we walked to our usual restaurant under the sycamores, the darkness and quiet of the neighbourhood with its ornate old brownstones and occasional modern apartment buildings reminding us both of the London we'd grown up in, though with that wilder atmosphere of even the most genteel New York neighbourhoods; the pervasive sense of more reckless lives being lived under more unpredictable conditions. We'd agreed early on in our friendship that this quality was what gave this city its edge over London, and was one of the reasons why we preferred to live there.

'My treat this time,' Marco said as we entered. 'I'm in the mood for a celebration.'

The place was packed, with a good roar of happy voices blasting out through the door. The maître d' greeted us warmly and led us to a corner table. Busboys hurried over, eagerly plying us with ice-water and crostini as if we'd crossed deserts to get there and were in urgent need of resuscitation. A waitress, new since we'd last visited, asked if we'd like to hear about the evening's special cocktails.

'We'd *love* to hear about them,' Marco said with his quick, raffish friendliness. The two had some jokey back-and-forth about the absurd ingredients of some of the drinks and Marco talked me into getting an artisanal gin decoction with pickle brine and smashed strawberries. He ordered two bottles of wine, to be opened right away, whipping out a pair of reading glasses to examine the menu and tucking them back in an inside pocket the instant he was done.

He was evidently his old self again. The Brexit vote had happened while he was in London, and he described how he'd taken advantage of the collapsing pound to go on a spree at Selfridges where he'd picked up some new outfits, including the dandyish rust-coloured cashmere jacket he was wearing. (I don't mean to portray him as an opportunist, just to convey the unguarded tone we relaxed into when it was only the two of us.)

'Look ...' He opened the jacket to show me a silk lining patterned with bright fishing lures.

'Very nice.'

Just then the waitress came back with our cocktails.

'Is that a Ted Baker?' she asked.

'Good guess!'

'I love Ted Baker.' She ran her thumb over the fabric with quick, easy familiarity. 'It's gorgeous.'

We ordered our food and got straight into the details of his London trip. I'm always interested in the minutiae of such stories and I pushed Marco to remember everything he could. He seemed to enjoy being pushed, even when the details didn't reflect well on him. Most people use self-deprecation as a clever way to look good, but the stories Marco told against himself seemed genuinely intended to make him look bad, and I had some respect for that.

The idea that had come to him that night in our guest room arose from our conversation earlier in the day. It had to do with Julia's university boyfriend – the apparent cause of her change of heart in Marco's bedroom.

'His name came back to me,' Marco said. 'Gerald Woolley.'

'I know that name. Isn't he an architectural critic?'

'He may be now. Yes, I think that was his subject. Don't tell me he's become famous ...'

'He's fairly well known, in that world.'

'Your dad knew him?'

'Yeah, but he was banned from our house after praising someone he shouldn't have. Some postmodernist, no doubt ...'

Marco laughed – the embattled lives of the men and women of our parents' generation, with their lofty principles constantly requiring indignant defence, was a source of amusement to us both.

'Well, I suddenly remembered he'd written to me.'

'A letter?'

'Yes, an actual letter! Remember those? I'd totally forgotten about it till that night at your house. I was lying in bed scrabbling through the past for the zillionth time in search of any scrap of evidence that might help prove my version of events—'

'I'd been thinking you might try to track down that cameraman.'

'Oh, I did. He's dead. He must have been in his forties when I worked with him, so – a drag but not totally surprising. Anyway, the boyfriend's name popped into my head and for some reason I seemed to be seeing it handwritten in ink on cartridge paper, and I remembered this letter he'd written me. Julia had told him about our affair, and he wanted to meet.'

'You?'

'Yes, me.'

'To fight a duel?'

Marco chuckled, filling our glasses.

'To discuss the situation, see what sort of person I was, what my intentions were.'

'That must have been quite a meeting!'

'It didn't happen. I don't think I even answered him. I imagine I dismissed him in my mind as a chump who didn't merit the effort of a reply from someone as busy and grand and generally superior as myself. No doubt I was further puffed up by the fact that I was shagging his girlfriend. That's the way I was in those days – very arrogant, very contemptuous. I also took it for granted I was going to be massively famous one day and that biographers were going to be beating a path to my door, so I kept every scrap that had anything to do with my life or career. Every press cutting, every contract; everything short of bus tickets, basically, and probably some of those too. And certainly every letter. I stopped after I moved here, but I'd packed it all up in my parents' attic when I left London, and no one's touched it since.'

'Nice!' I said.

A busboy cleared our appetisers and the waitress appeared with our main courses – mine was a pasta dish with chorizo and clams in a bright orange sea-urchin sauce.

'How were your appetisers, gentlemen?'

'They were extremely rich,' Marco said.

She looked upset.

'But we like rich,' he told her.

'Oh, good. Me too.'

'Then we'll consider allowing you to join our club.'

She gave a laugh with a flirty ripple to it that seemed genuine enough, even allowing for the transactional aspect of these exchanges. Marco gazed after her for a moment as she left; not leering, but with an impassive reflexiveness, as if he were unaware of it. There was nothing of the ageing roué about him, except, in some lights, a slight antique colouration in his teeth, which were also crowded and uneven, like mine: little crooked monuments to 1970s English dentistry.

'So the letter,' I said.

'Yes.'

'You found it?'

'Yes. Here, you can read it.'

He brought up a picture of the letter on his phone. It was written in a neat, legible hand on unlined writing paper, with the date in small roman numerals at the top. I scrolled through it.

Dear Marco (if I may),

I believe you know who I am. I hope you will forgive this intrusion, but I am trying to settle a matter of great importance concerning the future: my own but also that of our mutual friend Julia Gault, and perhaps yourself too. As you know, Julia and I have been together for several years and have been planning to get married after I finish my doctorate. I don't need to tell you that Julia is enormously attracted to you and has possibly fallen a little in love with you. Obviously this has been painful for me to discover. It is painful to acknowledge too. But I accept that these things happen, and I ask you to believe that my greatest concern here is for Julia's happiness, not my own. I want only what is best for her, and since she is in a state of some confusion about her own feelings at the moment, I feel I should try to bring some clarity to the situation myself. To that end I would like to ask you to give me an hour or so of your time.

I realise I have no right to question you about your 'intentions', and that anyway Julia is free to do as she pleases, regardless of what those intentions may be. But it would be enormously helpful to me to meet you in person, and sound you out on this delicate matter. I assure you I bear you no hostility: quite the reverse. I have long admired your work in television, and I am more than prepared to accept Julia's high opinion of you, expressed to me in a long and very honest conversation we had yesterday, in which she described you as an exceptional human being: 'exceptionally decent as well as exceptionally talented'.

I do hope this request will not sound too strange to you, and that you will consider granting it. I would be greatly honoured.

Yours,
Gerald Woolley

'That's quite a letter,' I said.

'I know. Even better than I remembered!' "Exceptionally decent as well as exceptionally talented." How extremely helpful is that?'

I was referring to the letter's honesty and candour, not its practical utility, but I let that pass.

'I mean, I know victims sometimes send weirdly affectionate messages to their attackers,' Marco continued. 'The Ghomeshi case fell apart because of that. But this is her talking to a third party, not me. And look at the date. That's after the Belfast programme was aired, meaning *after* that night in the hotel. "Exceptionally decent" – i.e. not some fucking caveman. You can imagine how relieved I was to find this!'

He'd brought the letter to the *Messenger* in person as soon as he unearthed it, taxiing across London to their offices near the Embankment. The elaborate security in the lobby made it impossible to surprise Sauer as he'd have liked. Reception had to call up with his name. An assistant had to come down to verify that Marco was who he said he was. A photo of him had to be taken and printed onto a pass. But none of this diminished the pleasure of confronting his nemesis.

'I knew I had the fucker!'

'What was he like?'

'Bland. Early forties, I'd say. A bit overweight. Gingery hair and eyebrows. Puffy face without a lot going on in it. He started out in that ridiculous flowery mode of his, telling me what a pleasant surprise it was to meet me in person. He even complimented me on a programme of mine he claimed to've seen as a student. I shoved the letter at him. You should have seen him as he read it. He was trying to look unimpressed, but these giveaway signs were twitching all over him. He was swallowing, darting his little tongue out to wet his lips, drumming his fingers on the desk … When he was finished he cleared his throat and sort of tucked his chin into his neck, looking at me with this weird expression that I think was supposed to be gently reproving, as if he'd caught me trying to pull a fast one. He started questioning the authenticity of the letter, arguing that I could have written it myself, or that Gerald Woolley might be somehow in cahoots with me after all these years.

'I didn't bother arguing back – just told him he could think what he liked and that if he still wanted to go ahead and publish the piece, that was his call but he could expect a robust reaction from me. He'd gone bright pink in the cheeks by this point. "I'll show it to Legal, if it'll make you more comfortable," he says, still trying to sound like he doesn't believe it'll make any difference. I told him I wasn't going to leave the original but that he could make a copy if he wanted. He said in that case he wouldn't bother, since he was only offering for my sake. I got up to leave, basically calling his bluff. I'd just turned my back when I heard him say in this strangled voice: "All right. We'll make a copy." So that's what we did. I didn't hear from him after that. In fact, I haven't heard a word from him since. He's apparently too much of a prick to let me know they've pulled the piece. But they have.'

'How do you know?'

'Julia told me.'

'What?'

'Yeah. She called me at my parents' house a couple of days later – Sauer must have told her about my visit. I recognised her voice immediately even though she sounded like she'd been through the wringer a few times, which no doubt she has.'

He paused, looking a bit blank suddenly, as if he'd lost his thread. Or possibly he was just exhausted.

'What did she say?' I asked.

'Oh, I don't remember exactly. Something about me being vindictive, wrecking her one chance at getting back in the game, I don't know. She wasn't very coherent.'

'She must have known you weren't going to like the article ...'

He shrugged.

'I guess she hadn't considered it from my point of view. Maybe Sauer never told her I was putting up a fight. Though he did get her to change that one line. Well, who knows? Anyway, that's how I learned they'd pulled the piece.'

'It must have been weird, talking to her after all these years ...'

'Extremely weird.'

'Was she ... was her point just that you'd stopped her getting published, or was it still about the – you know – the accusation itself?'

He looked nettled for a moment, but then nodded sombrely as though to acknowledge an obligation to satisfy my curiosity. I was his appointed auditor, after all.

'Well, both,' he said, clearing his throat.

'So you talked about it? The accusation?'

'I mean, nothing new. She said what she'd written was true and that she had a right to publish it, and I told her it wasn't and she didn't. That's basically all.' He closed his lips, breathing in through his nose, his fierce features expressing the affronted dignity that I'd come to recognise as his way of showing pain.

After a moment, he added: 'But I guess hearing her say it, hearing her actual voice in my ear telling me I'd made her do something she didn't want to do, was different from reading it in Sauer's email.'

'You mean more ... real?'

'Something like that.' He smiled drily. 'She hung up on me before we could get too deeply into it.'

The waitress came to refill our glasses, and he paused, observing her with his coolly appraising eye as she poured and withdrew.

'Look,' he said, 'I don't get satisfaction from the thought of Julia being upset, however much she maligned me. That I can promise you.'

I believed him, and said so.

'On the other hand,' he said, 'defeating Sauer after the shit he put me through – that was pure joy!'

I raised my glass. I wasn't certain I'd extracted every significant nuance of his conversation with Julia, but I felt I'd pushed him as far as I could without spoiling the atmosphere.

'Well. To victory,' I said.

'To victory!'

We finished the bottle and Marco ordered crème brûlées and Gorgonzola with Vin Santo and then some grappa. I'd drunk more than I wanted, but I was experiencing a resurgence of that irrational negative reaction I'd felt when he first told me the news, and I thought alcohol might help suppress it. I didn't understand this lurking animus. He'd been wrongly accused. He'd defended himself; fought back single-handed against a national newspaper, and won. Why would I begrudge him his feeling of triumph? It wasn't as if I had any reason to doubt his version of events. And I didn't doubt it. There just seemed to be some resistance on my part to actual rejoicing. Had I internalised the campus outlook, I wondered, with its endless, tedious refinements of anxiety over power and privilege? I suspected this must be the case: these virtuous attitudes have a way of insinuating themselves even as you resist them, as if the very act of resistance creates the pathways they need to establish themselves in your psyche.

Back at his house he smoked a cigar in his partitioned living room with its mismatched charity-shop furniture and odd remnants of ornate wood panelling. (He'd bought the building, a former Single Room Occupancy with warrens of tiny rooms on every floor, long before gentrification had spread to the neighbourhood, and was defiant about not restoring it to its pre-SRO condition, or in any other way tarting it up.)

I made my excuses as soon as I politely could, and staggered upstairs where I had the sparsely furnished top floor to myself. Passing his bedroom on the second floor I noticed several pairs of scuffed leather ankle boots, all stylishly pointed at the toe as if to address an idea of locomotion inseparable from that of impalement, lined up in pairs against the wall, and a sort of cheap amusement passed through me, the hostility of which I preferred not to examine too closely. I was feeling surfeited, bloated – not just with food and drink but teeming, incoherent thoughts. My head started spinning as soon as I got into bed. The ceiling tilted ominously. A vivid sense of the viscous orange sauce on my pasta came back and for a moment I thought I was going to throw up our celebratory dinner. I held it down, just, overcome by the still stronger urge to sleep.

7

The summer passed, and in September I resumed my regular weekly stayovers at Marco's house. Alicia, his daughter, had moved in recently, along with her partner. Hanan was also staying there, having given up the lease on her own apartment. She was a Lebanese-born Australian, with a background in finance, who'd got into film after raising money for a documentary on the looting of antiquities in war zones, and divided her time between Sydney and New York. She always seemed a bit absent when I met her. Polite but distracted. I attributed this to the remoteness of her origins from the little world of Brooklyn, which I imagined must have seemed a bit frivolous to her; a village of pampered neurotics. But it might just as easily have been jet lag, or a lack of interest in me personally (she did seem to have trouble remembering why I came to stay at the house every week). She and Marco had a quiet, undemonstrative relationship. She was quite a bit younger than him, but they seemed content, and well matched. She'd taken over the money side of his *Crime and Place* series, which was by now officially in development after preliminary financing had been agreed on by a consortium she'd put together. The household was livelier than usual, and Marco seemed to be thriving in it.

True, he had a lingering, somewhat morbid tendency to talk about his 'ordeal', but he'd been badly shaken by it, so perhaps that was natural enough. Sometimes it was the moment of victory he'd want to relive, and he'd go back over his meeting with Mel Sauer with voluptuous relish, as if there were still vital juices to be sucked from its memory. Sometimes it was the dread that had come before; the sense of imminent ruin. Meanwhile he'd become more obsessed than ever with the assault and harassment scandals that seemed to be breaking just about every week in the news. The stories triggered violently contradictory responses in him, all of them transparently visible as he sat at breakfast in his shabby blue bathrobe, reading the *New York Times*. The progressive liberal in him would rejoice in the fall of some dinosaur mogul or smug college jock, drunk on their sense of unassailable omnipotence.

But then, as he began reappraising the story from the point of view of his own experience, misgivings would seize him. Might the accusations be false? Or at least exaggerated? Or over-simplified? If the truth happened to be complicated, could that complication ever be addressed by a process that recognised only the strictly differentiated categories of predator and victim? Was it possible to get a fair hearing in the current climate, where a good chunk of the populace seemed to have come to a tacit agreement that it was better that a few innocent men should be ruined than a single guilty one go free? He'd remark on his own quickness to condemn accused men; his willing – even exultant – participation in the ritual of public denunciation that these stories offered, and he'd shudder at how close he'd come to being the victim of that quickness and willingness himself. Then, as if catching himself sliding into sympathy with that week's proven sleazeball staring at him from the pages of the *Times*, he'd frown and toss the paper aside, muttering: 'Fuck this asshole anyway.' And then a week or so later the whole cycle would start up again.

'I'd like to make a documentary about these men,' he said one morning, jabbing at the paper. 'I think I could get them to talk, and I think they'd have interesting things to say about what it means to be disgraced in this era. They're all very different, of course, but collectively they comprise an interesting anthropological phenomenon. They're guilty, I don't question that, except in a few instances, but they're also functioning as sacrificial figures. We're entering a phase of political theatre not unlike what you had in China and Russia back in the day. The morning denunciation. The noon denial. The evening firing squad. Or in our case just the firing — so far. I'm thinking of "The Tarnished" for a title. How does that sound?'

'How about "The Abusers"?' Hanan said. 'Or "The Harassers"?'

She'd been sitting quietly next to him, working her phone and combining precisely measured amounts of grain and seed into her cereal bowl, seemingly uninterested in his words. It occurred to me that she still didn't know anything about his own troubles in this department. I remembered his remark about not wanting to 'put her to the test'.

'That's not the aspect of their stories I'd want to focus on,' he said.

'There is no other aspect.'

She pointed to his newspaper, where a picture of Roger Ailes, all chins and jowls and baldness and bad skin, stared out. 'You think people want to hear about how unfairly he's been treated?'

'That's not what I'm saying.'

'It isn't?'

'No!'

He frowned, staring at the photo, and one could practically see the heavy machinery of his interest in this topic grinding through its cycles.

His daughter, Alicia, emerged from the basement with her girlfriend, both of them groggy from a night on the town. 'Morning, Daddy,' she said sweetly, stooping for a kiss on the forehead. The tones and habits of childhood were still second nature to her. I wondered if it had ever crossed her mind that coming nonchalantly to her father's breakfast table in a T-shirt and shorts with a female lover who, from the pale tuft of beard at her chin, seemed (though Marco hadn't dared ask) to be switching gender – whether she'd considered that all this constituted a momentous breach with several thousand years of tyrannously inflexible social convention, especially concerning the behaviour of marriageable girls. No doubt it had; she was well informed and curious. She'd graduated from Vassar that summer and had a place lined up at Cornell for a masters in International Relations. But she certainly wasn't burdened by the knowledge. She had the aura of inhabiting an entirely benign cosmos that had always and ever been thus.

As if finally subdued by the combined effect of his daughter's innocence and his girlfriend's scepticism, Marco put down the paper and dropped the subject.

But later that morning, after they'd all left the house, he started up again, arguing that the condition of being 'tarnished' was somehow intrinsically fascinating and worthy of study, and propounding, at some length, a theory that the older a man was, the more vulnerable he was to accusations of harassment, and the less likely to be given any benefit of the doubt, for the simple reason that it was repulsive to imagine older people having sex under any conditions at all.

I listened with my usual non-committal expression. As I said, I wasn't required to agree or disagree, just to provide him with an audience. Also, I genuinely didn't know what I thought. My opinions about these cases were as unstable as his, lurching between an icy willingness to condemn every accused man without further questioning, and what appeared to be a perverse, atavistic loyalty to the patriarchy that would take hold of me like a temporary seizure, and from which I would emerge stunned at myself. I didn't trust any of them.

The documentary idea seemed to fade, but Marco's agonisings over the subject persisted. They dominated our conversations at dinner when we went out after my class. And they were what prompted him into dragging himself across town for events such as that talk at the Irving Foundation, on rape and memory.

After the talk ended, Marco and I took the subway back to Brooklyn. We discussed the presentation for a while. Marco made a caustic comment about the slide-show, likening the installations to the dioramas at the Museum of Natural History, and from there we got on to the topic of a new phenomenon I'd noticed among students, namely a growing reluctance to discuss anything to do with sex.

'They'll fall into this embarrassed silence whenever I raise the subject, which is problematic, since that's what drives most of literature.'

'Sex?'

'Well, sex and money. Death too, though death they're okay with, especially if it has to do with Female Character Sacrifice, which is something they can get righteously indignant about. Money's tricky since characters who have any are presumed *a priori* to be villains, which makes nonsense out of most nineteenth-century novels. But sex is impossible. They'll just clam right up, and if you try to draw them out you start feeling like some pervy creep in a park.'

In the crowded A train with its noisy teenage school-kids primping and posing and flashing their smartphones like mating plumage, I told him about a class I'd taught on *Anna Karenina*, in which I'd tried to get the students to isolate the psychological principle underlying the opening descriptions of Anna, where Vronsky meets her and starts shifting his allegiances towards her, away from Kitty Shcherbatsky. I'd drawn their attention to Kitty's extreme virginal reticence, and then pointed them to the contrasting passages where Vronsky and Anna dance the mazurka together, and where Anna takes the train through the blizzard back to her husband in Petersburg. I wanted them to grasp the particular quality of awakened sexuality in Anna that draws Vronsky to her, and the way Tolstoy frames it as something at once powerfully life-enhancing and highly dangerous. I'd told them to look at the phrases he uses to describe Anna in that first meeting; those repeated images of barely contained 'animation'; of natural desire swelling up against the straitjacket of a dead marriage. Look at the ominous notes of painful pleasure on the train back to the husband she's about to betray, I'd told them, where she feels *as though something were being torn to pieces*, but at the same time finds that feeling oddly exhilarating. I'd wanted them to feel how Tolstoy himself felt the iron law of social convention twisting his heroine's amazing carnal vitality away from life and onto the path of destruction – the deathward track that supplies the gruesome terms for the big scene of sexual consummation, with its charnel-house imagery of murder and hacked bodies, its terrible mixture of 'shame, rapture and horror'. But I couldn't get anywhere. The more I talked about Kitty's inviolable virginity and Anna's awakened desire, the more stubbornly silent the students fell, and the more embarrassed they all looked.

Marco chuckled. 'Why do you think that was?'

'I assume because the whole subject has just become so fraught. They're terrified of saying something that another student might find offensive or, you know, "triggering". There are serious consequences for doing that now – actual legal consequences. So they prefer not to say anything at all. Somehow we've recreated the taboos of the Victorian era. Different reasons maybe, but the same anxious squeamishness around the whole topic.'

Marco was shaking his head.

'I don't think so. I don't think that's it at all.'

'What is it then?'

'It's you, pal.'

'Me?'

'It's because you're old! Not as old as me, maybe, but old. They don't want to listen to some balding geezer with the flesh beginning to sag under his chin – no offence – talking about desire and virginity and the life-enhancing power of awakened sexuality. Of *course* they find it embarrassing!'

I considered this, trying to ignore my wounded vanity. It hadn't actually crossed my mind as a possible explanation for these awkward silences, but I had to admit it made a depressing sense.

'This is as per your theory of why older men are vulnerable to accusations of harassment?' I asked.

He nodded.

'Same deal. Similar, anyway. Older men are going the way of older women. Maybe even overtaking them in terms of perceived repugnance. Power and status aren't enough to blind people to the liver-spots and age-warts and wrinkles any more. Plus there's a punitive element: societal revenge. We've finally been unmasked as the real villains of history.'

We got off the subway and ambled through Clinton Hill past the old pre-gentrification bodegas with their faded carnival bunting, and the glass-fronted newer establishments, gleaming complacently in the sunshine. Marco appeared to be in an expansive frame of mind. He moved at a leisurely pace, hands in his jeans pockets, his open coat of russet suede hanging in folds either side of him, doubling the width he took up on the narrow sidewalk so that every time we came to one of the thick old blotchy plane trees with gnarled roots breaking through the paving slabs, someone had to stand aside and wait for us to pass.

'Speaking for myself,' he said, 'I'm reconciled to growing old. I embrace it. I'm actually happier, on balance, than I've ever been. I felt that way before this crap with Julia started, and I'm starting to feel it again. It does have something to do with sex, I think, in a negative way. I've discovered I like not being at the mercy of physical desire the whole time. I don't lust in the abstract any more; only when occasion demands it, i.e. in bed with Hanan. It's very nice. I don't feel I have to make a conquest of every attractive woman I encounter. I don't have that ridiculous idea that their attractiveness is somehow specifically directed at *me*, which leaves me much freer to enjoy all the secondary effects of desire – the pleasure of a good conversation, a good meal, a nice painting. I've come to appreciate all that, as well as all the little ordinary chores and rituals of life, things I barely noticed before or else regarded as drudgery. Going out in the morning to pick up an espresso and smelling all the neighbourhood smells of cooking, or spring blossoms, or diesel fumes; bumbling off to the gym or a board meeting at the Cinema Collective; watching people going about their lives ... I never imagined such humdrum things could be enough to make life worth living, but they're more than enough. If I were religious, those are the things I'd want to give thanks for. As a matter of fact, I'd say it's almost worth becoming religious so as to be *able* to give thanks for them. They fill me with gratitude, and an urge to express that gratitude ...'

I thought of pointing out to him that this 'humdrum' life of his was what most people would consider the height of leisure and luxury, but I refrained: I disliked falling into the role of purveyor of cold water in his company. Anyway, it wasn't as if he didn't already know it.

We reached his house and climbed the steep steps to his front door. There was a commotion going on inside. Alicia and her partner, Erin, were in the first of the adjoining reception rooms with Hanan, all of them laughing loudly. Alicia had a shiny black device strapped on over her eyes attached by cable to a monitor with a stereoscopic image of what looked like the inside of a fairground House of

Horror. She was leaping with shock, staggering back as if the floor had just collapsed beneath her, flailing her arms as if to fend someone off (a man with six-inch fingernails and a face like Freddy Krueger had appeared on the monitor), all the while shrieking with terror and dissolving into giggles. Erin stood behind her, catching her as she fell and keeping her from banging the wall as she jerked sideways from her imaginary attackers. Hanan explained what was going on: the mask was a virtual-reality headset. We stood with her for a bit, laughing along, and then Marco noticed a light flashing on the answering machine by the sofa in the next room. He went in through the open archway.

'Could you guys be quiet a moment?' he called out. 'Please?'

Alicia took off the headset, and we lowered our voices. The voice that came spilling out as he hit the playback button silenced us completely. It was high-pitched, unsteady, and filled with a bitter rage so intense it was as if some tormented spirit from the underworld were manifesting itself in the cosy shabbiness of that parlour room.

'Yes, this is a message for Marco Rosedale. Marco, I want you to know you haven't succeeded in silencing me. It's Julia here, by the way, Julia Gault. I've found a publisher for my memoir. I'm sure your pa*pa* knows her, if you don't. Renata Shenker. She's going to publish the whole thing. As a book. Whitethorne Press. *The* Whitethorne Press. Anyway, I'm making some revisions. I'm going to say you raped me, Marco. Yes. This time I'm going to say it. Because you did. You raped me.'

Marco hung motionless for a moment, bent over the end table as if trying to convince himself the message was just the result of some freakish malfunction of the answering machine. Straightening up, he turned back to the archway and looked at the four of us with a stunned, almost dreamy expression. His daughter had flushed pink. Erin was staring off to the side with an odd smile. Hanan faced him, her eyes glittering as if a mass of thoughts were already firing in rapid succession behind them.

'Who was that?' she asked.

Marco seemed unable to answer. He gazed blankly at her, the hawkish set of his features lending a helpless, irrelevant dignity to the shock imprinted on them. I felt his discomfort so acutely that I found myself trying to think up some innocuous explanation for the message. Wrong number ... Different Marco Rosedale ... Crank call from an old friend with a twisted sense of humour ... Before anything plausible came to mind, however, he spoke. His voice was surprisingly calm.

'I'll tell you,' he said. 'I'll tell you the whole story. I was hoping not to have to burden you with it, but I see that's no longer an option.' He turned to his daughter. 'You too, sweetheart.'

He beckoned them into the living room. Erin retreated tactfully down the passageway to the basement stairs and I went up to the spare room. I remember feeling surprised and impressed by the stoic courage he appeared to have found in that excruciating moment. But I feared for him all the same. The voice on the machine, so familiar to me and yet so changed, had disturbed me profoundly. It seemed to me Marco was up against a more formidable antagonist than he, or I, had quite realised.

Part Two

Part Two

1

Later that fall my mother had a serious stroke. I flew to England to be with her and my siblings. She'd left instructions not to be kept on life support, and after nine days she died in the hospital.

As far as I can tell, the emotions prompted in me by these unexpected events had no impact on my reactions to Marco's story as it continued unfolding, so at the risk of appearing callous I will keep them to myself. In a more practical sense, however, the events themselves did have some effect. For one thing, they brought me to London.

In the mass of things needing to be done in the immediate aftermath of my mother's death, the task of contacting her friends about the funeral fell to me. Her address book was an enormous grey spring-binder, creased and dilapidated, but still bearing the faded insignia of my father's old firm, where it had originally been prepared. It contained a thick sheaf of old printer paper – the kind you had to pull apart along the perforations after each printing job – interspersed with newer sheets of miscellaneous size, added as need arose. In the years since my father's death my mother had done her diligent best to keep it up to date, scribbling or whiting out obsolete addresses, writing down the new ones in her increasingly unsteady hand, adding email addresses and mobile phone numbers as those things came into existence, crossing out the names of deceased friends with an eloquent single line of ink (apparently she couldn't bring herself to consign them to total oblivion with the white-out brush), and inserting an occasional more recent acquaintance, sometimes on a thin snippet of fresh paper pasted onto the overcrowded original sheet.

Going through it was an unsettling experience. The names of my parents' friends, living and dead, already had a certain talismanic significance for me. Together they brought back a powerful aura of that vanished world which had come to seem about as remote, in my eyes, as that of the ancient Greeks and Egyptians, and almost as heroic. That much I could have predicted. What I hadn't reckoned on was finding myself back in the force field of Marco Rosedale's saga. It hadn't exactly been at the forefront of my mind since my mother's stroke, so it was a surprise to be confronted by the names of so many of its principal players as I turned the pages.

Marco's parents, Alec and Gabriella Rosedale, were there, their unchanged information testifying to a rare marital and geographic stability. Renata Shenker, proprietor of the Whitethorne Press, was there, along with her neatly crossed-out late husband Otto. And Julia was there too. She and my mother had of course been close once, but that was at a time before even this ancient tome had been compiled; before personal computers and perforated printing paper had been invented. She'd faded from our lives, and I was under the impression that she and my mother had lost touch.

But there she was, with a whole inserted page to herself, full of scribbled-out addresses and phone numbers and email addresses, many with question marks or the words 'not sure' written beside them. The most recent address was of the house in Maida Vale from which Julia had been evicted after refusing to leave (the owners she'd been house-sitting for were friends of my parents). That was a little over a decade ago, and it appeared my mother's efforts to keep track of her former protégée had exhausted themselves after this.

We weren't planning a big funeral, just family and close friends. Julia, who at one time would probably have been considered both, no longer fell into either category. And yet I found myself trying all the phone numbers on her page. I was aware of an element of idle curiosity in this. The thought of seeing her in person, or at least of talking to her, after all that had been going on with Marco, intrigued me. But I felt a little furtive as I dialled the numbers. I don't like to think of myself as a busybody, though that in itself doesn't seem enough to account for this dim sense of wrongdoing. Perhaps I was aware of the dangers of becoming implicated; of shifting from neutral observer of this drama into something more, shall we say, participatory. At any rate I was as much relieved as disappointed, when none of the phone numbers or email addresses worked. No doubt I could have got hold of Julia if I'd really wanted to, but I decided to take these failures as a sign that I should let the matter drop. I hadn't forgotten her voice on Marco's answering machine, and I could certainly see the benefits of not confronting its owner.

As for the other players in Marco's drama, his parents had heard the news of my mother's death through Marco and had sent a message asking to be informed about the funeral arrangements. Unlike Julia, they'd never been more than dinner party acquaintances of my parents, but nor had they ever entirely disappeared from my parents' lives, and after some hesitation I decided I wouldn't be stretching a point, or even indulging inappropriately in personal curiosity, by inviting them to the service and the reception afterwards. Renata Shenker presented no such difficulties: she was an old and much-loved family friend, and was one of the first people I called.

She arrived early at the crematorium on the damp, pale morning of the funeral, and we talked for a while in the cloister outside the chapel. In my early twenties I'd interviewed for a job with her. She ran a small publishing company that specialised in social science, European fiction and Holocaust memoirs (her husband had been a camp survivor). On my way to the interview I'd prepared clever things to say about Herbert Marcuse and Primo Levi, but she was more interested in my typing speed. She didn't offer me a job, but she sent me to an editor at another firm who eventually hired me, so I'd always felt indebted to her. I hadn't seen her since my father's funeral, almost twenty years earlier.

'You've lost your hair,' she said. 'Still, at least you haven't swollen up like me. I can hardly walk these days.' Having always been rather thin and wiry, she'd grown stout and short-breathed, and leaned with both hands on a metal stick.

'But you're still publishing books,' I said. 'That's the important thing!'

'Is it? Yes, I suppose it is.' She frowned, and then added darkly: 'When people let me.'

I had a pretty good idea what she was referring to, but I felt I should make a show of ignorance.

'What does *that* mean?'

She gave me a searching look. She'd always had a reputation for shrewdness, and for having her ear to the ground. Still, it seemed unlikely she could have known I knew anything about Julia Gault's memoir, much less that I'd become Marco Rosedale's confidant.

'Oh, nothing,' she said, shaking her head. 'There's always nonsense of one sort or another going on in the book world, as I'm sure you know. How are you? I'm sorry about your mother. I shall miss her. She had her ways, but I was fond of her, on the whole. I certainly didn't expect to outlive her. She always seemed so youthful. And of course she was considered a great beauty. Well, we all have to go.'

I knew her – knew her generation's spiky honesty – well enough to know she was being affectionate, in her own way.

An usher opened the chapel and I went in with my siblings to check everything was in order, directing Renata to a waiting room. She shuffled off, but reappeared in the chapel a minute later, looking upset.

'I think I'll wait in here, on second thoughts,' she said, squeezing into a pew at the back. I assumed the waiting room must have been crowded, though I hadn't noticed many people arriving yet. It wasn't until after the service, when she made a conspicuously hasty exit and told me she'd changed her mind about coming to the reception, that it dawned on me the Rosedales must have been in the waiting room, and that it was the sight of Alec Rosedale – Sir Alec Rosedale, QC – that had upset her.

It occurred to me at that point that I had in fact already made the shift from observer to participant in Marco's drama, and that my role, minor as it was, had already implicated me in the distress of at least one person: an elderly woman who had once helped me, and whom I admired greatly.

2

It was at my urging that Marco had finally told his father what was going on. I'd suggested it early on, and I pressed him again soon after that sobering phone message of Julia's announcing (among other things) that Renata was going to publish her memoir.

'You're going to need legal help,' I'd said. 'Why not get the best?'

As before, Marco was reluctant.

'He's not a libel lawyer, my dad. The reverse if anything. Free speech was always his thing; anti-censorship ... He defended a publisher in an obscenity trial once.'

'All the more reason to get his advice. He'll know the subject from both sides.'

'I don't want to drag him into this, though. At his age he deserves some peace. Also it's just so humiliating, getting my dad to bail me out. And it's embarrassing too. Can you imagine telling your father you've been accused of rape?'

'He's going to find out anyway, if you don't stop the book. Then you'll end up with the worst of both worlds.'

He hung his head. 'I know. But I can't tell him. I just can't do it.'

But eventually he swallowed his pride and called his father.

Far from being unwilling to get involved, the old lawyer had rallied at once to his son's defence. Elderly as he was – ancient, really – he retained a keen interest in political and social affairs, and grasped instantly the danger facing Marco.

'This will destroy you,' were the words Marco dourly reported him saying, 'unless we fight back and fight back hard. If we lose, you'll never make another film. You won't be able to publish articles in reputable places either. And don't expect your friends to stay loyal. This sort of thing is absolutely radioactive. But we shan't lose. I'm going to put a team together. Send me your correspondence with that man at the *Messenger*.'

From what I gathered, he shared his son's view that he himself was at least a part of the reason why the *Messenger* had wanted to run the original excerpt from Julia's memoir. Years earlier they'd published an article attacking him after his defence manoeuvres in a terrorist case at the Old Bailey almost caused a mistrial. Later, when his clients were exonerated and freed from jail, the editors were forced to run a grovelling retraction, prompting (so he believed) their everlasting enmity. I still had my doubts about this supposed vendetta; the scenario smacked of grandiosity to me, but in any case Sir Alec apparently took a particular pleasure in his son's victory over Mel Sauer.

'That'll teach them to go after a Rosedale!' he'd chortled, delighted at Marco's account of that incident. He seemed to regard Renata Shenker, however, as a more dangerous adversary. 'She's a tough bird,' he'd told Marco. He'd known her former business partner, who'd parted with her acrimoniously, and he used to run into Renata herself occasionally at social events in London.

'I doubt she'll back down as easily as the *Messenger*,' he'd warned his son. 'She'll know, or her counsel will, that a jury's going to look sympathetically on a spirited senior citizen running a high-minded little independent publishing company. It'll be expensive to go to trial, of course, and I don't imagine her pockets are deep, but they'll award her costs if she wins, and she'll probably have a bestseller on her hands too, what with the publicity these things generate, so she might decide it's worth the gamble. I don't mean to alarm you – I'm just thinking aloud – but we're going to have a battle on our hands.'

The battle was swift and, it appears, hard fought on both sides. Sir Alec, acting with a former junior from his days as a busy QC, as well as a team of solicitors and a private detective, had Cease and Desist letters sent to the Whitethorne Press and their printers, and an application for a preliminary injunction against publication delivered to the High Court. Marco's correspondence with Mel Sauer, along with a copy of Gerald Woolley's letter about Julia, were offered as a basis for the injunction, on the grounds that whatever compelling legal reasons had caused the *Messenger* not to publish, could be presumed to apply equally in the case of the Whitethorne Press.

All this I learned from Marco at my weekly visits to his house and, increasingly, over the phone. He'd begun calling me frequently. Though I wasn't his closest friend by any means, I believe I was still the only one he had confided in on this particular subject. My knowing Julia and some of the other people involved was obviously a part of it, but he was worried about gossip, and my *not* knowing anyone in his professional circle was probably just as important.

I don't think he talked about it much with Hanan either. He'd told me she and Alicia had listened sympathetically when he explained the situation after Julia's phone message, but I got the feeling he wasn't entirely confident in her loyalty. I assumed she must be weighing her options. On the one hand she'd just moved in with Marco — taken the plunge with their relationship — and reversing course would have been complicated at the very least. Also she was having visa problems, to which the simplest solution would have been marrying Marco, who'd acquired US citizenship himself through his first marriage, and I imagine she wasn't ready to give up on that prospect just yet. On the other hand there was everything her instincts as a rational woman of the world must have been telling her: that if things went badly for Marco, she could find herself encumbered with a piece of irrevocably damaged human goods that she'd have to be constantly explaining and apologising for, and dragging around with her like an invalid with some highly noxious disease.

It's possible, of course, that her air of disengagement was just a more emphatic version of what I'd sensed earlier: an essential remoteness from the culture of New York, in this instance its anxious, obsessive interest in the subject of sexual conduct. It's also possible my perspective on her was shaped by factors that had nothing to do with her at all. Earlier that year, for example, I'd seen the documentary about Anthony Weiner. I didn't make any connection at the time, but as I write now it seems likely I was seeing Hanan through the lens of Weiner's wife Huma Abedin. There were physical resemblances:

similar black hair and large dark eyes; similar pale-olive complexion set off by bright red lipstick. Gestural similarities too, particularly a certain way of taking up position in a doorway or far corner of a room, arms crossed, gazing at their partner with a look expressive of both tenderness and cool appraisal. (No doubt, by the same token, I was also viewing Marco partly through the lens of Weiner himself; at the very least Weiner's drama must have added a tint of its particular farcical goatishness to the general murk of errant masculinity shadowing Marco's own.)

I barely glimpsed his daughter during that time, though I'd sometimes hear her and Erin pottering around in the basement. The little grin on Erin's face during Julia's fateful phone message had struck me as faintly malicious, and I wondered if she was amusing herself in some devious way, turning Alicia against her father. That's unfair perhaps, possibly even a bit crass, but I know that among the many kinds of pain Marco was experiencing during those days was a sense that his daughter might indeed turn against him, with or without her lover's connivance.

He was in bad shape again; worse than before. With Sauer, he'd conducted his own defence, which at least gave him something to focus his energies on. Now, having effectively handed matters over to his father, he'd succumbed to a restless, powerless inertia. A manifestation of this was an uncharacteristically crude, even brutal, cynicism. He wasn't someone who monitored his own speech very closely, at the best of times. On the plus side this gave his more generous sentiments, when he expressed them, a refreshing air of sincerity. But it also exposed his less worthy impulses. At times he could sound pettily angry or mean-spirited.

'I'm beginning to think it's all just a land-grab,' he said at one low moment. 'Land-grab, power-grab, money-grab, all this public accusation stuff ... Yes, people get assaulted, and they deserve justice, but this isn't about justice. It isn't about mindless imitation either – I was wrong about that. It's about business; plunder. Well, fair enough, we all want our share, and I'm sure I've had more than mine. But let's not pretend this public shaming rigmarole has anything to do with justice or civil rights. I mean, am I seriously expected to feel a burning solidarity with those reporters, so-called, at Fox News, cashing in on having been treated like bunny girls all those years? Let them grab their millions in payback, and good luck to them. I'm all for it. But don't tell me it has anything to do with righting wrongs, or healing wounds. It's business! Pure and simple.'

'But Julia isn't demanding money, is she?' I said.

'True. Not yet. Not from me. But I'm sure if this memoir of hers comes out, she'll find some way of leveraging it. It'll be her official certificate of victimhood, which is money in the bank, as you know. It's like what a cab medallion used to be.'

'You really think it's just money motivating her?'

'Why else would she put all this effort into a lie? She's been broke for years, and now suddenly she realises she has a nice, juicy, privileged, straight white male she can take down. I'm a bounty-hunting opportunity, is what I am. A scalp. So are you, by the way, so watch out.'

Other times, however, in less rancorous humour, he'd admit at least the possibility of motives besides money for Julia's behaviour, and he'd speculate on what they might be.

'Could she be punishing me for not offering something more serious all those years ago?' he said on the phone one morning. 'Not pushing her to dump the boyfriend and ride off into the sunset with me? I know things fizzled out between her and Gerald Woolley in the end anyway ...'

I waited while he reflected on this.

'So actually, maybe *that's* what she's angry about,' he mused. 'Not my casual attitude in itself, but the fact that our fling screwed up her relationship with the guy she might have married. Do you think that could be it?'

'It's possible ...'

'I was definitely careless about people's feelings in those days. It never occurred to me not to make a move on someone just because they were involved with someone else. And then as soon as I was bored I'd cut out. That was the code back then: every man for himself. Every woman too, by the way. And Julia certainly gave the impression of being as tough as anyone else, in that department. But maybe she wasn't. Maybe it wasn't such a great code anyway. I'm certainly open to being persuaded that it wasn't. I think I half-knew it was problematic even at the time, though I won't pretend that slowed me down. The truth is, I regret a lot of things I did when I look back. I could be charming when I wanted, and I'm pretty sure I was fun and interesting to be around. But I wasn't kind. I wasn't interested in kindness. Kindness was for people who couldn't get laid, in my book. Sex was what mattered, not being kind. Maybe that's what I'm really being punished for, karmically speaking ...'

On the legal front, meanwhile, things were moving fast. Within days of his father's application, a temporary injunction was granted against publication of Julia's book. Renata, who shared the high-principled, somewhat pugnacious temperament of that vanishing generation, saw this as a challenge to her integrity as a publisher, and vowed to fight it. A court date was set. Sir Alec and his team mapped out a dual strategy, mustering arguments in readiness for a trial, if it should come to that, while also taking steps to expedite their preferred solution, which was to get Renata to back down before proceedings began.

For the trial strategy, he asked Marco for copies of a documentary he'd made for American TV in the nineties, about atrocities committed by Serbian forces against Bosnian Muslim civilians during the Yugoslav war. A segment of the film was about the notorious rape camps in Foča, and the lawyers seemed to think the footage might help cast Marco in a usefully ennobling light, illustrating an unimpeachable attitude to women. For the same reason, they also asked for copies of the segment about the girl being tarred and feathered, from the film he'd shot with Julia in Belfast.

Marco wasn't happy with any of this. He hated it, in fact: hated the suggestion it raised, that he had some ongoing morbid interest in the abuse of women; hated the idea of using his films for purposes of self-exoneration; hated being in the position of trying to censor a book in the first place.

'I don't seem to have much choice though, do I? Either I fight or I'm fucked, and these are apparently the only effective weapons I have to fight with. I have to win, too, obviously, though it's possible I'll be fucked even if I do.'

We were at his house during this last conversation, having an early lunch before I caught the train back upstate. Hanan and the girls were out, which inevitably meant a torrent of talk about his case. I asked about the other part of his father's strategy – getting Renata to back down. A pained expression crossed his face. Then he shrugged, and told me with the acid resignation that was increasingly his tone at that time, that his father's team was looking for ways to discredit Julia.

'Digging up dirt on her, basically. Apparently that's what you do. The assumption is that Renata Shenker's team will be doing the same on me.'

'They've seen that letter from Gerald Woolley?'

'Yes. But we need something stronger than that.'

'Such as?'

'Anything that'll make her look like she's unhinged, or a liar. Other false allegations of assault would be helpful, I suppose.'

'And what are they looking for on you?'

'Oh, dodgy bedroom behaviour, I imagine. Other women willing to corroborate her story ...'

'Are they likely to find any?'

'No. Not from anyone telling the truth. But ...'

'But ...?'

He tilted his head to the side, hawk-like, as if drawing a bead on some troublesome object.

'Well, I can imagine one or two women revising the past. Not out of malice, necessarily. Maybe not even consciously ...'

He cleared his throat. An odd expression – pained but also faintly amused – came into his eyes.

'Have I ever told you about my anthropology tutor at university?'

3

By this point in Marco's saga, something like a tacit
agreement had been established between the two of us,
that I was going to be, if not its official chronicler, then at
least a kind of semi-authorised literary witness. He knew
that the subject interested me. On one occasion he'd said
he was surprised I hadn't already written a book about a
predicament exactly like his. I'd explained the difficulty;
that in a made-up story you'd have to clarify in your mind
who was lying, the man or the woman, and that this
would inevitably read as a larger statement about the
relative truthfulness of men and women in general,
which in turn would reduce the story to polemic or prop-
aganda. In a true story, on the other hand (I'd added), the
question would remain specific to the individuals concerned and the particularities of their situation, which
would make it much more appealing, at least to me. He'd
smiled as if to say: 'Be my guest.' Between that and various asides of his over the months, along the lines of: 'I'm
sure you're taking notes on all this – just make sure
they're accurate!' I got the feeling that he accepted the
inevitability of my writing about it some day, and was
okay with it.

Needless to say, this complicated matters between us. He wasn't so naive as to think I would take everything he told me as gospel. As he himself had said when he visited me and Caitlin in the spring: 'You can't *not* have doubts.' He'd reiterated the sentiment many times since, and I took this to mean he understood that although I might be entirely sympathetic in my role as his friend and confidant, I was also going to be entirely dispassionate in my role as the teller of his story. Not a faithful amanuensis, in other words, but an appraiser of the truth.

In all our conversations he was careful to signal this awareness of my – so to speak – judicial independence, and his respect for it. But at the same time I could feel the constant pressure of his desire to keep me in line with his version of events, and I realised I needed to be vigilant in maintaining my objectivity. I'm sure Marco was aware of this, and adjusted himself accordingly, which of course added yet more layers to the already complex and potentially treacherous transaction being conducted between us.

I was more than usually aware of all this during our conversation about his affair with his tutor at Cambridge. I'd heard rumours of this as a teenager, when it formed part of the general legend of conquest and precocious charisma that trailed after Marco even then. I hadn't known the details though, and what he told me now fleshed out the story in unexpected ways.

The tutor's name was Maeve McLanahan. She was twenty-nine; quite a bit older than Marco at the time. She'd written a book about a matriarchal Amazon tribe she'd studied for her doctorate, which had found a wide general audience owing to its graphic details of sexual customs in the primeval rainforest. From Marco's description she was a tumultuous character; easily moved to raucous laughter, though also easily angered, with a fondness for drinking brandy during tutorials, which she conducted wearing jeans and sweaters and an old sea-captain's hat.

'She wasn't what I thought of as my type, which was pretty conventionally feminine at that time,' Marco said. 'Anyway, it wouldn't have crossed my mind to think about a teacher in that way. That wasn't a fantasy of mine. She was the one who initiated things.'

'She seduced you?'

He paused a moment.

'I'd say more like helped herself to me. There was nothing slow or simmering about it. She basically ordered me back to her flat one afternoon, told me she fancied me, and took me up to bed.'

He paused again, as if to let some implication sink in, and this time I felt that slight controlling pressure exerting itself against me, along with a corresponding stirring of my own defences.

'Not that I wasn't into it,' he continued. 'I was just a bit surprised. I'd never been with a woman that frank about what she wanted. It was confusing at first because what she wanted turned out to be the opposite of what you might expect, or at least there was something deeply paradoxical about it. She wanted to be totally in control and yet at the same time she wanted the sensation of being taken by force.'

Again I felt a sharpened attentiveness bristling inside me.

'I'd never encountered that before, and it took me a while to get the hang of it. But she was a very determined teacher. She'd get furious if I overstepped some invisible mark, or equally if I *under*stepped it. But when I got it right, the results were spectacular. I've never had sex like that with anyone, before or since. It was delirious.'

'For her too?'

'I think so. She used to call me her Nijinsky.'

'After the horse?'

'No! The Russian dancer. I reminded her of some ballet he was in. Something about a faun.'

'*Afternoon of a Faun*?'

'Yeah. What is that?'

'It's a poem by Mallarmé. It was made into a ballet with Nijinsky. I think Debussy wrote the music. I sometimes have it on my syllabus, actually – the poem.'

'What's it about?'

I told him it wasn't exactly 'about' anything. 'I mean, there's a story of sorts, but it's highly ambiguous. A faun wakes from an afternoon nap and remembers an erotic dream about a nymph. A couple of nymphs, actually. And it's not clear whether the encounter was what we would call consensual, or even whether it was in fact a dream – it's possible he's remembering something that actually happened. Basically, it's a celebration of a certain phase of male desire where the intensity of feeling dissolves all the usual categories of reality. I teach it alongside Sylvia Plath's journals and Elizabeth Barrett Browning's sonnet about female desire, "How do I love thee? Let me count the ways …"'

'It's about rape?'

'No … I don't think so … It's very tender and delicate. Paul Valéry thought it was the most beautiful poem ever written, at least in French. There *are* flashes of brutality, but the language creates a kind of pagan, pre-moral atmosphere in which—'

'What is a faun anyway?' Marco interrupted. He never had much patience when I waxed pedagogical. 'Is it the same as a satyr?'

'No. Those are cruder—'

'They're the ones with the hairy goat legs and the enormous rampant dicks?'

'Yes. Fauns have something more shy and elusive about them. They live in enchanted forests, as far as I remember. You could say they represent male desire in its youthful, innocent form, when it's all just wonder at the magical new kinds of pleasure that arrive with puberty. Whereas satyrs embody something worldlier, more corrupted. Lechery, I guess, as opposed to desire.'

'So she was being complimentary then.'

'Your tutor? Definitely.'

'Well, anyway, she was certainly extremely interested in — what you said: the combination of brutality and tenderness.'

It appeared this old professor of his had come to consider herself not only his academic instructor but also his tutor in matters of erotic technique. On breaking off the affair (which she did after a few weeks, as brusquely as she'd started it) she assured Marco she'd taught him an infallible method for arousing women, and guaranteed him limitless success with future lovers if he applied it.

'I believed her. Why wouldn't I? She was this sophisticated woman who seemed to know everything there was to know about sex, while I was this nineteen-year-old ... faun.'

He fell silent.

'Did you try it out?' I asked.

'Yeah. A couple of times, with girls my age.'

'And?'

'Well, it worked, sort of. Or anyway, no one objected. But I didn't feel good about it. In fact, I felt pretty awful. I made a conscious decision never to use it again, and I didn't. It was ancient history by the time I met Julia.'

I asked him what, precisely, 'it' was. An uncomfortable look appeared on his face, but then he nodded in that defiantly reasonable way of his, as if to assure me I had every right to ask.

'I suppose you could call it a sort of stylised sexual aggressiveness ... Or not aggressiveness, more just a kind of play-acting of confidence. Brutish confidence. You know the way gangsters in movies say: "I got this", when they're volunteering to take care of some tricky situation? That was pretty much the mental attitude behind it.'

'I got this?'

He nodded.

'Yeah. As in, you don't have to worry, I'll make this happen, for both of us. Anyway, you ask if Renata Shenker's lawyers are likely to find other women to corroborate Julia's story, and the answer is, I hope not, but I'm a little afraid one of those girls might look back and decide it wasn't all as harmless as they thought at the time. Actually, I'm more than a little afraid. I'm having serious cold sweats about it.'

I wasn't sure what to make of this story. It seemed believable enough, but it smacked also of pre-emptive defence; calculated insinuation. I wondered if Marco's real motive for telling it was to plant the suggestion that he, too, had been victimised in his turn; sexually manipulated by a person in power. If so, did that mean he was moving towards an admission of guilt concerning Julia, and coaching me to present his excuses for him if and when I ever got around to writing about him?

That same afternoon he took me into one of the small rooms off the corridor on the second floor of his house. It was a sort of junk room, piled high with photographic equipment and dusty old computer parts. Opening the drawer of a metal file cabinet, he lifted a stack of dog-eared papers.

'See that?'

I peered in, and flinched back.

It was a gun, a handgun, black and blocky, with a square barrel and curved indentations along the handle.

'Jesus, Marco!'

My shock seemed to please him. He gave a grim smile.

'I got it when I first moved here. The neighbourhood was rougher then. There were a lot of break-ins. Joan made me buy it.' Joan was his ex-wife, Alicia's mother. 'It's a Glock, which is what the cops here carry. Needless to say I never had any use for it, till now.'

'You're planning to shoot someone?'

'Possibly.'

'Who?'

'Can't you guess?'

'Julia?'

'Yeah, right, I'm going to smuggle it onto a plane and shoot her through her letter box. No, dummy, guess!'

'I've no idea.'

He glared at me.

'I think you're being obtuse.'

I was. I'd guessed what he meant but I didn't want to acknowledge it. I'd known only one person in my life who'd killed himself, a school friend who'd jumped from a building. He'd led a fairly desperate existence from the age of fifteen when, for reasons he never discussed, he walked out of his parents' comfortable home in Highgate and moved into a squalid bedsit where he lived like some Dickensian waif, betting on horses (for which he had a certain gift), eating tinned soup and trying to keep up with his homework. Uncomplaining, unassuming, introverted to the point of not being able to look even his friends in the eye, he'd come to embody my idea of what it was to be 'a suicide', which was to say someone about whom the surprising thing (at least in hindsight) wasn't that he killed himself, but that he kept going for as long as he did. Marco, secure on the foundations of his happy and privileged upbringing, hale and vigorous even under the stress of his resurgent ordeal, could not have been less like him. I knew rationally that there were plenty of different reasons why people killed themselves, but I couldn't take him seriously as a candidate for that particular act. He was too vivid even in his dejection; too solidly anchored in life.

'Marco,' I said, as gently as I could. 'I mean, come on!'

'What?'

'You have a daughter ...'

'It'd be for her sake, mainly, if I do it,' he said.

'That's ridiculous.'

'My sake too, obviously. I don't have the temperament to live as a pariah. I'm too attached to the things I'd lose. I like working. I like being on panels and juries. I like being invited to dinner parties at people's houses. I like having an intelligent, glamorous girlfriend. I like knowing my daughter and her friends feel comfortable around me. I care what the world thinks of me. Maybe too much, but that's the way I am. I don't have your appreciation for solitude, or the wilderness.'

It was an eloquent speech, and it touched me, but at the same time its very eloquence affirmed my sense of his fundamental robustness.

'I understand,' I said. 'But still . . .'

He stood close, eyeing me fiercely from under the sharp angle of his brow. I knew he was waiting for me to be properly appalled – for *his* sake; not just his daughter's – at what he was contemplating. I couldn't bring myself to oblige him, though. There seemed to me something maudlin about the situation, melodramatic, that shouldn't be indulged. And I couldn't help feeling that slight pressure again; a not-so-subtle attempt to reinforce his image in my mind as a figure of tragic honour and pathos, and to lay claim to the role of victim in this story. I didn't necessarily dispute either point, but I didn't like the feeling of being coerced.

'I'm sure you'll win this battle, Marco,' I said.

He slid the drawer shut and turned away with a look of such unmistakable hurt that I felt at once ashamed of my coldness, and spent the rest of the day trying to make up for it.

4

But I was right about him winning the battle, even though it came about for reasons so unexpected as to seem absurd; farcical almost.

I was already in London, at my mother's hospital bedside, while this next set of events was occurring. As I say, I had more pressing things on my mind than Marco's troubles, and Marco was tactful enough to keep his distance. I heard nothing from him, in fact, until this particular chapter was over. He sent me an email: 'Just to let you know, Renata Shenker backed down. No need to write back, but I thought you'd want to be told. Hope you're bearing up okay. M'.

I was curious, naturally, and despite the drama unfolding in my own life, I emailed back to arrange a call.

He kept his tone carefully restrained when we spoke, but I could tell he was jubilant; revelling again in the joy of victory. Even the roundabout way he told me the story had something transparently gleeful about it. He'd obviously enjoyed himself thinking of the juiciest way to recount it.

'Have you heard of Hanna Reitsch?' he began.

'I don't think so.'

'She was an aviator. First woman to fly a helicopter. First woman to compete in the world gliding championships. Huge celebrity in her lifetime. Kennedy invited her to the White House. Nehru flew in a glider with her over New Delhi. In the sixties she lived in Ghana where she had an affair with Nkrumah. Died in 'seventy-nine. Anyway, Julia turns out to have been a big fan of hers, and it seems she wanted to write a book about her. This was after her TV career had gone belly up. Ditto her return to radio. She'd had a spell as partner in some short-lived gallery, then I think a brief debacle in PR, and then some time in the nineties she decided she was a writer. She did some magazine articles, fluff mostly, but then she got interested in this Hanna Reitsch woman, and started researching a biography. You're sure you don't know the name?'

'It does ring a faint bell.'

'You never saw that Carlo Ponti movie *Operation Crossbow*?'

'No.'

'Or *Hitler: The Last Ten Days*?'

'Nope.'

'How about *Downfall*?'

'With Bruno Ganz? Yes. Oh, right.' It came back to me: 'She was Hitler's test pilot.'

'Bingo. So Julia fires off a proposal for this book. The proposal gets read by a friend of hers who used to read for a publisher back in the nineties. Our investigator tracked this woman down and she told him about this proposal and the report she'd written on it. He found copies of both in the publisher's archives in Croydon. They make fascinating reading. It seems this new heroine of Julia's was an unrepentant Nazi – Kennedy and the rest notwithstanding. She wore the Iron Cross with diamonds that Hitler gave her, to her dying day. In her last interview she said, quote: "I am not ashamed to say I believed in National Socialism."'

'Julia didn't know that?'

'Oh, she knew it. That's the point. She appears to have found the woman's, uh, *constancy* altogether admirable. She positively gushes about it. Let me read you the last paragraph of her proposal: "I want to tell the tale of this heroic woman whose physical courage and astonishing technical skills were matched only by her refusal to betray her own principles. She was no more reluctant to acknowledge her belief in National Socialism, than she was to test-pilot a V-1 Flying Bomb; no more afraid of denouncing modern-day Germany as a 'Land of bankers', than she'd been to fly General von Greim out of the bunker under enemy fire in order to deliver the Führer's last commands to the Luftwaffe. I hope to write a book that will do justice to this brave, stubborn, uncompromising, altogether extraordinary individual."'

'Christ,' I said.

'Unbelievable, right? Our old friend Julia Gault, a Nazi sympathiser!'

I chafed a bit at that.

'Well, as you said, it's the constancy she's admiring, not the principles themselves.'

'I don't know,' Marco replied, suavely enough. 'She clearly has no problem with that phrase, "Land of bankers", which you have to admit has a certain Julius Streicher-esque ring to it . . .'

'But I mean, didn't you tell us when you came to visit that she was even further to the left than you?'

'That was when she was young. People adapt their politics to their circumstances. She certainly wouldn't be the first unhappy person to get lost in these particular woods.'

'You don't think it's all just clumsy wording?'

'Doesn't matter what I think, does it? What matters is what Renata Shenker thought when we brought it to her attention, and clearly she thought it was more than clumsy.'

'Well, Renata's husband was a camp survivor,' I said. Then I realised I'd been a little slow on the uptake. 'Oh, but you factored that in. I see.'

'We did think it might weigh in our favour. But even Julia's reader friend seems to have been shocked. Listen to her report. Here's what she says: "... I have to confess I fear my old chum might have gone off the deep end with this idea ..."'

'Okay, it's badly expressed,' I said, 'but I still think it's obvious what she's trying to say. She's admiring the woman's stubbornness, not her actual beliefs ...'

'Maybe, maybe not. Either way it did the trick.'

I didn't respond. I didn't want to quarrel with Marco, and I wasn't even sure why I was defending Julia in the first place. I had to admit I found her interest in this *Überfrau* from the Third Reich depressing, regardless of where her sympathies precisely lay. But I suppose I wanted the fight between her and Marco to be about what happened or didn't happen in that Belfast hotel room. I didn't want to see her brought down by some stupid smear, even if it turned out to be deserved. Also, I didn't like the thought of dear old Renata Shenker being, effectively, blackmailed.

Marco must have taken my silence for disapproval.

'Look, all we did was send Renata a copy of both documents with a note saying she might be interested in taking a look. For all I know she was grateful to have had it brought to light *before* she went ahead and published. Might have been embarrassing for her if it came out after ...'

'Oh, I'm sure you'd have kept it decently under wraps,' I said.

'Now, now! Nobody threatened her. We certainly didn't force her to dump the book.'

'I'd say it was a foregone conclusion, given who she was married to. Not to mention the Whitethorne Press being a major publisher of Holocaust memoirs.'

He chuckled.

'What can I tell you? We turned out to have the more powerful victim card, and we were damned if we weren't going to play it. But don't forget it was Julia who created it in the first place.'

'Yes. And her so-called friend who put it in your hands.'

'The reader? Ex-friend, I should have said. One of many ex-friends, it would seem. She seems to have a gift for alienating people, poor Julia.'

Yes, poor Julia, I thought. Nothing seemed to work out for her. I felt sorry for her in spite of everything. Her voice on Marco's answering machine echoed in my ears, distress and rage blended in it indistinguishably: *I want you to know you haven't succeeded in silencing me ...* It seemed to me that whatever force was impelling her forward in this course of action, whether it was a real thirst for justice, or a deluded sense of injury, or just the pure malice and greed Marco believed it to be, she was clearly powerless in its grip, and clearly suffering.

'How did she react?'

'Julia? No idea. Not my concern. My position at this point is that Julia Gault can rot in hell.'

'Well, I'm glad it's finally over,' I said. 'Congratulations.'

'Thanks. We'll celebrate again when you're back.'

I got off the phone, confused and dissatisfied, and thoroughly perplexed by my own lurching sympathies.

5

That was where things had stood when I met Renata at my mother's funeral a week later.

Needless to say, she hadn't been remotely 'grateful' at having her author's misstep of twenty years back brought to her attention (or, more accurately, shoved in her face). I suspected she'd have pressed ahead with the book if it hadn't been for the thought of her dear departed Otto turning in his grave. I don't think she was afraid of public opinion, but she'd been devoted to her husband; they'd built the Whitethorne Press together, and it was surely the case that he wouldn't have wanted her mixed up with an admirer of some member of Hitler's inner circle. I pictured her in that little office I'd visited in my twenties, sighing heavily amid the stacks of manuscripts as she weighed her options and made her reluctant decision to ditch Julia's ill-fated memoir. Well, Sir Alec Rosedale had judged his opponent nicely. But he was known for that, of course.

I saw him at the funeral and again, later, at the reception we gave at my mother's house. He and Gabriella were standing at the back of the drawing room by the old Dutch spinet my father had rescued from a burning building during the War, talking with a group of other elderly people.

My instinct was to avoid him if I could. Not that I'd taken Renata's side against him – I was trying to maintain a scrupulous neutrality – but on a personal level it would have felt treacherous to have a friendly conversation with him, having just parted from her.

But Gabriella spotted me, her angular, well-preserved, carefully made-up features lighting up in an oddly excited smile. She tugged at her husband's arm and he too smiled when he recognised me – less dramatically, but still with an odd eagerness, as if we were much better acquainted than we really were.

Detaching themselves from their group, they squeezed through the packed room towards me. There was no possibility of avoiding them.

After offering their condolences, they brought the subject around to Marco, telling me how pleased they were that he and I had become such good friends, and how deeply touched Marco had been by my support.

Gabriella did most of the talking. Even though she'd spent most of her long life outside the world of fashion, she was still invested, in my eyes, with the glamour from her distant past as a runway model. Her firm, balletic gestures and severe upright carriage were impossible not to notice, as she stood before me, wafting a strong scent of roses. She wore a tailored jacket of ruched black chiffon with a large emerald brooch that brought out the grassy green of her eyes; the same colour that glinted, in certain lights, among the browner hues of her son's. Her voice had the trace of a Milanese accent, its liquid sibilants and refined vowels giving it a sort of furtive, corrupted, beguiling sensuality.

'Marco says you've been a brick, an absolute saviour. He speaks of you often. I can't tell you how grateful we are. Of course, we all feel very sad for this crazy woman, don't we, Alec? And I hope she's getting the psychological help she so obviously needs. But as a mother, I can tell you there were times when I wanted to go to her house and strangle her!'

Alec stood beside her, nodding at intervals, frail-looking with his wisps of spun-sugar hair and shrivelled pink cheeks, but with a gleam of alert intelligence in his eyes. His wren-like face had always had something impish about it, I remembered; an air of mischievous innocence that, from the research I'd done on him for my unwritten book about these characters from my parents' world, belied a ferocious legal mind and a willingness to go to unusual lengths to win a case. Perhaps because I knew this, I had an odd feeling that under the appearance of a fragile old man conserving his energies by letting his younger wife do the talking, the reality was closer to that of some discreetly powerful sovereign carefully monitoring an ambassador to whom he had entrusted a precise and delicate task.

Caitlin and our children, who'd flown in the day before, came up, and I introduced them. Again the Rosedales' faces brightened with intense, eager smiles. Gabriella gushed over my son and daughter, complimenting us on their looks. Even Alec became effusive in his mild fashion, spreading his hands and making an elegant speech to the effect that even though both my parents had sadly departed, he hoped the younger generations would maintain the tradition of family friendship with the Rosedales, especially now that Marco and I had become so close.

The vague discomfort I felt throughout all this I attributed, at the time, to my lingering sense of treachery towards Renata. Later, after confirming with my siblings that the Rosedales had indeed never been especially close friends of my parents, I wondered if the whole exchange hadn't been contrived as some kind of performance on their part — a piece of theatre for the benefit of the various social circles represented in that room, engineered to demonstrate that our family was firmly in the Rosedale camp, just in case Marco's story got out.

No doubt I was guilty of some grandiosity myself in this conjecture. But it played into something I'd been thinking about ever since my conversation with Marco on the phone. He'd been elated, understandably, and I didn't begrudge him that. But it was obvious to me that he didn't seriously believe Julia was any kind of closet Nazi or anti-Semite, and that he knew he'd won his battle on what amounted to a clumsy choice of words. I didn't even mind that, in itself. What bothered me was that he seemed perfectly okay with it. I wanted him to at least put on a show of wishing he could have had an opportunity to win by fairer means. But apparently it didn't trouble him in the least that the question of what happened in that hotel room had been answered by means of legal transactions and manoeuvres, aided by a threat of blackmail, rather than the diligent proving or uncovering of an objective truth.

I thought of that glib remark of mine that Marco had latched onto back in the spring: *the onus of belief is on the believer*. It wasn't actually something I believed at all. If anything, the opposite. I was, in my heart of hearts, an absolutist. Reality, for me, wasn't a 'construct' arrived at by some Darwinian battle of competing human interests and ideas. It wasn't a prize awarded to whoever fought hardest, or dirtiest. It was something that existed outside the human mind, and independently of it. Whatever happened between the couples in those rooms – Marco and Julia in Belfast, Dominique Strauss-Kahn and the maid, Nafissatou Diallo, at the Sofitel in New York; Assange and the Swedish women – was an actual occurrence, fixed in time and unchangeable; not some quantum state of infinite potentiality. I couldn't accept those stories as variations on Schrödinger's cat, alive and dead simultaneously until its box was opened; their protagonists at once guilty and innocent, victim and false accuser. Nor could I accept them as fables on the limits of the knowable. The truth might be hard to bring to light, but that didn't mean it didn't exist, because it did exist: fixed in its moment, unalterable, and certainly not a matter of 'belief'.

I was still ruminating on these thoughts a couple of days later, when the phone rang in my mother's living room and to my surprise I found myself talking to Julia Gault.

6

In the shock of hearing Marco's accuser in my own ear, I barely took in anything she said at first, beyond the fact that she'd read my mother's funeral announcement in the paper, and seemed to think she owed us an explanation for why she hadn't come. A concert seemed to have been involved, or the organising of a concert. Southwark Cathedral. Syrian refugees. I was aware of condolences being offered, and of offering the conventional responses in return.

'I haven't seen your mother for years,' she said, 'but I've always felt close to her. She was one of the few people on this planet who understood me.'

Her voice, somewhat high-pitched, as it had been on Marco's answering machine (though without the fury), had a sing-song intonation that I didn't remember from the past. Otherwise it was much the same, with its distinct mixture of flattened Midlands vowels and crisp, Oxbridge emphases – a rare blend of the regional and the imperial that, along with her intelligence and good looks, had made her a natural candidate for a career in TV.

'Now remind me,' she said, 'are you the one who went off to America?'

'I am.'

'I remember you! You were shy.'

'Very shy.'

'I think I used to make you blush.'

'You did. You probably still could.'

She laughed. 'But I suppose now you've conquered America you're one of those insufferable men who swagger about as if they own the world and everyone in it.'

'That's me. Master of the Universe.'

'Well, lovely to hear your voice after all these years.'

'Yours too.'

We chatted on for a while. She seemed eager to talk, or at least in no hurry to get off the phone. I got the feeling she was guilty about having disappeared from my mother's life, and glad of an excuse to reconnect with our family. As the surprise of hearing her voice wore off, I began wondering how to bring up the topic of Marco. I was aware that this might be an opportunity to go a little deeper into his story – get closer to its central chamber, so to speak – and I knew I'd regret it, from a professional point of view if nothing else, if I didn't pursue it. But just blurting out that I knew Marco Rosedale seemed a bad idea; crass, and potentially confrontational.

'Well, I hope it won't be another hundred years before I talk to you again,' she said, winding down. 'I've enjoyed it.'

'Likewise.'

'You know, I'd love a photo of your mother. Do you have one you could send me?'

'Of course.' Inspiration struck: 'Or I could give it to you in person ...'

'That would be nice!'

'I could meet you somewhere in town, if you like ...'

'Come to tea,' she said decisively. 'Are you free tomorrow?'

I was. Caitlin and the kids had flown back the day before and I was staying on for a few days to start clearing out my mother's house.

'I warn you, I live miles from anywhere. You'll have to change trains about six times. I spend my entire life changing trains.'

She gave me an address in a part of London I'd barely heard of and never visited. The journey involved stretches on the Docklands Light Railway as well as the Tube. It was raining when I arrived, and the walk from the station along wet streets, with no shops or pubs to relieve the monotonous stretches of residential developments, was bleak. She lived in a brick apartment building with pinched, jutting balconies overlooking a row of one-storey houses behind a long wall. She buzzed me in, and I took the lift five floors up to her flat. She was waiting in the doorway, wearing a mauve wool dress with a loose polo neck. Her face was lined, and her blonde hair had faded, but otherwise she seemed remarkably unchanged from when I'd last set eyes on her, fifteen or twenty years earlier. We shook hands first and then kissed on the cheek, laughing at our awkwardness.

'Here we are!' She showed me into a light-filled but sparse living room furnished with a wicker sofa and chairs with floral cushions tied at the corners.

'I'll put on the kettle.'

She went into a kitchen alcove partitioned by a countertop – empty except for a small toaster. I sat on one of the wicker chairs, looking around.

What was I expecting? Signs of derangement? Not exactly, but the neatness and ordinariness of the place surprised me. So did the bareness. Somehow I'd imagined her as a hoarder – of objects as well as memories, injuries. From conversations with my mother, I knew she'd been involved with plenty of interesting people in her time – politicians, diplomats, a minor rock star or two – and I'd assumed I'd find her surrounded by the memorabilia of a life that, even if it hadn't turned out quite as expected, had certainly been eventful. But the few shelves were almost empty, and the walls had nothing on them at all.

She brought in the tea. I gave her some photographs of my mother, and after looking through them she began reminiscing about her.

'I remember how we became friends. I was at a drinks party just after I got my first job in television. I was complaining that I had no one in London to go shopping with, and she offered to go with me. Just like that! We had a lovely afternoon traipsing around the West End, and then she took me to tea at some posh hotel where we talked about everything under the sun – art, politics, religion, my boyfriend, your father, everything. Even you! I seem to remember she was worried you were taking drugs.'

I laughed, and she flashed a rakish smile: 'Well, who wasn't, of course? Anyway, for the next few years she was like a second mother to me, my London mother ... I feel terrible for losing touch with her. I always have. There was a reason – I'm sure you know it. But it's my fault all the same. I miss her ...'

I did know the reason. At some point in their friendship my mother had introduced her to a man in London, a young American. They'd embarked on an affair. He'd proposed marriage, and with my mother's encouragement they'd begun making plans for a wedding – a lavish do at St George's, Hanover Square, with half of London's cultural establishment on the guest list. And then abruptly Ralph, the American, had called the whole thing off. Though Julia couldn't, and didn't, blame my mother for the debacle, she appeared to have found herself too sore to continue the friendship. The episode had always interested me, not only for its melodramatic aspect ('Julia Jilted!' one of the tabloid headlines ran at the time), but also its contribution to the layer of pathos that was paradoxically what brought about the climax of her television career—her brief apotheosis—gilding her already complex aura with a final burnish of tragedy that, by whatever mysterious alchemy of luck and fashion, impressed her TV bosses as precisely the quality they were looking for in their new current affairs presenter, whose face would soon be beamed every night into a million homes up and down the country.

I'd written copious notes on her for that abandoned project of mine: memories, observations, stories I'd heard from other people, ideas for scenes I wanted to write. I'd looked through them on my laptop before coming this afternoon, and the images they'd stirred, together with the more recent impressions conjured by Marco's drama, gave me a peculiar sense of being among a multitude of Julias, from different times and places, in different aspects and moods. Julia and my mother gossiping quietly on the sofa in our house in London while my sister looked on, excluded. Julia visiting my father in his office as a young arts reporter, noting with private amusement his brusque way of talking to his secretaries and receptionists, while obstinately failing to flirt with her. Julia at nineteen up a tree with a girlfriend at a Blind Faith concert in Hyde Park, shouting out: 'God, Steve, you are a beautiful man!' in a voice so infectiously enthusiastic the good-humoured crowd below her took up her words as a kind of mass chorus, like a football chant. Julia as an absence from our home, a diminishing echo and source of perplexed regret, of troubling rumours. Julia as Marco's problem, his seemingly indefatigable persecutor, her disembodied voice spilling out of his answering machine: *I'm going to say you raped me ...*

I'd made up my mind to tell her I knew Marco, and to try to get her side of the story. But it was no easier in the flesh than on the phone. I prevaricated, asking what she was doing with herself these days. She told me about a charitable organisation she'd joined, which raised money for refugees. In a roundabout way she led me to understand that she was one of the public faces of this organisation, and although she spoke of the role in a self-deprecating tone, I got the feeling she was proud of it.

'The way I see it, if I can turn the tiny bit of fame I once had to good use, then why not do it? I like being useful to other people. I wish I'd learned that about myself earlier on in life ...'

Images of her from the past continued surfacing in my mind as she talked, blooming and dispersing. I remembered reaching to lift a wire for her on a country walk in my teens, not realising it was electrified, my yelp of shock prompting a peal of laughter from her, followed by an unexpected touch on my shoulder of magical tenderness and sympathy. I remembered the party at our house where my mother first introduced her to that young American, Ralph Pommeroy, and the expressions on their faces as they circled each other in those first moments: Ralph's a little stunned as if he thought he might be dreaming, Julia's mirthful, with that air of being deep in some private revel while at the same time alertly conscious of her own effect.

'And you?' she said. 'What have you been doing all these years?'

I told her about my life in America: writing, teaching, living out in the woods with my family.

'How romantic!'

'It was nice.'

'Was? It's over?'

'No, but the kids have left.'

'Ah.'

She crossed her legs and tilted her head back a little, the broad planes of her cheeks catching the waning daylight from the balcony window. She was still striking to look at; beautiful by any measure, with her handsome head like something sculpted for a Roman fountain. And in fact I'd listed attributes of certain goddesses in the notes I'd made, copying out lines from Homer on Athena's daylight-sharpening powers, her 'slate-flecked silver eyes', as well as a passage about Artemis from Camille Paglia: 'Artemis is pre-Christian purity without spirituality ... She has nerve, fire, arrogance, force ... She is pristine. She never learns. In her blankness and coldness, she is a perfect selfhood, a sublime energy.'

'Tell me about your wife ...' she said.

I don't think she was remotely interested in Caitlin, but the act of making me talk about her seemed to remind her of an aspect of herself that hadn't been called into play until then. A look of sidelong amusement came on like a light in her eyes. She nodded occasionally as I talked, but didn't offer any comment when I finished. A car went by below the balcony window, sizzling on the wet. Lights glittered in a distant, solitary tower block, as if signalling to us. It was still raining.

'Shall we move on to something stronger?' she asked as I trailed off into silence. 'Whisky? A glass of wine?'

'Some wine would be nice.'

She took the tea things into the kitchen. From the back, sheathed in the soft fabric of her dress, she looked like a woman in her thirties. I found myself trying to decide what I thought of her: what I, in my older self, thought of her in hers. *Julia as flight from nature*, I'd written in those notes; *abandonment of the old, animal, earthbound human archetype...* Elsewhere: *The world becomes clarified in her presence but also diminished, as if digitised, immolated in a cold fire...* Was that 'cold fire' still burning? If so, did it still exert any lingering fascination over me? I reminded myself I was there to investigate Marco's story, not to revive some ancient plot-line in my own. And yet the question pressed itself. Was I still susceptible to her in any way? I wanted the answer to be yes. One doesn't like to lose the capacity for enchantment.

She came back with the wine, and pulled her chair closer to mine, touching my glass with hers.

'I do remember you,' she said. 'I remember hearing you play your electric guitar up in your room. Your parents used to groan whenever it came on, but I enjoyed it.' She leaned confidentially towards me. 'In fact, I sometimes wished I could go up there and hang out with you. I'm sure you'd have rolled me a nice fat joint if I'd asked.'

'I'm sure I would!'

She smiled.

'I seem to remember there was a Hendrix song you used to play rather beautifully ...'

'"Little Wing"?'

'That's right! One of my favourites!'

I was stunned. I thought I'd long ago raked over every last ember of memory having to do with my teenage crush on Julia, but somehow I'd forgotten the little sonic bouquets I used to send down the three flights of stairs from my bedroom whenever she arrived at our house. I'd taught myself the intricate fingering of that song specifically for the purpose of impressing her.

'You know, I met Noel Redding once,' she said. 'I had a thing for musicians in those days. I'd never say no to a party where there was a chance of a real live rock star making an appearance.'

'Didn't you once get a chant going at a Blind Faith concert?'

'You've heard that story?'

'You were up a tree, in the version I heard.'

'It's true!' she laughed, putting her hand on my arm. 'With Francesca Leeto. Is that who you heard it from?'

'Yes.' The Leetos were family friends. 'I was collecting anecdotes for a novel about my parents' world.'

'A novel? How wonderful! Was I in it?'

'There was a character somewhat based on you.'

'Really?'

'Well ... you were a part of that world. A big part, for a while.'

'I'm flattered! Or were you going to make me into one of those twisted characters no one likes?'

'Of course not — you were highly sympathetic!'

She looked pleased; more pleased than my flippant answer seemed to warrant. Clearing her throat, she asked: 'How did I end up? Happy, I hope, and extremely rich!'

'Oh, I didn't get that far. But I'm sure you would have.'

Her flecked grey eyes widened for an instant, searching mine. It struck me, as it never had in the past, that she was insecure; that it actually mattered to her how, to what precise purpose, someone who called himself a writer might adapt her existence for the purposes of a story.

'Well. It must be fun to make up stories about real people,' she said, resuming her poised air. 'You can make them do whatever you want, can't you? Fall in love, inherit a fortune, become a Buddhist or a junkie or God knows what ... I'd like to end up in a nice little cottage in the Cotswolds, if you do write your book, with hollyhocks and plum trees and two or three handsome farmers for lovers, preferably with wives they have to get home to before daybreak.'

'I'll arrange it.'

'Ha! And interesting friends like you to come and visit, of course.'

'Of course.'

She gave a contented sigh. I got the sense of an impressionable spirit; more susceptible to things than I'd imagined.

'And what was your role in all this going to be?' she asked. 'One of those detached observers like what's-his-name in the Powell books?'

'Nicholas Jenkins.'

'Yes, Nicholas Jenkins. I always found him rather cold and dull. I hope you weren't going to portray yourself like that.'

'Actually, I think I was.'

'No! It wouldn't be accurate. You're a lot more fun.'

'Well, I'm glad you think so.'

She narrowed her eyes in a look of mock provocation.

'And would I still be able to make you blush?'

I was enjoying the flirtatious tack she'd taken, but even as I laughed and tried to think of a suitably suave reply, something – some confusion, or irritation with myself – flared inside me.

'Listen, Julia, I've been wanting to tell you,' I heard myself say, the words tumbling out in a sudden, clumsy, headlong rush, 'I'm a friend of Marco's. Marco Rosedale. I see quite a lot of him in New York.'

7

It seems even clumsier now, that declaration, than it did at the time. Brutal, almost. But then in hindsight practically everything I said seems tinged with brutality.

The effect on Julia was instant and extreme. She seemed to recoil from me, physically, flinching back into her chair, all the little nuanced tensions of amusement on her face slackening at once, giving way to a look of hurt shock, followed by anger.

'Is that why you're here?'

'No.'

'Did he send you?'

'No.'

'He sent you, didn't he?'

'No. I'm here because you invited me.'

'Why didn't you tell me you knew him?'

'I've been wanting to. Ever since you called. It's just – not the easiest thing in the world to bring up.'

'What isn't?'

'Well ... The whole story.'

She gave me a hard stare.

'You've heard it then.'

'Parts of it. His side, obviously.'

'What does he say?'

'Well, mainly that he didn't, you know …'

'Rape me?'

I nodded. She looked down, her lips moving for a moment without sound.

'What I'd like to know,' she said, raising her head again, 'is why the *fuck*, in that case, he thinks I'm saying he did?'

I'd decided by then that I was going to be absolutely frank. I felt guilty for not having told her right away that I knew Marco, and it seemed to me I owed her a full account of everything he and I had discussed. More pragmatically, I also sensed I was as close to the heart of the story as I was ever likely to get, and that in my role as its custodian, so to speak, I ought to do whatever I could to keep pushing forward. Frankness on my part, it seemed to me, would be as good a method as any to provoke frankness on hers.

'He has a few theories,' I said.

'Such as?'

I looked at her as levelly as I could.

'Money, principally.'

She breathed in, long and slow. I saw a muscle clench in her jaw.

'Money?'

'He seems to think you … you're in a position of needing to make money.'

She gave a mirthless smile.

'Well, it's true. I am. Who isn't? Not him, I suppose, with his money-bags father behind him. Anyway, so what?'

'That's why he thinks you wrote that thing,' I said. 'Or one of the reasons.'

She closed her eyes, shaking her head slowly.

'Yes, okay, money. I need to make it, just like everyone else. I wrote a memoir, which by the way is mostly not about Marco Rosedale, though I'm sure he thinks it's all about him. It's about the same world as your book, by the sound of it, only it isn't made up. I didn't *write* it for money, I wrote it in an effort to get myself out of a deep emotional and professional rut. But I certainly hoped to get a decent sum for *publishing* it. I showed it to the *Messenger* and they offered me what would have been a year's rent on this place just for that little bit about Marco. I was surprised it interested them, frankly. I mean, who cares about Marco Rosedale? And it's not as if his behaviour was so unusual either. Half the men in London were like that, I said as much in the piece. Still, I'd have been happy to take the money if the *Messenger* hadn't been so pathetically afraid of upsetting him.'

'You think they should have ignored that letter?' I asked.

'What letter?'

It hadn't occurred to me that she might not have been told about Gerald's letter. I braced myself.

'Well … Marco found a letter from your boyfriend at the time.'

'What boyfriend?'

'Gerald Woolley.'

'Oh, God! He found a letter from Gerald Woolley?'

'Yes.'

'To me?'

'No, to him. Marco. He showed it to the guy at the *Messenger*. Mel Sauer. That's what changed their mind.'

'Gerald wrote a letter to Marco?'

I nodded.

'When? Recently?'

'No. At the time of your ... thing with Marco.'

'Oh, for heaven's sake! Saying what?'

'Asking to meet him. You'd told Gerald about your – your feelings for Marco, and he wanted to talk it over with Marco, man to man, I guess.'

'You're joking!'

'The letter quoted things you said about Marco.'

'What things?'

'Well ... Very complimentary things.'

'Not possible.'

'Calling him an exceptional human being, exceptionally decent ...'

'Not *possible*!'

'He showed me a picture of it. Apparently it was sent just after the Belfast programme was broadcast. So after – you know – the night in question.'

I was trying to get it all out as quickly and straightforwardly as possible, to spare her any unnecessary anguish. But from the waves of pain registering on her face, it appeared my responses were striking her as something more in the nature of poisoned arrows than the simple expedient frankness I was intending.

'Let me get this straight,' she said. 'Gerald and Marco held a meeting to decide who I belonged to and now Marco's using the letter to try to prove I'm a liar – is that what you're telling me?'

'Well, they didn't actually meet. Marco never answered the letter. And to be fair to Gerald, he did acknowledge you were free to do whatever you wanted.'

'Jesus Christ.'

'I know. Very ahead of his time.'

'How come Mel Sauer never mentioned any of this to me?'

'I have no idea. What *did* he tell you?'

She shrugged. 'Something about Marco being more aggrieved than they'd expected, even after I toned it down, and the story not being a big enough deal to be worth a legal fight. I didn't question him because it confirmed what I thought anyway, though it made me furious that Marco thought he had any right to be aggrieved. That was actually when I first twigged that I'd written something important. I mean, I knew it was somewhat titillating, but I'd imagined people would just read it as a funny sketch of seventies sexual habits, which is how I'd thought of it myself. I didn't think of it as anything serious. Not till they tried to stop me publishing it.'

She refilled her wine glass, gesturing at the bottle to indicate I could help myself, which I did. Her hand shook a little as she raised the glass to her lips. She narrowed her eyes suddenly.

'I see! So that's why Renata Shenker changed her mind too! She told me it was because she couldn't deal with all the Cease and Desist letters Alec Rosedale was firing at her. Apparently he was going to force her into bankruptcy. But they must have shown her Gerald's letter. Yes. I see now. Dragged her into their nasty little cabal. That's the real reason why she pulled out. Very interesting. *Very* interesting.'

'Well, no, actually,' I said, realising I was going to have to break another unpleasant piece of news to her. 'It was something different in her case.'

'What?'

I fortified myself with a large sip of wine.

'I think it was some correspondence about a book you wanted to write. On a German aviator.'

'Hanna Reitsch?'

'Yes. They got hold of your proposal, along with the report from the original publisher's reader – a friend of yours, I believe.'

'Andrea Merton? Not that she's still a friend of mine, by the way. But go on.'

'That's what they showed Renata. That's why she backed out.'

Julia looked even more bewildered than before.

'I'm confused. What on earth could that book proposal possibly have to do with ... *anything*?'

I did my best to explain. It all sounded a bit far-fetched. Julia was looking increasingly agitated. She stood up before I'd finished, and began pacing about, biting at a nail.

'So Renata Shenker thinks I'm some kind of Nazi sympathiser? That's why she pulled out?'

'I don't know what she thinks.'

'What do *you* think?'

'I don't think you're a Nazi sympathiser. For what it's worth, I don't think Marco does either. But the way he sees it, he's fighting for his reputation—'

'Fuck him!'

'I mean, I think you were trying to praise the woman for not being a hypocrite, but I could see how someone might take it the wrong way. Especially the widow of a camp survivor.'

'Oh, rubbish! You'd have to be a lunatic to think I was in any way sympathising with her political beliefs. She went to prison for them, rightly, *obviously*, but then built a new life for herself. That's what interested me about her. I was interested in people who've had to start afresh in life. I'd done a whole series of articles on second acts. The book proposal came directly out of those.'

'I didn't know that. Marco only read me the parts where you seemed to be praising her for not recanting her National Socialist principles.'

She flung up a hand.

'Of course I wasn't praising her.'

'Also for calling Germany a land of bankers.'

'God almighty!'

'I mean, to be fair, even your friend, or former friend, seemed to find it strange. She said in her report she thought you might have gone off the deep end.'

'Andrea?'

'If that's—'

'She's the only person who saw it. She told me it'd be a tough sell so I didn't show it to anyone else. I've often wished I had. That's one of the things I write about in my memoir, by the way – my chronic lack of self-confidence.'

'She didn't tell you it came over as, you know ...?'

'No! Nobody tells me anything, apparently. Except you.'

'I'm sorry to be a bringer of bad tidings.'

'Though here's something even *you* probably don't know, which is that I had a fling with Andrea's husband. He was a junior minister under Blair and some photographer snapped us in his limousine. That's why Andrea's so keen to dish on me, no doubt.'

'Huh.'

'Not that it makes any difference. I'm sure Alec Rosedale would have got some other dirt into his grubby little mitts if this hadn't shown up. Or rather, twisted some other perfectly innocent thing to make it look like dirt. That's what those people do, isn't it?'

'Lawyers?'

She gave me an angry look.

'Yes, lawyers.'

Dusk had fallen outside. The rain had slowed. Yellow lights gleamed blurrily below us. Julia leaned against an empty bookcase.

'So. Money. What else? You said Marco had a few different theories.'

I shrugged. A slight weariness had fallen on me. 'Does it matter what he thinks?'

'It matters to me. Tell me.'

'Well. He thought maybe you were punishing him for not offering you a serious relationship.'

'Rubbish. *Rubbish!* What a fucking arrogant bastard!'

'But actually, then he changed his mind and said he thought it was more that he'd somehow ruined your relationship with Gerald.'

'My God! You seriously believe that? As if I could possibly have any regrets about Gerald Woolley. Other than letting him cling to me as long as he did. Your mother thought he was an utter drip. She's the one who persuaded me to ditch him for that American of hers.'

'The one you—'

'Got jilted by. Yes!'

She gave a harsh laugh.

'That's someone I do regret losing, by the way. Ralph Pommeroy. Just so you don't think I've become some man-hating harpy. I loved that man with all my heart.'

'I'm sorry,' I said.

She switched on a bright overhead light and sat back down in the chair facing me, clamping her temples between a finger and thumb.

'What else? What other *theories?*'

'Something about repetition, imitation,' I said. 'Doing it just because so many other women are doing it.'

'Accusing men of rape?'

I nodded.

She considered this for a moment, then tilted back her head.

'What ... exactly ... is wrong with that?'

'I guess he thought it made the accusation less, you know ...'

'Original?'

I smiled, and she gave a faint smile back, just a flicker really, but it made me feel she hadn't altogether merged me into Marco, for which I was grateful.

'Raping people isn't exactly original either, is it?' she said.

'True. But listen. Julia ... I want to ask you something.'

'Yes?'

'I mean – tell me if I'm out of line, but ...' I broke off, unsure how to put it.

'Go on.'

She was gazing at me intently from the flimsy wicker chair. She seemed exposed at that moment, unguarded; the bareness of the little flat expressive, suddenly, of an acute and anxious vulnerability.

'Well ... What actually happened in that hotel room?'

8

The question hung in the silence for an uncomfortably long time. I began to wonder if, in my growing fascination with the story, I'd allowed myself to lose sight of a certain basic decorum or tact. But when she finally spoke, there was no particular rancour or even discomfort in her voice.

'I've told you,' she said mildly. 'What happened is that Marco raped me. What else matters?'

'I suppose I'm trying to understand how it came about. I realise it's not my business . . .'

She gave a little movement of her head and the gesture seemed to express a tacit permission to probe. At any rate, I decided to take it as that, and she didn't seem to object.

'You'd gone up to his room with him?'

'Yes.'

'Voluntarily . . .?'

'Yes. And yes, I lay down on his bed voluntarily, and yes, we started kissing and touching and all the rest of it, voluntarily.'

'And then . . .?'

'What do you mean?'

'Did something happen, to change your mind?'

'No. I just realised I didn't want to screw him.'

'Do you remember the reason? Not that there, you know ...'

'Not that there has to be a reason. Quite. But there was a reason, and I do remember it.'

'Was it Gerald?'

'No. Well, yes, partly. That's certainly what I told Marco.'

'He ... disputes that, by the way.'

I began to explain that it was the timing he disputed, not the remark itself, but she silenced me with a dismissive wave.

'Who cares what he says? Anyway, there was something else too.'

'Yes ...?'

She turned, facing the black window. I caught her eyes in her reflection.

'It was because it wasn't me he was screwing, or trying to screw. It was someone else. And I didn't like that.'

'You mean ... in his mind?'

She nodded, turning back to me.

'I assume you know why we were in Belfast?'

'For that IRA film, right?'

'That's right. Well. We'd spent the day in a flat with a view onto an alley where we'd been told by some disgruntled ex-OIRA man that the Provos were going to tar and feather a girl who'd been out with a British soldier.'

She paused, seeming to lose herself in the memory. Another long silence passed. She'd drunk enough, it appeared, for her sense of time to have become somewhat elastic.

'Marco told me.' I prompted her: 'He said it had been gruelling.'

'Did he?' A glimmer of sarcasm showed in her eyes. 'Well, it certainly was for the girl. They dragged her screaming from a car, stripped her to her underwear and tied her to a lamp post with her hands behind her back. She already had black eyes and bruises all over her face but she was struggling as hard as she could the whole time. Two enormous women shaved her head and then a man who'd been warming a pot of tar with a blowtorch poured it over her and someone else dumped a sack of chicken feathers over her. They hung a sign around her neck saying: "Soldier Doll" and drove off. It was the most horrifying thing I've ever seen in my life. I was sick with guilt too, for not intervening. Not that there was anything we could have done, from where we were. When we got back to the hotel that afternoon I had to have about six whiskies just to begin to calm down. I was drunk by then, obviously, but I can tell you sex was the last thing on my mind. Still, I'll admit that when Marco started in with the little caresses and kisses it certainly gave me something new to think about.'

'He said it wasn't the first time you and he ...'

She gave me a sharp look.

'Of course it was the first time! It could only have happened because I was drunk, and that was definitely the only time I got drunk with him. He wasn't the kind of boy you'd take that kind of chance with unless you were certain you wanted to end up in bed with him. Believe me!'

'So you'd never had any physical contact with him before?'

'No. It was the first time – and the last, needless to say.'

She seemed to have accepted me, by now, as a kind of designated interrogator, as if I'd been appointed by some impartial agency to adjudicate the matter. I pushed forward, armoured in the sanctioned iciness of the role.

'Actually, Marco thought it might not have been the last time either.'

'What? Rubbish! Utter rubbish! How could anyone possibly believe that?'

'He wasn't sure. He just thought there might have been other occasions.'

'Well, he's sorely mistaken.'

'You did go on working with him, though?'

'Yes. I wasn't going to give up my career. Why should I?'

'And you never said anything about it at the time? Never reported it? Not that not reporting it means nothing happened, obviously ...'

She gave a grim laugh.

'You *have* been well trained, haven't you? You men all act like you've come through some sort of Maoist indoctrination programme nowadays. I bet Marco's the same. I bet he doesn't go around raping people *these* days. Assuming he even could, any more.'

'But just so I have it right, you didn't tell anyone at the time ...'

'Oh, for heaven's sake. As if anyone would have taken any notice if I had. There was no such thing as rape in those days, once you'd got into bed with a man. I didn't even think of it as rape myself, at the time. The word didn't enter my head.'

Her candour startled me. I could hear Marco laughing mirthlessly at the admission, as if she'd just self-evidently wrecked her own credibility. *See what I mean?* I imagined him saying, his voice dripping with cynicism.

'But so he was thinking of someone else ...'

'He was thinking of the girl.'

It took me a moment to catch on.

'The one they tarred and feathered?'

'Yes. There was something he did – holding my wrists together behind my back, very tightly – that made me realise. It turned him on. Especially when I struggled.'

I thought, naturally, of Marco's affair with his tutor.

'You're saying he was getting off on some kind of S and M thing?'

'Oh, I don't care about that. It's that he wasn't thinking of *me*, wasn't seeing me, even. I didn't like that. It offended me.'

'So you tried to stop him?'

'Yes! I said I was sorry but I didn't want to go on. I told him about Gerald. I couldn't have explained the other thing, even if I'd wanted to. I didn't understand it myself until recently. I probably didn't even realise I was offended. Not that it would have made any difference. Telling him about Gerald certainly didn't. If anything it just spurred him on. Anyway, it was all over very quickly, as they say. *Very* quickly.'

I nodded, absorbing the casual pragmatism she seemed to be admitting to. Apparently she saw nothing odd in adapting her emotions to fit her evolving perspective on the event.

'But you stayed with him, all the same,' I said.

'What?'

'You spent the night with him. That's what he says. You were there the next morning when the cameraman came to wake him for the flight home.'

'Oh. Well, yes, that's true. But what of it? I was drunk and I passed out. But I'd have stayed anyway, probably. I'm not going to pretend I was conflicted about that, at the time.'

'But I mean, if he'd just forcibly … you know … why would you stay in his bed?'

'I told you. I couldn't articulate what I'd experienced, at the time. I didn't tell myself: *I've been raped.* I knew something I didn't want to happen had happened, but I didn't know how to think about it. It wasn't as if I was lying bleeding in a ditch, or tied up in a dungeon. It's taken me a long time to see things for what they were. That's not unusual, by the way, and I'm not going to apologise for it.'

'No, of course.'

She shook out the last drops of wine into her glass and went to open another bottle. I got up to pee. In the cramped bathroom a leaky tap hissed into a basin. There was a meagre clutter of jars and half-squeezed tubes. I wondered what it must be like for Julia to live in a place like this. It wasn't a dump, exactly, but it had a peculiar cancelled atmosphere, as if it had been deliberately chosen for its lack of any qualities that might suggest the idea of a home.

I realised, washing my hands on a cracked slip of soap, that I'd decided she was telling the truth. Or at least telling me truthfully what she remembered. There was always the possibility of false memory, I supposed, though I'd never really accepted that as a concept. I was temperamentally opposed to it. I don't share the contemporary relish for questioning the reliability of the human mind as a processor of reality. At any rate, taking stock of things as I stood at the mirror with its reflection of the door on which a worn grey towel hung like an abstracted grimace, I noted the absence of doubt inside me. I'd been planning to press Julia on the question of whether that fateful evening was the first or last time she'd been to bed with Marco, but it seemed a minor quibble suddenly; not worth pursuing. And as if freed from some internal prohibition, my mind went to that other room, the hotel room in Belfast. I seemed to see it with stark clarity; a functional seventies box with a bed on which Marco with a drunken grin was ignoring Julia's change of heart, her ineffectual attempt to push him off; forcing himself onto her, into her, the act compressing its own colossal implications to a blackness too dense for either of them to comprehend as they rolled apart. It was like one of those vitrines we'd been shown at that talk at the Irving Foundation: one figure sated, indifferent; the other staring out at the washbasin in the corner, the fly-specked light, the row of boots lined up against the wall, wondering what had just happened.

'So ... What are you going to do now?' I asked, returning to the living room.

Julia was once again seated on the chair facing mine. A new bottle of wine stood on the table between us. She'd refilled both our glasses. I'd have liked to eat something before drinking any more, but food didn't seem to be on the horizon.

'About Marco?'

'Yes.'

'What I've been trying to do all along.'

'You mean ...?'

'I'm going to publish my book.'

'You have a publisher?' I asked, surprised.

'No, but I'm going to find one. Renata Shenker isn't the only fish in the sea.'

'Have you ... sent it out?'

'Not yet. I thought I might try to get an agent this time. Perhaps you can suggest someone?'

I stammered something about being out of touch with the English literary scene. 'I could probably find you some names, though ...'

She must have noticed my lack of conviction.

'Are you against me publishing it?'

'No, no. Of course not. But ... I mean, I do wonder if you've ... if you're aware of the impact it'll have ...'

'On?'

'Marco.'

Her eyes flashed wide.

'Why should I care what impact it has on him?'

'No reason. Just that ... I mean ...' I looked for a neutral tone. 'It will destroy his life.'

'Well, that's just too bad, isn't it?'

'Do you *want* to destroy him?'

'No. I don't actually care what happens to him, to be honest. But I have a right to tell my own bloody story! Don't I?'

'Of course. But he will be destroyed. As long as you realise that. He'll be finished as a journalist, a film-maker. His personal life will be wrecked. He'll ...' I could hear my voice rising. I appeared to have shifted from the role of impartial magistrate, now that I'd accepted her version of events, into something more like Marco's advocate. I was surprised at this, though the surprise didn't change anything. I'd drunk enough to feel the gap between my acting self and my observing self. 'His life will be over, for all intents and purposes. I'm not saying that's necessarily unfair. Maybe it's exactly what he deserves. I'm just ... pointing it out. I mean, since you say you don't actively want to destroy him ...'

The expression on Julia's face seemed to suggest she hadn't considered this aspect of the situation until now. I continued, cautiously encouraged.

'He's very open to self-criticism, you know. He told me he regretted a lot of his own past behaviour with women. He felt bad that he hadn't been more considerate, empathetic. We had one conversation where he spoke very frankly about growing older and not being so governed by his libido. He said he was a lot happier. He admitted he used to feel compelled to make a conquest of every woman he encountered, but now that's gone, and he says it's actually liberating.'

I repeated, as accurately I could, Marco's spiel about the autumnal pleasures of life that he'd begun to appreciate: pottering off to the gym or bakery, savouring the aromas of the local restaurants and vegetation. She listened, clutching her glass of wine without lifting it.

'I'm telling you this in case you think he's still a danger to other women. I mean, if that's part of the reason why you feel it's important to publish your—'

'It has nothing to do with it,' Julia burst out. 'I don't give a damn what he does to other women. He can rape his way across the entire fucking planet as far as I'm concerned. There's one reason and one reason alone why I intend to tell my story, which is that he raped *me*. It *happened*. And I'm not going to be made to shut up about it.'

Evidently I'd misconstrued her attentive expression. I felt suddenly out of my depth; bewildered by her seemingly implacable tenacity, but also by my own apparent compulsion to defend Marco, or at least plead for mercy on his behalf.

'He has a gun in his drawer,' I heard myself say. 'He showed me. He said he'd use it.'

'On me?' She looked momentarily fascinated.

'On himself. If you publish.'

'Oh, for God's sake.'

'I'm just trying to convey how desperate he is.'

'I told you. That's not my concern.'

'He has a daughter ...'

She glared furiously at me.

'I don't care. I don't *care*.' She slammed down her glass of wine, which miraculously didn't snap. 'Why should I care? Would you care, if you were the one who'd been raped?'

I looked away, thrown off my guard.

'Would you give a fuck whether or not your rapist had a daughter?'

'Probably not.'

She gave a curt nod.

'He will fight you, though,' I said. 'He'll fight you as hard as he can.'

'So what's new?'

'Well ... as long as you think it's ... worth it.'

'What do you mean?'

'I'm just saying, in his mind, he's fighting for his life. It's you or him, basically. One of you ends up terminally discredited. Lying rapist or lying Nazi. That's unfortunately the logic of the situation. And it could be you, Julia. He'll show every publisher in London that letter from Gerald Woolley, along with the stuff about Hanna Reitsch. His father'll make sure they all get copies, along with injunctions and writs and all the rest of it.'

She looked at me with sudden intense dislike.

'Now *you're* trying to threaten me!'

'What?'

'You don't believe a single word I've said, do you?'

'I do!'

'Then you don't care!'

'The point is, no one can prove it either way. That's the nature of these things. And without proof he'll always be able to raise the possibility that you're making it up. Especially given the circumstances.'

'The circumstances?'

There was a brief pause, in which both of us seemed to reel a little at the suggestion that had slipped out of me.

'You mean my going to his room, voluntarily?'

I made an attempt to backtrack, though I didn't feel entirely in command of myself at that moment.

'Well, it's a factor, I mean, the world being what it is . . .'

She tilted her head, seeming to reappraise me.

'You don't believe it was rape, do you, even if everything I say is true?'

'I do,' I protested, trying to sound like myself. 'Of course I do.'

'You don't. Not real rape. Not in a way deserving of real consequences. You think I should just shut up about it, don't you?'

'Not at all,' I said with a weird, glib feeling, as if I'd become my own communications director. 'But I don't think it's going to be easy to find a publisher, with those documents doing the rounds. They're pretty incriminating.'

'I'll publish it myself, in that case!'

'You'd self-publish?'

'Why not?'

'Well, that's your prerogative . . .'

'What are you saying?'

'Nothing . . .'

'You think he'd try to stop me doing that too?'

'I imagine so. If he can find a way.'

Her fury seemed to falter; she looked vulnerable again, uncomprehending.

'I'm not even allowed to self-publish? Christ almighty! *Christ* almighty!'

I had a feeling I should leave. I didn't appear to be in control of what I was saying, or even thinking. I seemed to see myself in front of some grim-visaged campus committee, trying to account for this weird surging impulse to act as Marco's surrogate. I stood up.

'What are you doing? You're not leaving, are you?'

'I should get going.'

She stared, blinking, with a peculiar, unseeing look as I went over to the door and reclaimed my jacket.

'What if I can prove it?' she said with an abrupt wild jerk of her head. 'What if I happen to have proof that what I'm telling you is true? Because it so happens I do. Cast-iron proof!'

I should have told her I didn't need proof; that I already believed her. But I didn't; couldn't. Perhaps it was the still tenuous nature of that belief — it hadn't quite solidified into an irreversible conviction. Or perhaps it was just the timing of her offer. I have a professional resistance to last-minute twists, surprise endings, and this sudden offer to supply one offended my sense of literary propriety. I looked down without answering, and began buttoning my jacket.

'I'd have put it in the memoir,' she went on, speaking rapidly, 'except I knew it would be too controversial. Too explosive. Do you want me to tell you what it is?'

'It's up to you,' I said.

'Do you know what people like Marco have in common?'

I continued buttoning my jacket.

'*Form*,' she said, her voice high and breathy. 'It's never just a one-off. There's always a history. And Marco's no exception. I happen to know that, for a fact.'

I looked up; curious in spite of myself.

'Did he ever tell you why he moved to America?' she asked.

'No ...'

'Well, *I'll* tell you.'

She paused theatrically.

'He was banished.'

'Banished?'

'Yes.'

Her face, like her voice, had changed; acquired a defiant brightness.

'Yes. He was caught with a fifteen-year-old girl. That's statutory rape. Her mother found them in bed and told him he had a week to leave England, for *good*, or she'd go to the police. So now you know.'

She waited for me to react.

'Huh,' was all I could think of to say. The story sounded absurd. I felt a sort of cringing awkwardness on her behalf, and a strong urge to get out.

'It was the mother who told me. I'd tell you her name, but she asked me not to, out of consideration for her daughter. There's a lot of stigma for women who admit to being victims of sexual abuse, as I'm sure you know. It's true, though. Perhaps I ought to have put it in the memoir after all. I could have used pseudonyms. What do you think? I still can, of course ...'

'That's your call,' I said, probably rather coldly. 'If you think it'll help you, then you should certainly put it in.'

She flinched. She must have caught the scepticism in my tone. The brightness fell from her face like a mask. She looked dazed.

'It was good seeing you, Julia,' I said. 'I'm sorry if ...'

'Must you really go?'

'I should, yes.'

We managed a pro-forma kiss on the cheek. It was still raining outside. I was cold, hungry, exhausted. Even before I crossed the river the whole encounter was acquiring a spectral quality, as if I'd dreamed or imagined it. I made a deliberate attempt to fix its key features in memory: I had a feeling I was going to need to recall them at some point. Some effort of concentration was required. It was never a neutral matter to be back in London, and I found it hard to focus on other things as I inched home across the city. I liked to think of it as a changeless place, stalled for ever in the same drizzle and gloom I'd left it in decades earlier. But of course there was always some new development: flashy new buildings like the ones coming in and out of view from the Docklands train – Gherkin, Cheesegrater, Walkie-Talkie; new ticketing rigmaroles to figure out on the Tube, new announcements on the platforms in new kinds of voices, the trains themselves smashing out of the tunnel mouths at newly aggressive speeds as if charged with the task of obliterating all memory of the newly interminable wait preceding their arrival. Contrary to what I'd always maintained, the city I'd abandoned seemed suddenly more anarchic, vivid, tumultuous than the one I'd moved to. And by some odd alchemy of transference, that wildness seemed to spread back into the images of Julia and Marco I'd formed when I lived there, Londoners to their fingertips at that critical juncture in their lives, and I had a vertiginous feeling of being caught up in a more turbulent drama than I'd fully grasped, with larger protagonists, gripped by stronger forces.

*

The phone rang early the next morning. I was awake, just, but still groggy from the night before. I dragged myself into my mother's study, which we'd stripped almost bare, and picked up the flimsy plastic receiver with its coiled white cord that twisted itself back into the same tight knots each time, however often one unravelled it.

'I'm so glad I caught you. Listen ...'

It was Julia. She spoke with a nervous fluency, as if she'd been rehearsing her words.

'I shouldn't have said that nonsense about the fifteen-year-old girl. I made it up. It was stupid of me and I'm sorry. Not that I think you believed me. You didn't, did you?'

I tried to be diplomatic.

'The part about Marco being banished was a little hard to believe ...'

'I know. Banished! What a ridiculous idea! I don't know why I came out with it. Well, I do. It's one of those stories you make up when you're really furious with someone. I've been cooking it up in my head for ages, imagining telling it to the police, or a judge, or another newspaper editor. It helps me deal with the absolute hatred I feel towards Marco for trying to shut me up. Sometimes I get so lost in the fantasy, I believe it myself. Anyway, when you told me he'd try to stop me self-publishing I was so upset and angry I just blurted it out. I wanted you to take my side. But I didn't realise how completely mad it would sound till I said it out loud. I've been up all night torment-ing myself for being such an idiot.'

'Ah, I'm sorry to hear it ...'

'Everything else I told you was true. That I can promise you.'

'Right.'

'I felt you believed what I was saying, up until then ...'

'Yes.'

'And you still do ... right? I mean, nothing's different there ...'

'Of course,' I said.

There was a longish pause in which the brevity of my answer seemed pointedly emphasised. I braced myself for a more concerted interrogation. But she just gave a soft, surprised laugh.

'All right. Well, goodbye.'

She hung up, and for a moment the bareness of my mother's office confused itself in my mind with the bareness of Julia's apartment, so that I seemed to be back there, seeing the dazed expression on her face again as I left. I stared down at the phone, wondering why I'd withheld the reassuring phrases she clearly wanted to hear. Was it that I felt I'd been put through one hoop too many? Possibly. Nobody likes being jerked around. I certainly sensed I'd become *entitled* to that feeling, if it should prove in some way useful. Calling me up to admit to the lie hadn't exactly cancelled the lie out. In a way it seemed to have made things even murkier. The word 'tainted' came into my mind. Julia's entire testimony, I told myself, had become 'tainted'. It was a powerful formula, I realised. It allowed me to detach myself from her version of events without committing myself to the position of outright disbelief. Why I should find this desirable, I couldn't have said precisely, and yet I did. It seemed to offer obscure advantages.

9

I flew back to the States two days later. I'd missed a couple of classes and scheduled a make-up for a Monday in October. On the drive home from the airport I called Marco to ask if I could stay an extra night.

'Of course. In fact, why don't you come on the Sunday? I'm having some people over to watch the debate. It's going to be a blast. Disguster's last stand!'

He sounded like his old self again: cheerful and expansive. I thanked him, accepting the invitation.

'And don't forget you and I have some celebrating to do. We'll go out after your class. My treat again.'

I began to protest, but he insisted.

'I owe you! You've been an incredible friend. I wouldn't have got through this without your support.'

I was debating, as we continued chatting, whether to mention my visit to Julia. I didn't want to risk spoiling his mood. On the other hand I was going to have to tell him eventually, and it might seem odd that I hadn't done it now.

The traffic was slow on the throughway – weekenders heading upstate for the foliage. Fall had arrived, making its usual splashy entrance of pinks and magentas, as if it wanted you to think some season of vigorous growth was coming in, rather than just the prelude to winter.

'See you Sunday then,' Marco said. 'Eightish, or come early if you can. Lots to catch up on!'

'Marco, listen, I have to tell you something. I saw Julia in London. Your Julia.'

There was a brief silence on his end.

'Oh?'

I explained how her invitation to tea had come about. 'Obviously I could have made some excuse, but I have to admit I was curious ... For your sake as well as mine.'

I thought he might object to the last part, but he didn't seem to.

'Of course. What did she have to say?'

I described the meeting. Marco listened with uncharacteristic restraint; not interrupting to dispute Julia's version of events, not snorting incredulously as he usually did when he disagreed with something, not reacting at all to Julia's candid admission that she'd only recently come to regard the episode in the hotel as an assault. The only sound he made was when I told him she was still determined to publish her memoir — self-publish if necessary — at which point a long, anguished groan escaped from him.

'No ...! No, no, no ...!'

I was surprised at the strength of his reaction. Not that I expected him to be indifferent, but the self-publishing idea had seemed fairly unthreatening to me; a very minor setback in the context of his overall victory.

'I told her you'd still try to stop her,' I said. 'I'm pretty sure she isn't going to do it. But even if she does, who's going to see it? Nobody reads those vanity press things, do they?'

'Oh, it'll get read. She'll put it online, start some kind of social media campaign or whatever ...'

I hadn't considered that. All the same, I thought he was overreacting.

'It would still be libel, though, wouldn't it?' I said. 'I mean, you could still sue ...'

'Sue what? The internet? Even if I could, she clearly doesn't give a fuck. She obviously has nothing to lose.'

The exuberance had sluiced out of his voice. Clearly I'd wrecked his mood.

'I'm sorry ...' I said feebly.

'Ah, God, I am so tired of this! I am sick to death of it! She's like something out of a zombie movie. Every time you shoot her down she bounces back up.'

'I do think I might have scared her off, Marco,' I said. 'I mean, she definitely got the message that you'd go on fighting to the bitter end.'

'Thanks. But in all honesty I don't think I could face another round. I'd rather just ... throw in the towel, I guess.'

I'd intended to tell him the business about the fifteen-year-old girl, thinking he'd appreciate hearing that Julia had admitted fabricating at least one story. But I decided that on balance it could wait.

'Speak to your dad,' I said, as soothingly as I could. 'I'm sure he'll have some ideas.'

He muttered some vague response, thanking me again for my support, and we said goodbye. The conversation left me feeling uneasy and dimly at fault. The whole situation seemed to have reached a point where it gave a duplicitous cast to everything that entered its orbit. I didn't want to think about it. I turned on the radio. The election coverage was in full spate. There'd been fresh allegations about the Republican candidate's treatment of women, this time on the set of his TV show. It was impossible, of course, not to relate this to Marco's drama. He must have been thinking about it himself, given his interest in all the stories of sexual malfeasance floating around in the press. The candidate's spokeswoman came on: *these outlandish, unsubstantiated, and totally false claims* ... I thought of the formula I'd adopted for Julia's account of what had happened in their hotel room: that useful word 'tainted' ... I was aware of something suspiciously convenient about it. I could see, a little too clearly now, how it allowed me to preserve my friendship with Marco without having to struggle with my conscience. I don't claim to have a particularly fine conscience. 'Well trained', perhaps, in Julia's acid phrase, but not especially active. I don't dream at night about human betterment (mostly I dream about getting my hair back). But I'd have trouble accepting the hospitality of a man I believed to have committed rape. Easier to believe Julia's story was 'tainted', or at least to suspend judgement, and she'd handed me an excuse for doing just that.

Three or four days passed; end-of-summer days, with the asters straggling a dusty blue along ditches, goldenrod turning ochre on patches of open ground. Caitlin was in talks with our old editor about the possibility of another travel book, this time in northern Spain. I had work of my own to catch up on. We'd go our separate ways in the morning, reconvening on the terrace at mealtimes. I made a point of cooking things we never had when the children were around. Tempeh, wholewheat pasta; broccoli raab: minor consolations of the empty nest.

One evening, a flock of wild turkeys came out of the scrub in the meadow, crossing the lawn below us as we ate dinner. There were four or five adults, with a dozen-odd lighter-coloured poults stepping cautiously in single file behind them like novices behind a group of black-shawled nuns. Caitlin gripped my hand as they passed, watching with the rapt look these visitations from the animal kingdom always produced. I remembered the smashed eggs we'd seen that spring, and my own role in that calamity. The hen must have had another brood, or perhaps these were the offspring of a different bird. Skirting the feeders without investigating the pools of spilt grain, they entered the colonnade of white birches at the edge of the meadow and disappeared into the forest beyond. They were of a size, already, to be safe from all but the larger, rarer predators that still prowled around in these woods: coyotes, the odd solitary bobcat.

'We should catch one for Thanksgiving,' I said – an old joke that always made the kids squeal when they were little. Caitlin gave a tolerant smile, squeezing my hand.

We talked about my meeting with Julia. Some faint but persistent qualm had been nagging at me – a sense of having missed or glossed over something. I trusted Caitlin's reactions more than my own. Her instincts, unlike mine, had an intact purity about them. The life she'd made for herself since we moved to the country and had children had left her comparatively unmaddened by the toxins that seemed to have saturated public discourse on every subject these days. Crucially, she'd been preoccupied with other things during the years when our friends took en masse to social media, and she'd never acquired a taste for that neurotic activity. Also, though she was thoroughly American (Minnesota farmers on one side, Chicago professionals on the other), she was free of that paradoxical and – to my mind – quintessentially American combination: the love of scolding and the hatred of being scolded. If anything she had it the other way around: she rarely set herself up in judgement of anyone, but she actively sought out people's criticisms of herself, and listened to them avidly. I knew that whatever she might have to say about Marco and Julia would spring from a clean source.

She heard me out – patiently, though also, I felt, somewhat unwillingly. She was fond of Marco: I knew that, just as I knew that the convolutions of an English-woman like Julia Gault were unlikely to engage her sympathies. At first I put her slight air of impatience down to a reluctant but growing conviction that Marco had in fact committed a grave wrong. But I was mistaken. It was apparently Julia's role in the story, not Marco's, that troubled her. Julia's revisions of her own feelings about the past, far from conveying a compli-cated authenticity (as they had for me), struck her as highly suspicious. The candour that I'd found so com-pelling merely seemed expedient to her. That absurd lie about Marco's 'banishment' was plainly damning, while the phone call the next morning was self-evidently manipulative.

'She must have realised she'd overplayed her hand. That's all that was about. She was just trying to get you back on her side ...'

I didn't entirely disagree with her, and yet I felt an obli-gation to play devil's advocate.

'You don't think she could have been telling the truth about the other stuff, even if she was lying about that?'

Caitlin shrugged. 'She's someone who lies. What else is there to say?'

Perhaps I shouldn't have been as surprised as I was by her verdict. I knew from her policy with our children that she had no tolerance for lies, so perhaps I should have foreseen that she'd react the way she did. And it's possible I *had* foreseen it in some way; that I was counting on her to give me the permission I couldn't quite give myself, to put Julia's accusations into a permanent moral quarantine, and continue my friendship with Marco as if nothing had changed.

At any rate the conversation brought a change of mood that continued through the weekend. I felt calmer, less inclined to torment myself about possible ulterior motives for what I did or didn't believe about Marco, and increasingly able to think of my coming reunion with him that Sunday without misgivings.

It was the kind of liberated mood that, in my case, often builds towards a state of mild euphoria, feeding on any stimulus that strays into its orbit. The burned-out beauty of the Indian summer with its rustling bracts and burrs, its sweet, pervasive scent of dried grasses and leaf-mould, became a part of it, as did the dawning realisation that Caitlin and I were not after all going to be spending all our days and nights grieving for our departed children. Even my work fed into it. I'd put Mallarmé's *Afternoon of a Faun* back on the syllabus for the literature seminar I was teaching, and remembering my conversation with Marco earlier in the year, I'd tracked down a film of Nijinsky's 1912 ballet based on the poem. The ancient footage was grainy, ghostly; fragmented to a point of near-abstraction, with phosphorescent images of the faun and nymphs flickering in and out of focus. It was hard to follow, even knowing the story of the faun's dreamlike encounters with the nymphs. But purely as spectacle it captured some quality of delight that made a powerful impression on me: Nijinsky in his dappled skin moving like a reclusive forest animal; his gestures, at once cryptic and familiar as some language one had always known but never heard spoken, seeming to arise out of a wellspring of elemental joy. I remembered something D. H. Lawrence, that maligned genius, had written about the figure of the faun. It was in his book on the ancient Etruscans, an account of a civilisation dedicated to a celebratory vision of life, utterly unlike that of the lugubrious Romans who supplanted them. I looked it up: 'They can't survive, the faun-faced men, with their pure outlines and their strange non-moral calm. Only the deflowered faces survive ...'

They can't survive, the faun-faced men ... The words were in my mind as I drove down to New York that Sunday afternoon. Inevitably, in the mood gripping me, they seeped into my thoughts about Marco. Was it possible, useful, to look at him, as his old tutor had, through the lens of the faun, that mythic incarnation of a masculine sensuality radically unlike the militaristic 'Roman' version that had replaced it, marching down through the generations in its heavy muscled armour all the way to the pornographic ideal of our present era? I thought of Tarquin, that archetypal Roman, with his 'rage of lust' as he forces himself into Lucrece's bedchamber in Shakespeare's poem. Was that Marco? Or was he one of the faun-faced men who don't survive? Perhaps he was both; had been one, had become the other. In any case the question brought in its wake the sense of a hunted, hounded innocence that I found hard to shake off.

It struck me that I hadn't, for one second, believed Marco unreservedly, and that this placed me among those doing the hunting and hounding ... I remembered my wariness when he first told me about his troubles; that triangulating impulse of mine, which instantly added to the two of us a third figure in the shape of Public Opinion, wagging its finger and warning me: *Be careful.* I remembered my hesitation in rejoicing with him at his moments of apparent victory; my lukewarm words when I finally did ... The memories displeased me. I didn't like the portrait they painted: a study in craven equivocation. Marco himself seemed, by contrast, magnanimity incarnate. I thought of his insistence, from the beginning, that he didn't expect me or anyone else to take him on trust: 'You can't *not* have doubts ...' Even his subdued response the other day, as I'd described my meeting with Julia, seemed, in this new light, a part of that same tact, which itself appeared positively heroic as I considered it now. No hint of reproach for my evident belief that there really must be two sides to the story; no attempt to influence me against Julia's version of things, or even ascertain whether I found it credible. Only that poignant gratitude for my 'support' ...

How little I'd done to earn that gratitude! How little 'support' I'd actually given! True, I'd sympathised with the public aspects of his situation; the various kinds of ruin and disgrace threatening him, but I'd never considered the peculiar private agony of being innocent and not being believed. For a moment I seemed to see it squarely, feel on my own nerves the pain of realising that not even the one friend he'd chosen to confide in could give him the assurance of unqualified belief. I remembered my refusal of empathy when he showed me that gun; the grim look on his face when he saw I wasn't going to take him seriously. I felt ashamed of myself, and then immediately a little worried too. What if he really had been thinking of blowing his brains out? And what if my report from London the other day had pushed him over the edge? I heard his voice again, thick and low: *Ah, God, I am so tired of this! I am sick to death of it!* ... An image came to me, of him staging some terrible act of self-immolation in front of his guests tonight. Unlikely, I told myself. Marco wasn't the histrionic type. All the same, in the flux of this restless, remorse-filled enthusiasm, it seemed to me that some gesture of solidarity was called for.

I happened to be on Route 17 just then. There was a discount liquor store in one of the malls along the highway where Caitlin and I often stopped for supplies. On impulse, I pulled off into their parking lot, marched through the automatic doors into the glittering interior, and before I could change my mind, bought a bottle of expensive vintage champagne. It would make a suitable *mea culpa*, I thought, carrying it back to the car; an eloquent statement of confidence in Marco's ultimate victory.

A peculiar clarity seemed to distil itself in me as I drove on. I was in front of that campus star chamber again, only this time I was on the offensive, attacking my interrogators with the icy fluency one commands during these purely imaginary exordia. They were reactionaries in the guise of progressives, I informed them; puritans whose obsession with female victimhood masked impulses as controlling and infantilising of actual women as the code of gentlemanly 'chivalry' that the pioneer feminists had diagnosed two centuries ago as the male sex's insidious means of female subjugation. I accused them of trying to bring back shame as an instrument of social control, of wanting to recreate a world in which a word, a rumour, an anonymous posting, could once again destroy an entire life. They'd trapped themselves, I declared, in the escalating logic of hysteria that ends, unfailingly, in the witch hunt ... I was aware of flaws in my own logic; weaknesses, exaggerations, but the awareness had little effect on the sense of exuberant vindication. It was as if the visions of some feverish genie had started wafting out of the wrapped bottle on the seat beside me, and into my brain.

10

I'd intended to arrive early at Marco's but I hit traffic at the Holland Tunnel and again at the Brooklyn Bridge, and by the time I got to Bed-Stuy the party was in full swing.

Alicia's partner answered the door, wearing a long green apron over her jeans, with the words *wi-cook.com* printed on it.

'Hi, Erin,' I said, pleased with myself for remembering her name.

'Actually, I go by Eric now.'

She stared up with a mild but steadfast look. The tuft of beard at her chin, or his chin, was neatly combed and trimmed. His hair, shaved at the side, glinted in the street light.

'Ah, okay,' I said, trying to project an attitude of nonchalant approval. 'Right!'

It seemed to pass muster. At any rate a hospitable smile spread over his face.

'Come on in. Hey, champagne! Would you like me to put that in the refrigerator? I'll tell Marco you brought it. He'll be super happy.'

I hung my pack in the entranceway and followed him in.

'I'll get you a drink,' he said, still smiling solicitously. 'Gin and tonic, right?'

I nodded, a little surprised at his affable warmth.

There were thirty or forty people packed into the suite of dimly lit rooms, with a din of excitable voices making themselves heard over loud music. I glimpsed Hanan in a sleeveless white top at the far end. Alicia, wearing the same caterer's apron as Eric, came up with a tray of canapés – elaborate confections that looked like combinations of sushi rolls and cream puffs. I asked about the matching aprons. She gave her bubbly laugh and told me she and Eric had started a catering and party management company.

'This is our first gig. Daddy invited all his most important friends, so we're trying to make a good impression!'

'Well, these certainly look impressive,' I said, taking a canapé. It had a custardy texture; I tasted shrimp in it, and horseradish, and possibly banana.

'Delicious!'

'Thanks!'

She hovered, unpractised at detaching herself.

'I thought you were going to grad school,' I said.

'Oh. We want to see how things go with the business first.'

I remembered a conversation we'd had when she was still at Vassar. She'd told me she hoped to work at the State Department one day.

'You don't want to be a diplomat any more?'

'No, I do, but right now I kind of feel this is more important. Eric needs to make money.'

It wasn't my place to inform her she had her priorities wrong. Instead I embarrassed myself telling her the story of Nancy Reagan's reply to the diplomat who asked what she thought of Red China – 'I think it's all right on a yellow tablecloth' – to which Alicia responded with a puzzled laugh that made me feel at once old, condescending, sexist and mildly deranged.

I caught sight of Marco in the next-but-one room along, where the giant TV was splashing colour on people's faces. He didn't look as gloomy as I'd been expecting; certainly not suicidal. In fact, he looked remarkably well: holding court in an untucked lime shirt with a half-dozen energetically gesticulating men and women grouped around him. Eric, passing them with my drink, paused to tell him something, pointing in my direction. Marco looked towards me and raised a hand in greeting, giving Eric's shoulder a friendly squeeze as he let the hand drop.

'Your dad looks well ...' I said to Alicia.

'He's great. He actually took the weekend off, which he never normally does. We've all been hanging out together.'

Eric came up with my drink.

'You need to keep circulating, girl,' he said to Alicia, cuffing her on the back. She laughed, and they went off.

I looked for someone to talk to. The guests were a mixture of mostly white people in their fifties and sixties and a more diverse younger set – Hanan's friends, presumably. They weren't ostentatiously glamorous but they had an air of relaxed confidence very unlike the mid-level freelancers and adjuncts I mostly hung around with. It would be a powerful thing to have a crowd like this on your side, I felt, taking in their well-made outfits and upbeat chatter. On the other hand they looked like they could give you a very cold shoulder if your stock happened to fall for some reason, or even looked in danger of falling. It didn't surprise me that Marco hadn't wanted to share his troubles with them.

I moved in his direction, passing the TV, on which pundits were pantomiming the scandalised incredulity that had become the default facial expression among commentators during this campaign. The cause was more misogyny; on this occasion leaked tapes of the Republican candidate bragging about assaulting women. Seeing me, Marco turned from the tight throng surrounding him and grabbed my shoulder, hugging me with unusual warmth.

'Really touched, *really* touched by the champagne.'

I smiled, glad he'd understood the gesture even though he clearly wasn't in any imminent danger of blowing his brains out.

'It's a new day, right?' he said, staring into my eyes.

I nodded, not sure what he meant. He gripped my arm.

'You heard the news, I assume?'

'You mean . . . about these tapes?' I gestured at the TV.

'What? Oh, well, yes, the guy's obviously toast, but no . . . Oh, hold on . . .' He detached himself from me. 'Chiara!'

A woman with vigorous features and hair piled in a dishevelled updo had appeared next to us. She and Marco embraced warmly and began speaking in Italian, Marco with his mother's sinuous Milanese accent. I realised I'd never heard him speak Italian before; it was like having an entirely new side of his personality revealed; subtler and more cunning than the one I knew. He broke off to introduce the woman; a film-maker who'd made a documentary about the trafficking of women refugees that had won great acclaim in Europe and was about to come out in the States. The Cinema Collective, of which Marco was a board member, was involved in its release.

'It's getting serious attention,' Marco said. 'Chiara's going to be on Charlie Rose next week, *and* Leonard Lopate ...'

They began speaking in Italian again. I moved away, wondering what Marco's news could be. Some major development with his own documentary, I guessed, judging from the happy atmosphere of his household. Across the room I saw Hanan leaning against a door jamb in a cluster of people, listening thoughtfully to their conversation. I caught her eye, and after a momentary blankness she smiled, flashing her even teeth.

'Oh, hello!'

We exchanged some pleasantries. I thought that would be that, but she stepped towards me, her coutured silk top catching the light in ripples like sculpted drapery.

'Actually, I wanted to talk to you.'

She spoke in a quiet, intimate tone, as if we knew each other better than we really did, and evidently confident that I would acquiesce in the change of register. It crossed my mind that she might be wanting to question me about that message of Julia's on the answering machine last month, and I realised I still hadn't asked Marco what he'd told her. But I was on the wrong track entirely.

'Marco says your wife gave up her career when you and she had children ... Is that really true?'

I was surprised: aside from the unexpectedness of the question itself, I didn't think Caitlin's existence had registered on Hanan.

'Well ...' I said, warily, 'she did continue working from home on other things ...'

I'd learned from experience that some people regarded Caitlin's decision to quit her career as an occasion to

deliver a stern lecture – to Caitlin herself, or to me if she
wasn't around – and I didn't want to hear one just then.

'Anyway, it wasn't based on any particular belief about
child-rearing. It was just that she preferred being around
the kids when they were growing up, and we were living
a pretty frugal life out in the country, so we could afford
it ...'

Hanan nodded.

'How does she feel about it now?'

She tilted her smoothly angled face up towards me,
closing her lips as she waited for my answer. Her interest,
which seemed genuine, puzzled me.

'She fluctuates. Sometimes she regrets it. Sometimes
not.'

'What are her main regrets?'

'Well, there's a big void now that they're gone, but she's
doing her best to fill it ...'

It occurred to me, suddenly, why Hanan was asking.

'Hanan, are you thinking of, I mean—'

'I'm pregnant,' she said.

I tried not to appear too astonished. She laid her hand
against her shoulder, her long red nails fanning out.

'It was an accident. But assuming I keep the child, I'd
love to talk to your wife.'

'Of course,' I said. 'I'm sure she'd be happy to talk any
time.'

She smiled, and turned back to the other people. I
wandered off to get another drink, trying to sort
through the many and somehow staggering surprises
contained in Hanan's words. How cosmically harmoni-
ous Marco's household had become since I was last
there! I supposed I was going to be adding the imminent patter of tiny feet to the list of things we'd be

toasting with that bottle of Krug. The thought trailed a slight caustic burn in its wake. An irrational annoyance at Hanan's questions seemed a part of it; as if she'd been trying to reduce Caitlin's difficult process of figuring out full-time motherhood to some kind of lifestyle option one could simply select like a new car or fridge. But it was more than that. There was some animus against Marco too. A resentment of his seeming invincibility; his amazing capacity for continually reviving and expanding his field of operations. And once again, as I saw this, I felt the dismaying pettiness of my reflexes. What was the matter with me, I wondered, that I could only fully sympathise with him when I thought he was on the ropes? Why did the prospect of Marco victorious, Marco the loved and honoured paterfamilias with his troops of friends, his unstoppable career, fill me with such peevishness?

'There you are. You vanished!'

I turned from the drinks table. Marco was in the kitchen doorway, standing with a switched-on look in his radiant shirt.

'Sorry,' I said.

'That's okay, but I wanted to hear your thoughts.'

'About ...?'

'About Julia,' he said, as if it should have been obvious.

'Julia?'

'You didn't hear?'

'No ...'

'I thought you must have heard.'

'What's happened?'

He stepped close to me, glancing over his shoulder.

'She killed herself.'

'What?'

'My dad called me yesterday. She jumped in front of a train.'

'No!'

He put his finger to his lips.

'I haven't told the gals yet. Not sure how they'll react.'

'I don't believe it! I was just ...'

'I know. I know. It's terrible.'

'I was just with her! She didn't seem ... I mean ...'

I stepped back, leaning my weight against the table.

'Beyond terrible,' Marco said quietly, glancing again over his shoulder. 'I feel awful. Really ... shattered.'

'When was this?'

'Night before last.'

He told me what the papers had reported. She'd jumped in front of a train coming out of the tunnel at Russell Square. A feeling of horror lurched through me as he described it; I felt myself cringe as if to ward off a blow.

'Poor woman,' he said. 'But ...'

He gave an odd, slow-motion shrug, hunching his shoulders high and holding them there.

'What?'

'Well, I just wish we didn't live in such an extreme, black-and-white universe, where the slightest transgression gets you vilified for all eternity ... Perhaps I wouldn't have fought her so hard. You know what I mean? Not that I'm going to blame myself for this. I'm just not. But maybe we'd have been able to talk it over, or something ...'

I wasn't sure what he was getting at.

'I mean, who knows, maybe I did do something I shouldn't have, back in that hotel. I know we were both totally hammered, so it's a possibility. A *possibility*. But it's not a possibility you can entertain in this particular universe. Not unless you plan to spend the rest of your life as a leper.'

'What are you saying?'

'Nothing. I'm just acknowledging that I can't pretend to know precisely what happened forty years ago in some cruddy Belfast hotel where two people, one of whom technically speaking was me, went upstairs with certainly every *intention* of fucking each other's brains out ... I mean, can I?'

He gave a peculiar smile. It seemed intended to be rueful, but some other emotion was hijacking it, warping it into something weirdly triumphant.

'You seemed pretty sure a month ago ...' I said.

'Well, you have to take a position, don't you? I *was* pretty sure. I still am. Seriously. But ...' He shrugged again. 'Anyway, look, I didn't mean to spring this on you. I assumed you'd heard. I thought that was why you brought the champagne.'

'No!'

He stared a moment. As was often the case with him, the workings of his mind were transparently visible on his face as he took in my appalled expression. I could almost see the cogs turning as he realised what he'd said. He nodded apologetically.

'No, of course not. Sorry – I'm not thinking straight. I'm in shock, I guess. You are too, by the look of it.'

He put a hand commiseratingly on my arm. I found it difficult to look at him at that moment. To my relief, Eric appeared, wiping his plump fingers on his apron.

'Marco, they're about to start the debate.'

'Ah, okay.' Marco resumed his normal tone. 'Let's get everyone in there, if we can. Otherwise we can bring another TV from upstairs. Turn off the music, would you?

And get that lazybones daughter of mine to top up people's drinks.'

'Will do!'

The boy strode officiously back into the main living room. He appeared to have changed personality as well as gender. There was no trace of the old malcontent in his new role as Marco's steward. His flourishing air seemed a rebuke to certain murky, residual prejudices lingering in me.

'We'll talk more later, okay?' Marco said.

I nodded.

He moved away, but then stepped back, gripping my arm again and flashing a conspiratorial grin.

'Think she'll stop persecuting me now?'

'Who?'

'Julia!'

His eyes scanned mine, searching for the smile of cynical humour we'd shared so often in the past. I could smell his cologne, and the bourbon on his breath.

'I wouldn't count on it,' I said.

He gave a loud laugh, evidently taking my unamused tone as ironic, and disappeared into the other room.

I went down the corridor and lifted my backpack off the coat hook, half-intending to keep going, out through the front door and back to my car. But aside from the fact that I could ill afford a hotel, I detected something artificial in the impulse, theatrical. I could sense already that it wasn't going to work to cast myself as a figure of blameless rectitude affronted by Marco's callousness. Whatever flaws I have in my moral make-up, the self-exculpatory urge has never been among them. All the same, I couldn't face going into the living room just then. I turned back towards the staircase. Alicia was coming the other way, carrying a tray of glasses. I held my pack up, pointing to the landing.

'Just putting my things upstairs ...'

She laughed, as if I'd meant to say something funny again. My daughter, two years younger, had the same habit of compliant laughter, and an urge to warn the girl against her own obligingness briefly seized me. Marco was probably right about me being in shock. I was certainly in a state of confusion.

Up in the guest room I sat on the bed and tried to comprehend what he'd told me. There was something unassimilable about it. It was at once too large and too remote to take in. Julia's face appeared in my mind, obstinately alive; staring at me again in the stark light of her living room. Again I had the feeling of having missed something. What, though? It wasn't as if I'd failed to notice she was unhappy. And I didn't think I'd glossed over any of my own stumbles or gaffes either. And yet I couldn't connect anything I'd observed to this staggering piece of intelligence. The violence of the act seemed a deliberate challenge, daring one to imagine for oneself a state of rage or despair of an intensity requiring nothing less than the impact of a hurtling train against one's frail body to alleviate it.

With an unpleasant inward jolt, as if something had been knocked loose inside me, I found myself remembering that in the notes for my abandoned literary project, I'd considered a possible suicide attempt for Julia. Not a serious one; in fact, a decidedly frivolous one, involving a dozen aspirins and a cunning plan concocted by her to make sure she was rescued. The idea had been to place it directly after the episode (drawn from life) in which she was jilted by her American fiancé, as a means of enhancing the quality of melodramatic self-absorption I'd allotted to her character. It disturbed me to recall it. Even without the brutal facts of this latest development to set it off, it seemed a strange thing to have invented. I wasn't so superstitious as to regard it as some kind of illicit magical tampering in her fate (it wasn't what had happened, after all), but precisely in its differences from the reality it otherwise so closely resembled, it seemed to confront me with some profound failure to comprehend her true character. I stood up, acutely restless; took out my phone to tell Caitlin the news, changed my mind, sat back down on the bed, and sprang up again, feeling suddenly cornered, and hurried back down the stairs.

A few of the guests were grouped around a small screen that had been set up in the front room, but most were packed into the main room with the big TV. I peered in through the arch. Marco beckoned me over, making a space next to him behind the old thrift-store sofa. Hanan was on the other side, squeezed up close with her hands linked over his shoulder in an uncharacteristically demonstrative pose. The debate was in full swing. There was a lot of raucous commentary from the guests, some of whom appeared to be live-tweeting the event, but the volume was up high and it was easy enough to hear what the candidates were saying. Distraction — my objective at that moment — seemed possible. One of the moderators was pushing the Republican on the things he'd said on the leaked tapes, and he was repeating the phrase 'locker-room talk' like a spell, as if it might ward off the general revulsion he'd aroused if he said it enough times. The guests were laughing, some imitating the schoolyard intonations of his voice, others mocking the lacquered fiasco of his hair. His crude attempt at turning the tables with an attack on his opponent's use of a private email server prompted loud booing. He looked at the camera, and from the scowl on his face – lower lip protruding, jaw clenched tight – it almost seemed he was hearing us.

'Look! He's making his Churchill face. The British bulldog!'

'Too bad he has such a wussy mouth!'

'Is it me or is there something obscene about it? Like it's a little anus that grew in the wrong place ...?'

'Wait, what's he saying? Quiet, everyone ...'

The man, towering over his opponent with the expression of an outraged mullah, was informing her that if he won the election he was going to get a special prosecutor 'to look into your situation'. The room exploded into angry jeers that all but drowned out the whoops of his supporters in the studio audience. I stared, fascinated in spite of myself. I'd been slow to take any serious interest in this weird, ivory-gold colossus who'd been destroying his rivals one by one throughout the summer. He'd been a fixture of New York, an established sideshow, since long before I arrived there in the late eighties, but only very recently had I begun to realise he was something other than just a buffoon; that he had his own sickened vigour, his own charisma even. Perhaps because he too had recently joined the ranks of powerful men accused of assault, his very distinct physicality had begun to acquire, for me, a heightened aura. He brought to mind those slabs of pallid humanoid flesh in Francis Bacon's paintings, enthroned on toilets in arid rooms with a molten dog for company; his lust for gold, detailed ad nauseam in the press, lending the image a tinge of jaundiced porcelain. Everything about him seemed at once gleaming and effluvial, like some Freudian idol we'd set up in order to load it with the qualities we most abhorred about ourselves before driving it out into the wilderness.

'He's going down!' someone shouted. 'He is *so* going down!'

He'd just threatened to jail his opponent and had retreated to his lectern like a bull withdrawing into his safe space, his *querencia*, looking at once menacing and cosmically aggrieved, as if nothing short of dominion over the entire universe could compensate for the wrongs done to him. That too, that titanically aggrieved air, was something I'd been slow to recognise; slower still to grasp its magical power over others, especially those with real cause for grievance.

'What a chump!' a woman on the sofa below me said.

'Dump his rump,' another person said.

People laughed, and soon everyone was coming up with rhymes: sump, slump, hump, pump his stump. There was a festive atmosphere, with a definite blood-sport cruelty about it, complicated by the fact that the quarry seemed only too eager to present himself as an actual monster. I drifted inward again. A phrase of Julia's came back to me: *He wasn't thinking of me...* I hadn't attached much importance to it at the time. It had seemed a bit trite, if anything; an easy formula she'd settled on to explain her change of heart up in Marco's room all those years ago. It wasn't that it had become any more profound, but it seemed to come at me suddenly from a different angle; one that put my own actions in a new light. *He wasn't thinking of me ...* For a moment I saw myself standing before her with a peculiar ruthlessness as I pursued my inquisitorial mission; facing her like some single-minded speculator surveying a landscape purely for its extractive possibilities ... Had I, too, not been thinking of her; not thinking of *her*? Absurd! I thought immediately. There was no comparison between my conversation with Julia in her flat and her encounter with Marco in that hotel bedroom. Here was a character flaw I most certainly did possess: a tendency towards morbid self-recrimination. I pushed the image out of my mind.

'He's stalking her! He's stalking her ...'

The Republican had appeared in the frame directly behind his opponent as she answered a question, his red tie stretching down the edge of the screen as he loomed into her space in what appeared to be a deliberate, and deliberately flagrant, attempt at intimidation. Again the room filled with cries of jubilant outrage. It really was like a bullfight, only with the Minotaur himself in the ring.

'Beautiful! That's it. Presidential candidate stalks his opponent on live TV. We're done. RIP, the Republican Party.'

'RIP. The whole white fucking billionaire patriarchy!'

'It's already going viral!'

I glanced at Marco. Was he experiencing any symptoms of identification with the beleaguered candidate? He didn't appear to be. But then, why should he? He was in the clear, I reminded myself. His accuser had been neutralised, silenced, undone. Hanan hung on his shoulder. I wondered if the news about Julia would affect this newborn tenderness of hers when she heard it. Probably not, I thought. She'd apparently made up her mind to believe in Marco's innocence. *The onus of belief* ... I thought again, blackly. It was as if I'd invented some spell of my own, for reducing reality to a question of where one's best interests lay.

'You okay?'

Marco's voice sounded in my ear. I must have been grimacing. I nodded.

'Don't torment yourself,' he said quietly. 'I don't think there's anything anyone could have done. I mean, if *you* couldn't figure out what was going on in her head ... You're the writer, after all!'

'Clearly I missed the story,' I muttered.

'Well, it happens. Anyway, not your fault.' He glanced surreptitiously at Hanan – her eyes were fixed on the screen – and turned back to me. 'She'd always been wobbly. Did I tell you she did a spell in the bin when she was at Oxford? Ten days in the Radcliffe under round-the-clock surveillance. We found that out even before we found out about the Hanna Reitsch stuff. So ...'

I said nothing. I didn't trust myself to speak without betraying an emotion I couldn't explain or justify.

'This is what matters now,' Marco said, gesturing at the TV. 'Right?'

I managed an accommodating grunt. I seem to have a large capacity for accommodation.

'We're going to win. Trust me. We're going to win big.'

'I know,' I said.

That at least was something we still had in common. I was as confident as he was in the Democratic candidate's imminent victory. She'd just reminded the audience of Tocqueville's old maxim, 'America is great because she is good', and it seemed to me still just about valid. Her opponent had faltered visibly in the interim. He was no longer swaggering so much as blustering; flailing even. Swaying on his thick legs, he gave the impression of some elephantine statue lassoed in ropes and about to come crashing down. The nightmarish possibility of his presidency was slipping, mercifully, into the realm of bullets dodged, disasters averted. Some day no doubt novelists would write dystopian alternate histories in which he won, but it was becoming clear, if one had any doubts, that in the real world rationality and basic decency were going to prevail, as they usually did, and that the arc of actual history was going to continue bending, in its imperfect way, towards justice.

It was some consolation, I supposed.

penguin.co.uk/vintage